THE ECSTASIES OF CREMORNE

Lizzie lay languidly on the large double bed, her blonde hair spread out in a golden mass across the pillow. She wore a loosely fitting white dress which seemed almost transparent in the bright sunlight pouring through the high windows.

'Why don't you take your jacket off, Bob?' she said with a mischievous twinkle in her cornflower blue eyes. 'And your vest and shirt, too. I promise you will feel so free without the restraint of unnecessarily covering your body.'

And to show that she practised what she preached, Lizzie loosened the strings and unfastened the hooks of her dress so that she was revealed in glorious nudity. Bob could not prevent a gasp of excitement excaping his lips as he drank in the firm swell of her bare breasts, each globe proudly uptilted and crowned by two large pink-circled aureoles with raised crimson nipples which acted as magnets to his greedy gaze . . .

Also available from Headline

Cremorne Gardens
The Temptations of Cremorne

Omnibus collections
The Complete Eveline
Lascivious Ladies
The Power of Lust
Follies of the Flesh
Forbidden Escapades
Hidden Pleasures, Secret Vices
Wanton Excesses

The Pleasures of Women
The Secrets of Women
The Delights of Women
Love Italian Style
Ecstasy Italian Style
The Lusts of the Borgias
States of Ecstasy
Wanton Pleasures
Amorous Liaisons
Lustful Liaisons
Hidden Rapture
Saucy Habits
Sacred Passions
Love Bites
Eroticon Dreams
Eroticon Desires
The Royal Scandal
Pathways of Pleasure

The Ecstasies of Cremorne

Introduced and edited by
Charlotte Elizabeth Cope-Hornington

HEADLINE

First published in 1992
by HEADLINE BOOK PUBLISHING PLC

10 9 8 7 6 5 4 3 2 1

ISBN 0 7472 3912 6

Typeset by Keyboard Services, Luton
Printed and bound in Great Britain by
HarperCollins Manufacturing, Glasgow

HEADLINE BOOK PUBLISHING PLC
Headline House
79 Great Titchfield Street
London W1P 7FN

The Ecstasies
of Cremorne

INTRODUCTION

The re-publication of the Cremorne chronicles –
Cremorne Gardens, *The Temptations Of Cremorne*
and now *The Ecstasies of Cremorne* [Headline Books,
London] – allows the modern reader unrivalled
access to the real-life romps of the notorious Cremornite fraternity, a secret band of turn-of-the-
century hedonists dedicated to the pleasures of the
flesh.

In the popular mind, the Edwardian age will be
forever fixed with long hot summers and golden
scenes of ladies in trailing dresses being punted
along the river by men in straw boaters and gaily
coloured blazers; of lively music-hall entertainments
with back-stage johnnies fixing assignations with
pretty chorus girls; of the bluff, shrewd Edward VII
whose robust sexual appetites were catered for by a
variety of willing women from the highest echelons of
Society.

After the stern, repressive years of suffocating
Victorian morality, the beginnings of a more relaxed
and understanding philosophy emerged with the dawn
of a new century. The world's very first blue movie, *Le
Tub*, was made in 1897 and Edwardian 'French'
postcards (very tame by today's standards but considered very daring when they first appeared) were

1

furtively purchased by an increasing number of young men. Any breaking of the old taboos was rigorously confined to members of the upper classes, however. As Steve Humphries commented in his fascinating history of sexual manner and mores in Britain between 1900 and 1950 *A Secret World Of Sex* (Sidgwick and Jackson, London): 'all the institutions that really mattered when it came to moulding the minds of young people . . . took a hard line on what was called "promiscuity". Only those who came from either very rich or very poor backgrounds managed to escape this control.'

It has always been the self-induced duty of the governing aristocracy to protect the lower order from their own base instincts. In 1905, when the events described in this novel took place, tremendous efforts were being made by the Establishment to segregate the sexes and promote a strict gospel of restraint and abstinence. These unrealistic attitudes led to a huge demand for 'horn books' such as the *Cremorne* series which led a resistance to the prevailing ethic. For every grave warning against masturbation, petting and intercourse, the underground books and magazines retorted that copulation was the most enjoyable activity in the whole wide world. They examined frankly the actual mechanics of sexuality of which the general public were deliberately kept in ignorance until the sexual liberation of the 1960s finally broke the mould of the old order.

Ostensibly the Cremornites were members of a London dining club set up in 1894 by a wealthy group of lively men-about-town. The truth is that membership was coveted not for the weekly Thursday luncheons, even though the lavish cuisine was prepared by Mrs Hetty Beaconsfield. Ninety years ago she was perhaps the most noted cook in the houses of London Society; her name appeared in *Cremorne Gardens*, as it does in this tale. In truth, men joined the society primarily for the wild parties held in the homes of its founders such as the raffish financier Sir Ronnie Dunn, the sophisticated European and friend of King Edward VII, Count Johann 'Johnny' Gewirtz of Galicia and Max Dalmaine, the latter gentleman being the editor of the monthly club magazine, *The Cremornite*, a scurrilously rude publication in which many saucy stories were recorded. Only recently has a complete set of this journal come to light, discovered three years ago in a refurbished Oxfordshire water mill near Witney. Although the front page cheekily bears the proud *imprimateur* of the Oxford University Press, it was probably composed on the Birmingham presses of Conrad Fingleyson, who made a lucrative living distributing illicit literature in the Midlands. In 1909, no longer able to bribe the previously compliant police forces, he prudently emigrated to France with a considerable fortune and two pretty twenty-three-year-old girls from his factory in Smethwick. He was then forty-seven.

As well as editing *The Cremornite*, Dalmaine (1852–1939) also penned most of the novels which appeared in serial form in the magazine until 1910, when his father-in-law Sir Jasper Muttlebury died leaving a huge inheritance of more than a quarter of a million pounds (almost half a million dollars). His wife wisely insisted on pulling Max away from the fleshpots of London to the quieter setting of their splendid country seat in Sussex.

Several of the protagonists who appeared in the two previous novels in the series appear in this third tale. They include the promiscuous Sir Paul Arkley who regards all the female servants in his household as fair game; his equally hot-blooded daughters Katie and Penny who show us that even in the depths of the country nubile young ladies might indulge in pursuits more exciting than pressing flower and exchanging polite conversation at tea with the vicar; and of course, our hero, the ever-lusty Bob Goggin. There is also a selection of other young people, male and female, all united in their eager quest for erotic joys. For let us be frank – Max Dalmaine's writing is clear and explicit even by the far more liberal standards of the 1990s. Sexual adventure presses hard on the heels of sexual adventure, yet the sheer energy and variety of the many encounters of the close kind ensure that this never becomes exhausting as he writes with a fluency and a refreshing, pungent vitality often missing in other Edwardian 'horn' books (as erotic novels were called during the early years of the twentieth century). It is fortunate indeed that copies of *The Cremornite* have survived to entertain all those broad-minded enough to enjoy the frankness and ingenuity of the magazine's extraordinary parade of erotic exhibitions.

The Ecstasies Of Cremorne, reprinted here for the first time in its full unexpurgated form, will amuse and intrigue a new generation of lovers of gallant literature as well as helping social historians towards a truer understanding of the manners and mores of Edwardian society.

Charlotte Elizabeth Cope-Hornington
Devizes
September, 1992

All thoughts, all passions, all delights.
Whatever stirs this mortal frame,
All are but minister of Love,
And feed his sacred flame.

Samuel Taylor Coleridge

CHAPTER ONE
Art For Art's Sake

'Ladies and gentlemen, we must follow the lead of Henri Toulouse-Lautrec and liberate painting from all its current taboos. He not only set up his easel in a brothel, lifting a corner of the veil that had concealed one section of society, but more importantly worked out a new technique of painting that later generations will, I am sure, use to typify his epoch. He never aimed at prettiness or tenderness for their own sakes – no, what he demanded was accuracy, and he set down on canvas exactly what he saw without evasions, without comment and without distortion.

'Nothing is more terrible than the truth and Toulouse-Lautrec lived his art – even if this meant shutting himself up in a variety of brothels, sleeping with many whores, jeering at convention and cocking a snook at respectable members of Society.'

Dr Osbert Radley-Thatcher, the senior lecturer at St Dominic's School of Art, an exclusive private academy in the heart of London's West End, paused for dramatic effect as he addressed his students. 'Do I shock you? Well, I do not expect my students to immerse themselves in such a noxious *milieu* as Toulouse-Lautrec. But in the painting you are preparing to submit for my critical examination in three weeks time, I want you to keep these ideas in mind.

Few of us may be blessed with the genius of the artist of whom I have just been speaking, but let us attempt to portray what we see with honesty and veracity. I look forward to seeing your efforts.'

And with those stirring words he marched out of the large lecture room. One of his most attentive pupils, young Bob Goggin, sighed as he put away his notebook. He looked around at his fellow students. Most ranged from the middle-aged to the elderly, and appeared to be sober representatives of the professional and upper commercial classes, unlike Bob whose lowly occupation was that of under-gardener at the palatial country seat of the Arkley family. His secret liaison with Penny, the luscious younger daughter of Sir Paul and the formidable Lady Laetitia Arkley, had led him to the hallowed portals of St Dominic's as Penny had persuaded her father Sir Paul, a self-styled patron of the arts, to give Bob three months' paid leave of absence during the Spring of 1905 to see whether his artistic career [see 'The Temptations of Cremorne' – *Editor*] could be better served by a course at this fashionable institution.

Although Sir Paul was not over-pleased to lose Bob's services even temporarily, let alone give the young gardener enough for board and lodging during his studies as well as paying the fees of one hundred guineas to St Dominic's, Penny approached her Papa at just the right moment. Right for her, one might add, but quite wrong for Sir Paul. At the time he was locked upstairs in his study with his trousers and drawers in a crumpled heap round his ankles, having his cock sucked by Helene, the nubile young parlour-maid who the Arkleys had just taken into service.

10

Rather than let the gorgeous girl release his pulsating prick from between her lips, Sir Paul would have gladly promised Penny almost anything to make her go back to the drawing room and leave the raven-haired Helene to complete her unfinished business. Alas, the poor girl could not swallow her master's copious creamy emission and no doubt the Chinese rug upon which she was kneeling to this day bears the stains of Sir Paul's spunk, but if space allows, the liaison between the randy baronet and the equally lusty serving wench will be chronicled in more detail at a later stage in this narrative.

So Bob Goggin was in a reflective mood as he prepared to leave St Dominic's. Am I out of my depth here, he wondered thoughtfully. Perhaps it would it be best just to return home, he said to himself, back to his native little town of Greenford where dear old Uncle Felix was forever promising a good job with prospects in his house-building business. Or there was the other option open to him – to return to Arkley Manor and live the simple country life in the beautiful Sussex Downs where Penny's luscious body (as well as those of several other girls) awaited his pleasure. But he decided against both these faint-hearted courses; nothing good is easy, he muttered as he locked his case and prepared to leave.

'Oh, I don't know about that,' a cheerful deep voice came cutting through his reverie. 'What about drinking? Now that's something that's very good and pretty damned easy!' Bob spun round to see the burly figure of Gary Hornby, one of the few students in the class of about his own age, standing behind him. 'Come on, young Bob, it can't be as bad as all that, what's troubling you?' asked this bearded, well-dressed gentleman, clapping a hand on Bob's shoulder.

'Something and nothing, I suppose. Perhaps it's just that when I look at some of the great pictures in the National Gallery and then look at some of my work I think, how do I have the audacity even to call myself an artist?' said Bob, with a little smile.

'*Phoeey*, you'll drive yourself crazy if you start comparing yourselves with the old masters,' said Gary Hornby vigorously. 'Of course neither you nor I will ever be another Velasquez, da Vinci, Constable or whoever – but we can still paint for our own amusement and if others appreciate our art, well, so much the better. Now, I insist on your coming to my club for a bite of lunch where a bottle of the house claret will soon put you right.'

Bob hesitated but the affable Mr Hornby pressed his invitation. 'Come on, don't be shy. I have been meaning to ask you to come out with me for ages. We're not complete strangers, you know – I was down at Arkley Manor last summer with Katie Arkley's old beau Clive Bull, the young financial wizard, for a tennis weekend. Clive's an old chum of mine from way back and he told me all about your dalliance with Katie's sister Penny. No, don't worry, my lips are sealed – on the understanding that you join me for lunch!'

His easy informality put Bob at ease and the younger man overcame his initial shyness and said: 'Fair enough, I'd love to have lunch with you. Is your club far from here?'

'No, only ten minutes' walk at most,' said Mr

Hornby and so they strode out together and made their way down Bond Street. 'I'll wager it was Penny Arkley who persuaded her Papa to fork out for your course at St Dominic's – am I right? Yes? I thought so, both the girls can twirl their Papa round their little fingers like most pretty daughters.

'I hope it gives you a leg-up, Bob, and gets you out of the Arkley's garden – Penny's very fond of you, you know. I've seen your work and you've certainly got more idea about design than I have, though that's not saying much.'

'Then why are you studying at St Dominic's? Are you a keen artist?' asked Bob.

'Not exactly,' cheerfully admitted his companion. 'I'm here because of my late maternal grandfather. He was the famous textile magnate, Sir Alex Luton. Now photography has always been my great hobby but the old boy had this fixation that I had the ability to be one of the greatest photographers in the world. When he kicked the bucket last year he left me a hundred and seventy-five thousand pounds in his will but only on condition that I took a summer course in fine arts at St Dominics. Well, I had planned to go to New York for a good summer's fucking with Molly Farquhar but for a hundred and seventy-five thousand smackers I'd stand naked all summer in the courtyard at Buckingham Palace and waggle my cock at the Queen's bedroom! Actually, I don't think she would mind too much as they say that between Lillie Lang-try, Lady Goldhill and Mrs Keppel, old Tum-Tum *[the nickname given to King Edward VII – Editor]* finds it difficult these days to give his wife more than his kind regards in bed.'

'Yes, I remember hearing about a wild party Sir Paul Arkley went to in Mayfair a few years ago given by some foreign gentleman at which the King was present when he was Prince of Wales,' said Bob.

Gary Hornby gave a short chuckle as they turned into Piccadilly. 'You must be referring to Count Gewirtz's Green Street orgy. *[see* 'Cremorne Gardens' *for an extremely detailed description of this affair! – Editor.]* They say that the prettiest chorus girls from the Alhambra music hall were queuing in line to be fucked by the Prince, whilst the opera singer Vazelina Volpe was sucking his balls. I also heard that Arthur McCann, the explorer, had a dildo shoved up his arse by mistake by one of the girls and he couldn't sit down for a week after. But how did you get to hear about it, Bob?'

'Another of the guests, the Italian violinist, Signor Bernardo Rubino, came down a couple of weeks later to give a recital at Arkley Manor. One of our parlourmaids heard him reminiscing with Sir Paul about what happened at the Green Street party.'

'It goes to show you that you can't keep anything secret these days. Oh well, so long as it's never written down I suppose the King will be able to sleep easily,' ruminated Gary Hornby as they reached the portals of the Rawalpindi Club in Albemarle Street.

Bob Goggin cast his eyes down his clean but cheaply made suit. 'I'm not really dressed for such a posh place as a West End club,' he murmured. 'Oh don't be daft,' said his new friend. 'We have a wide cross-section of members across the complete spectrum of Society, from members of the House of Lords to champion jockeys.' A uniformed flunkey took their hats, coats and cases and Gary signed in his visitor in a leather-bound book which was placed on a beautiful Louis XIV table in the hallway. 'There are a couple of quaint customs we have at the Rawalpindi about which I'd better explain,' said Gary as he guided Bob towards the bar. 'For a start, members never shake hands with each other or their guests.'

'They never shake hands?' said Bob in surprise.

'No, not with each other at any time and we never take our hats off to other members either. But it's handshaking we're out to stop. The whole business dates back from when right hands held daggers or could draw swords and to place your hand in the keeping of another was to clear yourself of any dangerous intention or ability. Well, that's all right as far as it goes but don't you get fed up with the hearty bone-crushing grip? Mind, it's hardly worse than the flabby unmanly touch of fingers which leaves such a bad impression. So we've decided to abolish the practice completely within these walls and between members of the club.'

'How interesting,' said Bob. 'Now are there any other strange rules I should know about? I don't want to put my foot in it.'

'There is a tradition about first-time guests' duties such as yourself,' replied Gary with a wolfish grin. 'But it's entirely optional. Let's have lunch first and I'll tell you later, but I don't think you will find the task too onerous.'

The club was crowded that day and as Gary had not made a prior reservation, the only available table was near the doors to the kitchen. 'Can't you get me a better table than this, Jackson?' he complained to the head waiter. 'I'm sorry, Mr Hornby, but we're very busy this morning. Anyhow, you know what they say in the East – *ober az me zitst bay'm tepl, es men besser.* I'll see you right, don't fret.'

When the waiter had left them Bob asked: 'What did he say? Was that an old oriental saying?' 'Not exactly, it means the nearer the pot, the better you eat and the vernacular comes from Aldgate East,' commented Gary wryly. 'Still, the grub's usually good here on Tuesdays when members bring in guest cooks from their homes. Today I think Lord Bellamy has the great Mrs Bickler preparing the luncheons so we should be in for a real treat.'

Jackson was as good as his word – after all, Gary Hornby was known as one of the most generous members of the Rawalpindi when it came to slipping staff gratuities for service above and beyond the high standards expected of all employees. The two men enjoyed the best of Mrs Bickler's prandial extravaganza, which comprised of caviare, tomato and basil soup, fillets of sole in a white wine, grenadines of veal with Italian cream, a superb coq au vin followed by ice-cream with a selection of fresh fruit including strawberries, pineapples and peaches.

This sumptuous meal was washed down not with the house claret but by two bottles of '98 Moet et Chandon champagne. Gary insisted on ordering two large brandies as they moved away from their table into the club lounge where comfortable seats by the window and a steaming pot of coffee awaited them. 'Thank you very much, Mr Hornby,' said Jackson with genuine thanks as he pocketed the half sovereign which had been slipped into his hand. After a quiet few minutes, during which the two men sipped their cognac, Bob poured out two cups of coffee and said: 'Gary, what is this second custom of the Rawalpindi Club regarding visitors which you mentioned before lunch?'

'Ah yes, *jus primae visitate*, as we call it. Well, old boy, the simple fact of the matter is this – did you see the pretty blonde girl who was in charge at the enquiries desk when we came into the club?'

'I'll say I did – what a smashing looker too if you don't mind my saying so,' grinned Bob.

'No, not at all – and Lizzie will be pleased to hear such a compliment. For she is central to the business of the little task we expect our visitors to perform. It is true that Lizzie is a bright, most attractive young woman but, alas, two years ago she suffered a great misfortune. Her husband, who is in the police force, was badly injured in an accident on Hampstead Heath when a runaway horse trampled upon him and, not to put too fine a point upon it, left him a eunuch.'

Bob winced and commented: 'How absolutely terrible! What a shocking fate to befall any man. I'm sure that Scotland Yard took up a collection for him, and that his fellow constables gave generously to make up a good sum.'

'Yes, though no doubt more money would have been collected and far more sympathy would have been evoked for Philip if he had been injured in the course of duty and not have been lying down on his back, licking out the cunney of Lizzie's younger sister Margaret, who was sitting on his face with her drawers down and sucking his cock at the time of the accident. In more normal circumstances he might

17

have been able to move away more smartly and so would have escaped such serious injuries.

'Anyhow, the point I am making is this – Lizzie is very fond of fucking and so after the accident the executive committee decided that all male visitors would offer their cocks to the girl who would be given the opportunity to suck and/or fuck them if she so desired. She has yet to turn down any first-time visitor to the Rawalpindi and indeed each time our mutual friend, Count Gewirtz, comes into the club he swears that it is his first visit! Oh, I mustn't forget to add that these charitable couplings are kept in the strictest confidence. Anyone who spilt the beans would be expelled from the Rawalpindi and blackballed from any other club in England.

'Well, Bob, are you game? I'll let you into a little secret – on my instructions, Jackson passed a note across to Lizzie and she would be very grateful if you would be kind enough to go up to room eighteen on the second floor and fuck her as soon as possible.'

'It's the very least I can do,' declared Bob, rising to his feet. 'But it would not be polite to leave you here –'

'No, no, I am in no way inconvenienced,' assured his host. 'I have an assignation myself at four o'clock with Lady Estelle Bunbury. Sir Michael is out of London until Thursday, which allows her to see gentlemen friends at her leisure. Gad, Estelle is a randy girl, Bob! She's almost insatiable. As soon as I come into her house, she's unbuttoning my flies and taking out my cock to suck. We always spend at least three hours fucking away like a couple possessed. I just do not know how such a slightly built girl can possess such a robust constitution because she is always ready for more when, quite honestly, I am at the point of total exhaustion. However, this is a problem with which I can happily live, though doubtless it must be one of the reasons why Sir Michael leaves town for recuperative trips to the country so often.

'Look, come to my rooms for supper tonight at eight o'clock. I am staying at Lady Colchfoster's London residence in Bedford Square.' With those words, Gary Hornby heaved himself up and made ready to make his way to Lady Bunbury's mansion in Belgravia.

So, feeling somewhat nervous, Bob made his way cautiously up the staircase to room eighteen as instructed. He knocked on the door and a sensuously soft voice bade him enter. He slowly opened the door and his eyes roved around the richly decorated bedroom, lushly furnished in the finest of silks and satins. But the *pièce de résistance* was the wide double bed upon which Lizzie was languidly lying. He stood still, drinking in the delicious beauty of the girl, her pert mass of light blonde hair, her exquisite cornflower blue eyes and tiny nose that set off generously wide red lips and a smile showing pearly white rows of teeth that would have melted the heart of the fiercest red-blooded man in England.

'Close the door behind you, Bob,' said this heavenly apparition, sliding off the bed and walking towards him. She was dressed in a loosely fitting white dress, though her feet were bare and the sunlight that poured through the high windows made the fine cotton of her frock almost transparent. Lizzie took his

hand and gently moved him forward to sit on the bed.
'Would you like some tea? Or maybe a glass of
champagne? Or an iced drink perhaps? I know we
should be thankful for such nice weather but it
becomes so stiflingly hot in town that wearing even
the lightest clothes becomes a nuisance. Don't you
agree?'

Bob cleared his throat and managed to blurt out a
reply: 'Yes, and it's especially uncomfortable for men
on a day like this when we are forced to wear vests,
shirts and jackets.'

'Well, don't be bashful, Bob, do take them off and
walk around *au naturel* and I promise that you will
feel so free and unshackled without the restraint of
unnecessarily covering your body which, I am sure,
would look even better undraped,' she dimpled
sweetly.

And to show that she practised what she preached,
Lizzie loosened the strings and unhooked her dress so
that it fell to the floor and she stood in glorious nudity.
Bob could not prevent a gasp of excitement from
escaping his lips as he gazed at the firm swell of her
bare breasts, each globe proudly uptilted and crowned by two large pink circled aureoles with raised
crimson nipples which acted as magical magnets to
Bob's gleaming eyes.

He stood transfixed, but the pretty girl acknowledged his timidity by moving towards him and
saying: 'Let us find out for ourselves' and offered up
her mouth to be kissed whilst her hands deftly unbuckled his belt and unbuttoned his trousers before
bringing out his hot, hard penis between her fingers.
She grasped the shaft and murmured: 'Oh, what a

perfectly proportioned prick! It's a real disgrace to keep such a lovely cock hidden away.' And as their lips met, she gently squeezed his stiff shaft, capping and uncapping the bulbous red knob as the handsome young couple exchanged a passionate kiss, their tongues filling each other's mouth, probing, rousing and caressing as Lizzie aided Bob to undress completely. His clothes fell in an untidy heap on the carpet where they were still standing, their mouths glued together as Bob suddenly lifted the trembling girl into his arms and carried her gently to the bed.

They lay there together, still kissing, his hands on her breasts, rubbing her erect red nipples against his fingers. Then her lips broke away to travel downwards, first grazing his nipples before moving downwards towards his throbbing cock. She began by kissing all around it and Bob whimpered as his shaft shook with every kiss. He looked down at the tousled mass of blonde hair between his legs as her wet tongue shot out to lick his rampant rammer and he groaned as her tongue continued to flick and tease the sensitive underside skin. She took pity upon the handsome youth and, after a quick dampening lick on his purple helmet, she opened her mouth and proceeded to suck in at least three inches of his twitching tool between her lips.

Lizzie adored sucking her lovers' cocks and Bob was in the seventh heaven of delight as her moist mouth worked up and down, licking and lapping his entire length, her hand grasping the base of his staff as she pumped her head up and down, keeping her lips taut, sucking lustily until she suddenly paused and pulled her lips away. Some pre-spend juice had oozed out of the tiny 'eye' on Bob's knob and her darting pink tongue instantly lapped it up. One of her hands now gently massaged his balls and the other clamped itself around his shaft as she jammed her mouth over the uncapped mushroomed dome of his pulsating prick and slurped lustily away on her fleshy lollipop.

The sensation was delightful for Bob and all too soon he felt the rush of sperm flowing up inexorably from his balls. With a hoarse cry, he jerked his hips upwards, sending a stream of gushy spunk crashing into Lizzie's throat. She gurgled delightedly and continued frenziedly to suck and with great gulps to swallow every last drop of his milky emission until his cock ceased its pulsing agitation. He sank back sated but his tool only shrank slightly into a semi-erectness as the gorgeous girl refused to release his wet shaft from her mouth. She washed his knob with her tongue as she rubbed his shaft between the palms of her hands. Perhaps it had been the enforced absence of Penny and his lack of opportunity to meet any other girl (except an occasional visit of the five fingered widow!) but in no time at all Bob's shaft was standing almost as high as before. It took but a few wet caresses from Lizzie's tongue before his cock was ramrod straight and straining for action.

Then, without a word, Lizzie fell back to lie beside him, arching herself like a sleek kitten as Bob scrambled to his knees to position himself between her thighs. He started his love-making by kissing her feet, her ankles, her calves and knees and then as he started to kiss her inner thighs, his hands massaging her divinely full breasts, Lizzie parted her legs as far as possible to fully expose her silky flaxen bush of pussey hair and the pouting cunney lips between which jutted out her excited erect clitty which stood out like a miniature cock. Bob buried his head between her legs and sucked deeply on her open cunt. He flicked his lips in and out between her cunney lips and then he brought down his right hand from her titties to roll her clitty between his thumb and forefinger. Lizzie squealed happily as he buried his face in her blonde brush, now moving both arms round to grasp her rounded buttocks as he flashed his tongue around her dampening crack. She squealed again as, inhaling the tangy feminine aroma from her pussey, Bob slipped his probing tongue between her cunney lips, flicking against her clitty as he licked rhythmically away in long, thrusting strokes. Love juices were now flowing from her and Lizzie moaned: 'Oh, fuck me, Bob, fuck me!' He looked up and saw that she was clutching and pinching her own nipples and Bob wondered if he had sent the sweet girl too far forwards towards the plateau of paradise.

So Bob pulled his head back abruptly and turned the quivering girl face downwards, grabbing a pillow to insert under her belly so that her hips and delicious bum cheeks were raised high in the air. He moved purposefully between her legs, nudging her knees further apart as he took his thick prick in his hand and slicked his fist up and down the glistening shaft as both her wrinkled little rear dimple and her cunt waited for his arrival.

Lizzie turned her pretty face towards him and said with a saucy grin: 'This will be nice – I just love being fucked from behind, Bob, but I'd prefer it if you would leave my bum-hole for another time. I want to

23

feel every inch of your big cock in my tight little cunney.'

'Your wish is my command, though as it happens I was always going in that direction as I never go up a girl's bum without first asking prior permission,' said Bob gallantly as he carefully guided his bared knob slowly into her sopping slit from behind, easing every inch of his shaft into her welcoming wetness until he was comfortably ensconced inside her and his balls were brushing the back of her thighs.

He now leaned forward so that his hairy chest was pressed against her back as he reached round and toyed with her proud breasts, holding them in a firm grip as he began to slick his shaft in and out of her juicy cunt. Lizzie moved her hips in rhythm with his thrusts so that with every plunge forward, Bob's shaft was fully ensheathed in her warm, clinging wetness. They enjoyed a most pleasurable fuck as Lizzie's wriggling bum spurred Bob on to faster and deeper thrusts, his shaft sliding to and fro along the lubricated walls of her cunney, though he was able to feel his foreskin being drawn backwards and forwards with every shove.

Lizzie's plump buttocks slapped sensuously against Bob's thighs as the throbbing and contracting of her cunney muscles on his enraptured shaft spurred him to further efforts. Bob looked with relish at his glistening prick see-sawing in and out of Lizzie's cunney, above which the little brown rosebud of her arsehole quivered and winked with each push. As they approached the heights, Bob changed the tempo of his fucking to one of swift, short jabs as Lizzie rotated her bottom lasciviously as he pulsed in and out of her squelchy cunt. They climaxed together as his cock squirted fierce jets of spunk which mingled with her own stream of pussey juice and their love liquids dripped down onto the sheet.

Bob fell on top of the trembling girl and they sank down onto the comfort of the silk sheets, totally exhausted, entwined in each other's arms to enjoy the divine lethargy that envelops body and soul after making love. Neither had noticed that whilst they had been engaged in their frantic fucking, Jackson the waiter had quietly entered the room and set up a table upon which he had placed a selection of dainty sandwiches, fruits, orange juice and a bottle of champagne in an ice-bucket (all provided by the ever-generous Gary Hornby) before making an equally stealthy exit. Although Bob had consumed a large luncheon, the worship of Venus and Priapus acts as a healthy stimulation of the appetite and the couple ate and drank their way through an informal tea, sitting up naked on the bed.

'Lizzie, there's something I would like to know,' Bob began but before he could complete his sentence the pretty girl shook her blonde tresses and giggled: 'I can read your mind, Bob Goggin, you don't have to continue. You are going to ask me what a nice girl like me is doing behaving in the way I do.' Bob looked shocked and smiled ruefully as he admitted: 'Well, I wasn't going to put it in quite so baldly but I suppose that would be the gist of what I was going to ask.'

'It's simple really,' sighed Lizzie. 'I was badly betrayed by my husband and until I find another man who I am very, *very* sure that I can trust, I am not going to let myself become involved with any man.

But until that happens I do not see why I should live the life of a nun. I am a healthy young woman with normal desires and as Philip is incapable of satisfying these needs, I must look elsewhere. Now I know how you men stick together, Bob, but you mustn't feel sorry for Philip. It is true that he was severely punished for his infidelity but he has only himself to blame for what occurred.'

'I know that,' said Bob sympathetically. 'Gary Hornby told me all about how Philip's philandering led to the accident on Hampstead Heath. Yet surely you would agree that fate dealt cruelly with him for just one mad afternoon of illicit nookie?'

'Ah, but you are only familiar with the very end of the story,' retorted Lizzie. 'Are you interested in hearing the full account of my intimate history? I'd like to tell you as I wouldn't want a nice lad like you to think badly of me.'

Bob hastened to assure her that he could never think ill of such a sweet creature and he settled down to hear Lizzie's confession . . .

She sipped at her glass of champagne and said: 'I was born and brought up in Chelsea. My dad was killed in a train accident before my second birthday but my mum married again, to a very nice neighbour whose wife had been fatally injured in the same crash *[probably the South Wimbledon disaster of 1886 – Editor]*. He had been left with a little girl even younger than me and with the compensation money my stepfather took over *The Dirty Duck*, a public house off the Fulham Road in Chelsea, which was patronised by many artists – this is how, by the by, I first came to hear of the Rawalpindi Club which has many painters, writers and musicians amongst its members. Anyhow, by the time I was eighteen years old I had been propositioned many times by customers and I'd posed for several of the artists, though never in the nude and always with my mother there acting as a chaperone. Mind, I'd slipped out occasionally to meet boy friends though I'd never gone further than kissing and cuddling though I'd let one or two slip their hands inside my blouse and feel my breasts and the more daring had taken my hand and made me rub their stiff cocks through the material of their trousers.

'Then shortly after my eighteenth birthday, when I was working full-time as a barmaid, I developed a crush on this handsome young policeman who would pop into the bar almost every day and was given a free drink. To be absolutely fair, he did offer to pay for his refreshment but my stepfather always insisted that whatever I served him was "on the house". This surprised me as we ran the bar very strictly and, on my stepfather's instruction, my half sister Maggie lettered and coloured a sign that read "Please do not ask for credit as a refusal often offends" which was displayed prominently by the till. When I tackled my stepfather about this he winked at me and said: "Lizzie my girl, always keep on the right side of the police and you won't go far wrong."

'So when the good-looking constable told me his name, which was Philip Greecer, and asked me if I would like to go to Walham Green music hall with him that evening, I was pleased and flattered by his interest. My stepfather had no objection and so off we went. Well, Philip was the perfect gentleman that night and even on our second date he only kissed me chastely on the cheek when we said good-night. But one afternoon on his day off he took me for a walk near Stamford Bridge and we finished up in his room at the station-house where he lived. We sat together and Philip kept staring at the front of my frilly blouse – it was a warm day and I had undone the two top buttons so he could see the swell of my breasts – but though he kept his arm round my shoulders he seemed to wait for some sign of encouragement before going any further.

'I wanted to kiss him but was unsure myself how to react. So I snuggled myself into his chest and rested my head against his shoulder. This lit the fuse! He lifted my face and kissed me so passionately on the lips which fairly sucked the breath out of my heaving lungs. In a trice his hand slipped from my shoulder to down underneath my arm and I felt it close gently over my breast. I made no attempt to pull away as the emboldened boy unbuttoned my blouse and shrugged it off me. He pulled down the straps of my chemise and let my bosoms spill out. For the first time my naked titties were exposed to a man's hands and oh, I have to admit that Philip was a smooth lover. As we kissed, his tongue entered my mouth and at the same time he ran his hands lightly over my bare breasts, tracing circles around my erect nipples with the tips of his fingers. Then he disengaged his mouth from mine and bent down to take one of my rosy little nips in his mouth and the wet friction of his tongue made me tingle all over as he licked and lapped it, making me shiver all over with pleasure.

'Now his hands were under my skirt and I could feel

28

them tugging at my knickers. I raised my bottom to let him pull them down and I felt incredibly aroused as he played with my pussey, rubbing and tickling until it became damp. Then he raised his head to kiss me again on the mouth as he put his left arm round me so that one hand could caress my breasts whilst the other remained between my legs. I crossed my thighs to trap his hand as he started stroking lightly on my bush with his thumb while his fingers probed the lips of my cunney. Then I quivered all over as his thumb found my magic button and he started to rub my clitty so beautifully and at that moment I was so incredibly aroused that I knew for sure that I would let him go as far as he wanted.

'I opened my thighs as his fingers parted the folds of my now very wet cunney and felt totally uninhibited as he pulled open my love-lips and rubbed his knuckles back and forth across the entrance to my now sopping slit. Then as he eased a finger into my cunt I sighed and raised my bum to push my pussey against his face, trembling all over as a thrilling kind of electric current surged through me. This one finger was soon joined by another and then a third as Philip began to finger-fuck at an ever increasing pace. What blissful agony as he toyed with my erect, pulsating clitty! I was on the verge of spending but the wicked man always cunningly stopped just in time. "More, Philip, more!" I gasped but the clever copper had other plans and he paused at this stage to unbutton my skirt and help me take off my chemise and my stockings so that I was now completely nude. He tore off his own clothes and scooped me up in his arms and carried me into his bedroom where he lay me down

29

gently on his divan and we exchanged a long, lingering kiss.

'By now I was completely carried away and I reached down to grasp his rock hard cock and rubbed my hand up and down his veiny shaft. Meanwhile Philip eased his hand back between my unprotesting legs and ruffled the soft down of my blonde muff before reopening my juicy crack. I let go of his prick as he placed his body between my legs and leaned forward to let his tongue flicker tormentingly along the length of my slit.

'"Oh Philip," I cried out. "Push your big prick inside me!" as he let the very tip of his huge red knob touch my dripping lips.

'"Are you certain, Lizzie? I can tell by my finger fucking that you've played with yourself, but I'll lay odds that you've never had a man's tool up your cunney channel. Now, my girl, both of us have to be sure that you really want it."

'"Yes, yes, yes!" I cried. "I want you to fuck me, Philip. Slide your big cock in my cunt, I want it more than anything else in the world." And to show that I meant what I said, I took his monster tool (the first naked cock I had ever handled) in both my hands and guided it towards my pussey lips.

'I was now so juicy that even Philip's enormous tadger slipped easily into my virgin love-hole as my own jism dribbled down my thighs. He slid his cock slowly into my cunney and met no resistance – the horse-riding lessons that Maggie and I attended to every Saturday morning had ruptured my hymen six months before – and Philip slipped in and out very deliberately which created a huge suction from my cunt. I was getting more and more excited and my movements were getting more and more agitated especially when he began fingering between the cheeks of my bum. At first I tensed up but after a few seconds I began to get used to it and as he pushed his cock harder and faster into my cunney, at the same time his finger pushed just inside my arsehole. His finger and cock worked together; while his shaft was all the way inside, his finger was outside my bum and then he would plunge it in up to the first knuckle as he withdrew his tool.

'This drove us both wild and I threshed around like crazy as Philip began pumping into me with great swinging thrusts as my buttocks arched up and he clasped my bum cheeks as we fucked away like people possessed. They say that imagination is more important than knowledge and though I was enjoying a cock in my cunt for the first time, I knew that by contracting my cunney muscles, I would feel even more of his gorgeous prick against the velvety walls of my vagina.

'I sensed his build-up approaching as his hairy balls slapped against my thighs which were soaking wet with my spendings. "Spunk into me, Philip," I heard myself call out as though another new Lizzie had taken possession of me. "Fill my cunt with sticky sperm, you randy fucker!" These lewd words carried him over the precipice and his prick began to throb violently before it shot out spasm after spasm of creamy spunk into my very vitals.

'How I enjoyed that first fuck! I screamed aloud as I climaxed immediately afterwards, my saturated clitty sending shudders of exquisite joy all over my body. What a sublime moment! I was in Paradise, swimming in a sea of pleasure, and the knowledge that I had finally crossed the Rubicon into womanhood, I am sure, added a piquancy to the fucking.'

The pretty girl paused to finish her champagne and Bob sat entranced by her articulate account of the loss of her virginity. 'Do go on, Lizzie,' he said encouragingly. 'You tell the story so graphically that just listening to the tale has given me a boner!' And he threw back the eiderdown to expose his tremendous erection which stood up in the air like a flagpole. Lizzie leaned across to plant a succulent wet kiss on his uncapped helmet before finishing her confession.

'I thanked Philip for his marvellous love-making but I was worried as his shaft was speckled with blood. "No need to fret, Lizzie," he assured me. "That is only the remains of your virginity." He tenderly wiped my still pouting pussey lips with a handkerchief which he said he would always treasure as a momento of the occasion.

'We fucked a great deal after that (although we were as careful as possible to miss the times that could cause my belly to swell up) and Philip taught me how to suck a cock which again was new to me. Then one afternoon my mother caught us in the act in my bedroom and Philip proposed to me that very evening. We were married a few months later and when he was transferred to North London, we were given a nice little police house near Chalk Farm.

'Now my half sister Maggie visited us every weekend because she loved to hire a horse and ride along Hampstead Heath. Looking back it was surprising that I did not think it strange that more often than not she would come up to the house when I had been called back to Fulham Road to lend a hand behind the bar. Yet my suspicions were not aroused until I returned home one afternoon and as I turned the key in the lock I herd a scuffling sound as if someone had been disturbed by my entrance. Philip came bounding down the stairs looking dishevelled to say the least in his shirt and trousers, his hair rumpled and his collar and tie missing. "Hello darling, we, I mean I didn't expect you back so soon," he said breathlessly. "Wasn't it busy at the pub?"

'"No, we were very quiet so Dad told me to go home," I replied and before I could say anything more, Philip added: "Maggie's upstairs, by the way, she's in the bathroom right now. I took her for a walk on the Heath and I'm just getting changed as I'm on duty at five o'clock. Time for a cup of tea first though, let me put the kettle on as you've been on your feet all day." His thoughtfulness and the deceitfully loving demeanour of my half sister smoothed away any thoughts of concern which might have lurked in my mind.

'And indeed, I may never have known that Philip was playing away from home if that very evening I had not decided to spring clean our bedroom whilst my cheating husband was supposedly walking the beat in Hampstead High Street. For wrapped in a copy of the *Police Gazette* was a love letter to Philip from that little minx Maggie, who had only just turned eighteen years old. She gloatingly describes all about the marvellous birthday present of an afternoon's fucking and sucking she received from him.

'Look, Bob, I have the letter here in the drawer of

33

the bedside table. Read it whilst I run a bath for us as I'm sure you feel as hot and sticky as I do after our lovely fucking. It will explain why I have not spoken to Maggie since the accident.'

She rolled over and passed Bob an envelope out of the drawer in question, kissing him on the end of his nose as he took out the cream sheets of paper and began his perusal of Maggie's *billet doux* to her illicit lover.

Bob began to read as follows:

Dearest Phil,

It is nearly midnight but I am finding it so difficult to sleep for my body is aching for the throb of your glorious cock in my juicy love-hole. How can I ever thank you for the lovely afternoon we spent together on the Heath? Now I must make a confession to you, darling, I have always been strongly attracted to you. Often when we have been alone I have been greatly tempted to lunge across the table, give you a long wet kiss and unbutton your trousers and get my hands around your delicious, thick cock.

Do I shock you by my candour? Well, I may only have celebrated my eighteenth birthday last Thursday but I have always enjoyed being fuck-ed ever since I was first introduced to the joys of love-making by old Cecil Osram, the grocer from Upper Phillimore Gardens who, unbe-known to my parents, threaded me in the back room of his shop almost a year ago. And I will freely admit that I was determined to seduce you ever since we got to know each other and when you welcomed my suggestion that we meet at your house after my riding lesson, I guessed that you would not be averse to a little naughtiness . . .

I planned the whole scenario with care. After I left the stables I took extra time to make myself as desirable as I knew how – and I knew at once I had succeeded when after you let me in and we were standing in the hallway. Oh, Philip, I will never forget the look on your face when I took off my coat and presented myself to you. There I stood, dressed only in a white singlet and tight, pale-blue riding trousers. I had pulled the broad leather belt as tight as possible so that when I bent down, as I did straightaway to pick up my handbag (which of course I had deliberately dropped), the denim would stretch tautly over the firm, full rounded cheeks of my strapping young bottom.

I was feeling so horny that I wanted you to fuck me then and there but I could hardly blurt out that my pussey was already juicing up, could I? So I told you that I needed to tone up my muscles after my ride and that would like to perform a series of exercises. 'Perhaps you would like to join me?' I said, and as soon as you agreed I knew that I had you in my thrall. 'I had better go upstairs and slip into something more suitable,' you said and I made my way into the lounge whilst you were changing. I stood with my back to the door facing the mirror and kicked off my shoes. Then I sat down and pulled off my socks and when I heard you coming down the stairs I scrambled to my feet and began performing my warm-up exercise, bending as far forward as possible so that my bottom cheeks would be stuck up lasciviously as you entered the room. I stayed bending forward in this position when I saw your reflection in the mirror and then I looked through my legs at you standing stock-still in the doorway. How strong and masculine you appeared to me, Philip, as you leaned back against the wall dressed only in your athletic singlet and football shorts, your arms folded across your muscular chest with a look of undisguised lust across your face.

I thought to myself how enjoyable it would be to run my tongue all over your body and I could feel my pussey begin to moisten as I continued my warm-up slowly, enjoying the sight of you watching me and your steely eyes told me that as you gazed at my wriggling bum that the warmest part of your body was the meaty bulge in your shorts that looked so inviting to my eyes. I ran my arms over my breasts after I touched my toes and then I hugged my ankles, peeking at you again from between my legs. The bulge was getting bigger, I thought, so I stood up straight and said coyly: 'Philip, I hope you won't mind but I would like to undress a little. It's so jolly hot in here that I'm perspiring before we've even prop-erly started.' In fact my pussey muscles had already begun to clamp together and I knew that the only way to calm them was by letting out the orgasm which was locked inside my loins. I rubbed my crotch with my hand but that only made things worse – so I looked you squarely in the face and said: 'I think I'll need you to help me relax. You will help, won't you?'

The excited brightness in your eyes made it obvious that there was no need to wait for an answer, so without further unnecessary words I unbuttoned my singlet and, raising my arms, tugged it off above my head. I heard you gasp as you caught sight of my bouncy, uptilted breasts which almost spilled out of their tight fitting bodice cups of white cotton. You let out a low growl of approval as I unbuckled my belt and rolled down my skin hugging riding trousers. I stepped out of them and your gaze was riveted on my matching brief knickers. At the front, where the white material was drawn into a narrow triangle between my legs, my swell of my pubic mound was clearly visible, the curly, thatch of pussey hair showing darkly through the thinly woven cotton.

I moved purposefully towards you and with one strong motion you grabbed me and mashed your mouth against mine. Our tongues met and wiggled deliciously against each other as you tore off my bodice and pressed my bare breasts against your manly chest. Then, still glued to each other, we wobbled drunkenly to the sofa and your hands roamed freely across my body. What thrills of erotic passion coursed through my body when your powerful hands squeezed my breasts and when your wet lips found my erect nipples, Oh! how lustily you sucked them inside your mouth and flicked the hard little cherries from side to side with your tongue. The palm of your hand now rubbed against my clitty so I lifted my bum to enable you to rip off my knickers. As you caressed me down there I could not help biting your shoulder as I felt the pent-up beginning of a spend breaking out from my ever-dampening pussey.

"Oooh!" I squeaked delightedly as you press-ed your lips even more firmly against mine and your hand wandered through my furry pouch, your fingertips tracing tiny circles around my cunney lips before your fingers parted the folds of my now sopping pussey and slipped into my love-channel. How quickly you made me spend, dipping your fingers in and out of my honeypot, rubbing your thumb against my clitty which drove me onwards to ecstasy. I remember franti-cally jerking my hips at a frenetic pace as I humped my cunt against your fingers and how I thrilled all over as I spent, the love juices pouring out of my pussey and over your hand.

But now the moment about which I had dreamed of for so long had finally arrived! I was going to be fucked by your big cock! I trembled all over as I sat up and pulled you up to your feet to stand in front of me. You guessed what I wanted you to do and you ripped off your singlet. I took hold of your shorts and eased them down-wards, letting out an excited gasp of joy as your gorgeous veiny pole sprang out in all its naked glory to stand stiffly against your belly. I passed my tongue hungrily over my lips at the sight of your throbbing monster and pulled you forward by your prick so that I could touch the shiny red knob of your cockshaft with my lips.

Oh Philip, can you remember the delicious emotions that coursed through your veins when I smothered your cock with smacking wet kisses, fondling it lovingly, rubbing its velvety smoothness against my cheeks before popping it into my mouth and closing my lips on your helmet, sliding its throbbing fleshiness against my agile tongue. I will never forget how you jerked your hips to and fro, fucking my mouth with your twitching tool, your breath coming in harsh gutteral grunts as I worked on your huge knob, easing my lips forward to take in as much of your enormous staff as I could. This really made you excited and you were moaning with ecstasy as I cupped your hairy bollocks, which hardened under my touch as your rigid rod pulsated convulsively. And then woosh! A veritable jet of juicy sperm hit the back of my throat and I swallowed all your tasty spunk until the fountain eased to a dribble.

"Maggie, you've been a very naughty girl," you murmured. "Now do you know what happens to naughty girls? They get their bottoms spanked!" And as quick as a flash you sat yourself down next to me, and pulled me across your lap, my rounded posterior wobbling as you smoothed your hand across it. No-one had ever smacked my bare bottom before and I winced at first as you slapped my neatly rounded cheeks lightly but rapidly until you said: "There now, your bum cheeks are as red as two rosy apples. I *do love the way your cheeks wobble as I smack them!" You continued spanking me until my bottom was tingling so deliciously that I cried out: "Oh, oh, oh, I am on fire, finish me off, Philip, finish me off by fucking me!" I twisted myself round so that I lay on my shoulders across your knees, feeling your rock-hard cock against my spine. You smiled and slowly slid round so that I now lay on the couch and you lay on top of me. My cunney lips were fairly aching for the magic feel of your cock and you thrust your strong tool straight inside, your balls banging against my bum as I wrapped my legs around your broad back and dug my nails into your shoulders. We lay motionless at first, billing and cooing with our lips until I began a slight motion with my backside to which you were not slow to respond. Your eyes shone with lust as you slowly slicked your iron-hard stiffness in and out of my squelchy honeypot. Then you lay still again, your throbbing cock embedded in my pulsing love channel and then you began to fuck me in earnest, pumping that rigid rammer to and fro and it only took seven or eight strokes before I was twisting away like a crazy woman, clawing your back with my fingernails as you raised the tempo of your thrusts.*

What ecstasy flowed through me as your gorgeous knob worked its way in and out of my welcoming pussey! How it seemed to swell inside my luscious sheath which received it so lovingly! How marvellously you fucked me, pushing that massive monster prick inside me so that in no time at all I screamed with joy as I spent copiously, coating your cock with love juice. I shuddered to my climax as you reached your peak and your frame shivered all over as you spunked so fiercely, washing the walls of my cunt with a flood of creamy sperm making my pussey explode into yet another amazingly powerful orgasm.

You stayed hard in my slippery cunney for a little while and then slowly withdrew, your astonishingly thick prick still hard and glistening with our mingled juices – but though we were both ready for a further round of fornication, you had to leave for work, so you were not given the opportunity to fuck me doggie-style which I now know is one of your favourite positions. Still, you only had to wait a week before we had a further chance to be alone. Oh dearest, I so yearn for the feel of your big cock inside my cunney that I can hardly wait till next Wednesday at noon! I've suggested to my father that we have to do our six-monthly stocktaking that day so Lizzie won't be back home until at least six o'clock which will give us plenty of time to fuck ourselves silly. And don't worry about my sister, Philip, a slice off a cut loaf is never missed.

All my love,
Maggie

Bob handed the letter back to Lizzie with a sigh. 'Your Maggie is a bit of a card,' he commented drily, 'though why your husband kept this letter is beyond

41

me. I suppose he probably enjoyed reading it whilst on patrol on a lonely night or in the police canteen on his tea break.'

'You're absolutely right,' said Lizzie as she put back the letter in the drawer, 'because I quickly found out after the accident that his colleagues knew all about Phil's philanderings. It seems that he was so proud of fucking his sister-in-law that he boasted about it to other bobbies and showed Maggie's letter to anyone who wanted to read it. So now you know why I am taking my pleasures in the way I do. Until our marriage is dissolved, I fuck for fun and frankly I am enjoying it so much I'm not sure that I want to get married again so quickly!'

Now Bob would have enjoyed a further fuck as his cock was standing as stiffly as a Guardsman after reading Maggie's lurid letter but in addition to making him randy, Maggie's salaciousness reminded Bob of his promise to Penny Arkley, his girl friend and generous benefactress, that he would write to her every Thursday afternoon. As he was dining at Gary Hornby's tonight, Bob told Lizzie that sadly he had better join her for a quick bath and then make his leave. The understanding girl kindly relieved his aching tool by tossing him off under the shower, her soapy fingers sliding up and down his shaft until a fountain of spunk jetted out from his knob like lava from a miniature volcano.

'Come and see me again any time you visit the Rawalpindi Club,' said Lizzie as Bob gave her a good-bye kiss. 'Let this be *au revoir* and not *adieu* for you know that you don't have to worry about being embarrassed by what happens in my bedroom.' The young man thanked her warmly for those words for he knew that Lizzie had no shortage of admirers. He left the Rawalpindi and walked back through Mayfair to Bloomsbury for his lodgings were tucked away in a side street fortunately not far from the posh house in Bedford Square which Gary Hornby had rented *[the Edwardians were given to letting houses for a few years or even just for the summer as was probably the case with Mr Hornby – Editor]* so he would not have to stretch his already strained finances any further for a cab home. He was fumbling for his key on the doorstep of Mrs Trenton's Private Guest House when the landlady herself opened the door. 'Good afternoon, Bob, how are you? I'm pleased you've come back because I am just going to the shops and you forgot to tell me if you wanted any supper tonight.'

'Sorry, Mrs Trenton, but I won't be eating in as someone at the art school has invited me out,' said Bob and the landlady, a buxom lady in her mid thirties, chuckled roguishly and said: 'That's nice, who's the lucky lady, one of those model girls who take off all their clothes for the students? Perhaps she'd like to turn the tables and see what you've got to offer.'

Mrs Trenton was always making slightly suggestive remarks like this and Bob grinned: 'There's no lady involved at all, I'm afraid, Mrs T. I've been invited to have dinner with a gentleman in my class at St Dominic's who lives in Bedford Square.'

'Oooh, dining with the toffs, eh? Well, I hope the gentleman concerned isn't one of those nancy boys because there are plenty of them around this part of town. So if I were you, I'd be sure to keep my hand on

my ha'penny, young man.' And with those words of
advice she brushed past him and Bob made his way up
to his room, where he dutifully composed a letter to
Penny, omitting of course everything that had happened after he finished lunch at the Rawalpindi Club!

He sighed as he affixed a postage stamp to the
envelope. Perhaps it takes you otherwise, dear reader, but an unexpected randiness such as Bob had just
experienced with Lizzie, often leads to a rather sober
state of mind. This was certainly true for Bob who
found himself for no apparent reason, in a bit of a
brown study. So he decided to post the latter to Penny
and to take himself down to Shawcross Street to the
public tennis courts where he could sit down on a
bench and watch a game. Thanks to Penny, who had
coached him in tennis as expertly as he had tutored
her in the finer arts of fucking, Bob played quite a
reasonable game of tennis, though so far, he had not
found any opportunity to don his white flannels. He
popped the letter into a pillar box and walked down
over Southampton Row to the small patch of green
where the Holborn Artisans' Lawn Tennis club –
which consisted of three courts and changing rooms
for both sexes – had been erected through a public
subscription and the generosity of Dame Valerie
Islington-Laurie, the socially-minded wife of a leading City banker, who, when it became apparent that
the amount collected was insufficient, doubled the
sum raised by the organising committee with a large
donation from her own pocket (though unkind gossip
rumoured that her long-time admirer Count Gewirtz
of Galicia had in fact stood most of the cost to put
himself in good stead with Dame Valerie, a noted

Society beauty). City clerks and shopworkers were the most frequent users of the excellent facilities, along with more than a few London University students from University College in nearby Gower Street. The daily presence of pretty girls dressed for tennis attracted a growing number of upper class mashers *[the Edwardian slang for rich young men about town – Editor]*.

Although the courts were available for public use, those wishing to play had to pay a small hourly fee when they wished to play and a nominal annual subscription for which a key was provided to the entrance gate. Bob had paid this modicum charge and so with his key in his hand he walked down to the entrance via the narrow side path between two rows of silver birch trees. Here he was brought up short by an extraordinary sight. Some ten yards in front of him, and oblivious to his presence, stood a youth, standing pressed against the fence of slatted railings which divided the tennis club grounds from the public area of greenery, his mouth open, his eyes glazed and he was openly masturbating with the fingers of his right hand rubbing against his bulging crotch. Bob recognised the fair-haired, fresh complexioned youngster at once. His name was Charlie Wilkinson, the sixteen-year-old nephew of his landlady who was staying at his aunt's house as a holiday treat that summer in exchange for helping Mrs Trenton out by running errands and performing other occasional small services.

Bob coughed discreetly and the lad spun round with a cry. 'Hello, Charlie, what the devil are you up to?' asked Bob good-humouredly. Poor Charlie blushed as he replied: 'Take a look through there, Mr Goggin, and you'll see for yourself.' Curious as to what on earth Charlie could possibly mean, Bob peered into the space afforded by a break in the hedge and gasped with astonishment. For on the grass of one of the tennis courts, unknowingly in full view of the two men, sat two girls, both fellow students of Bob's at St Dominic's. They also lodged with Mrs Trenton, which itself was no great coincidence for the landlady's establishment had been favoured with a recommendation by Bob's lecturer Dr Osbert Radley-Thatcher who we met at the very start of these chronicles and who we shall shortly meet again.

The older of the two girls, Susie de Vere Forrester, was sturdily built with long, firm legs and her curvaceous figure had attracted many a stare from male classmates at St Dominic's. Her strong features were softened by a pleasant smiling manner and gentle waves of reddish chestnut hair which she wore combed in silky waves down to her shoulders. Susie's swarthy colouring (her mother was Spanish) was in sharp contrast to the other girl in Bob's wide-eyed view, Amanda Crombleigh, whose slim, coltish frame was topped by golden-blonde hair which hung straight and loose over the pale oval of her pretty face.

Both girls were wearing white tennis dresses but no game – of tennis, that is! – was taking place. For Amanda was lying on the grass, her big blue-green eyes closed as she sprawled on her back with her legs apart whilst Susie knelt astride her. On her elbows and knees, Susie's face was above the open spread of Amanda's naked cunt, the fingers of her left hand

46

playing around the saffron cunney hair and her right hand holding what appeared to be a thick clay coloured tube shaped very much like a stiff penis, the rounded end of which she teased all around Amanda's pink pussey lips. Amanda wriggled her legs and her knickers, which were round her left ankle, flew off onto the grass as she writhed in delicious agony while Susie rubbed the side of the imitation cock all along her crack set in the dense crocus-coloured curls of her pubic triangle.

'Oh, don't do that, Susie, or I shall spend all over the model of Randolph's prick,' wailed Amanda, moaning gently as she writhed under her friend. Susie smiled to herself at this as she temporarily suspended the torment of Amanda's erect little clitty which had now poked through her slit.

'But I want you to spend, Mandy,' said Susie throatily. 'And I also want you to finish me off at the same time, there's a love!' And to encourage her friend Susie reached back and pulled her own dress up above her waist.

What a seductive view was now presented to Amanda's shining eyes, for under her dress Susie was wearing only a tiny pair of white knickers which contrasted so beautifully with the light brown tan of her long, agile thighs. The tight, white cotton perfectly shaped the charming little bulge of her honeypot through their gusset and she had without any doubt deliberately chosen a pair of briefs that were cut quite lasciviously high, laying bare much of the firm cheeks of her bum.

Susie moved her knees back so that she was now almost astride the blonde girl's face. Amanda rubbed

her hand between Susie's buttocks as she began to
lick the satiny surface of her thighs, coating them with
long, loving swathes of moisture. This made Susie
dive her own head down and begin to kiss all round
Amanda's pussey as she again began to tickle the
gasping girl's cunney lips with her dildo. This made
Amanda wild with desire and she fervently kissed the
warm cotton knickers where they couched the soft
bulge of Susie's cuntal pouch. The two male spectators heard her whisper: 'I'm going to pull your knickers down, Susie, for then I can taste you properly.'
In the event, she did not have to do so because
Susie was happy to oblige her, reaching back to
take the waistband and pull down her panties so
that they were drawn tight round the middle of
her thighs. Meanwhile she relentlessly continued
to manipulate the clay cock around Amanda's
golden haired cunney with wicked skill, teasing
and touching again and again driving the poor
girl to distraction until finally she inserted the knob-
end fully into Amanda's willing love-box. This really
set Amanda into frenetic action and she cupped the
globes of Susie's bottom, parting the fleshy buttocks
so she could now work her finger inside Susie's cunt
which provoked delighted cries of gratitude from her
partner. Wantonly her tongue now replaced her
finger as she grasped Susie's delectable bum cheeks,
one in each hand, her mouth pressed against the soft,
yielding flesh, wickedly probing Susie's slit with the
very tip of her pink tongue. And as Amanda rolled
her tongue around the other girl's sweet snatch,
Susie's head was firmly ensconced between Amanda's thighs, sucking and nipping at the tender clitty

in much the same way as Amanda was working on her.

They sighed and groaned together as they lay fixed in the tribadic *soixante neuf*, tonguing each other's cunnies, playfully licking and lapping to the mounting excitement of Bob and young Charlie. The latter could not contain himself and had taken out his not inconsiderable boner and was masturbating furiously as he gasped: 'Sod me, Mr Goggin, I'd give anything to be the meat in that sandwich.' Bob laid his hand on the boy's arm and said quietly: 'If you really mean that, then put your prick away and come with me.' Charlie looked puzzled but did as he was told and followed his mentor round to the club entrance. Bob unlocked the barred gate and the two of them walked across to where Amanda and Susie were still threshing around with great ardour, oblivious to the fact that Bob and Charlie were standing only ten yards away.

'A-h-r-e! I'm coming, Susie, I'm coming!' called out Amanda and Susie not only moved the dildo even faster in and out of the blonde girl's cunt but now slid a finger into her bottom-hole. Amanda thrashed around in a delirium of delight as the spasms of excitement ran through her body and she screamed as they culminated into a gigantic peak of orgasmic lust. When she had recovered she repaid Susie by nuzzling her lips between the girl's quivering cunney lips which were oozing love juice, her fluttering tongue darting in and out of the lovely hairy quim, slurping the love liquid from her pussey and filling the afternoon air with the scent of raw sex. She felt Susie's spend building up and she worked her tongue even harder whilst sliding her finger deeper and deeper into the girl's sopping muff until Susie howled with joy as she climaxed copiously in thrilling waves of pure pleasure.

They lay panting with exhaustion and it was not for a minute or two that Amanda noticed that they were not alone! She gave a little yelp and nudged Susie who sat up to see Bob Goggin sitting with his hands locked round his knees and Charlie Wilkinson, their landlady's teen-aged nephew, standing almost in front of them, his trousers by now down by his ankles playing with his erect shaft, capping and uncapping the bulbous red knob of his swollen joystick.

Bob called out: 'Charlie, I told you before, leave your widger alone, I'm sure that one of the girls might find a better use for it.' The girls giggled but did not contradict him when he added: 'Go up to them and let Amanda and Susie take a closer look at your stiffie.' Charlie appeared nonplussed but Bob gently pushed his legs forward and the lad warily approached the two tribades. Susie took his hot smooth-skinned shaft in her hand and said: 'You haven't used this for real fucking have you, Charlie?' 'No, miss,' he faltered shyly, 'but I should dearly like to try.'

'It would be a kindness to oblige,' said Susie thoughtfully. 'Would you like to fuck him, darling? My cunney is rather tender just now.'

'So is mine, and remember we will be stretching our pussies tonight,' said Amanda with regret. She paused for a moment and then her eyes lit up. 'However, I would have no objection to Charlie going up my bottom. His tool isn't too thick but it's of a good length for a bum fuck.'

This outspoken exchange appeared to worry Charlie who nervously stepped back a pace but Susie grabbed his shaft and massaged it gently in her hands. 'Don't be frightened,' advised the warm-hearted girl as Amanda scrambled over onto her hands and knees, pushing out the full pale moons of her arse, angling her legs to afford Charlie a better view of her wrinkled brown rosette. 'Have no fear, Charlie, the bum-hole can be a most pleasant channel of bliss,' said Susie cheerfully, bending down to take the lad's prick in her mouth to wash his shaft with her saliva. Then, with his cock in her hand, she guided the knob of his tadger between Amanda's buttocks. Charlie's face brightened as he pushed forward and he gasped with excitement as he felt his moistened bell-end enter the narrow orifice. His cock throbbed and bounced inside its tight sheath as if spring-loaded and it plunged to and fro quite easily as the blonde girl reached back and spread her cheeks still wider, jerking her bum in time with Charlie's rhythm. Fired by this virgin fucking, Susie lay down in front of the writhing pair and frigged Amanda's wet pussey to stir the blonde to the very highest pitch of excitation which allowed the girl to spend together in perfect accord with Charlie, as he exploded into her in a rush of liquid fire. He withdrew his still stiff weapon with an audible 'pop' as it bade farewell to Amanda's well-lathered nether-hole.

'M'mm, it looks as though there's a spark or two left in the embers,' remarked Susie as rubbed Charlie's cock between the palms of her hands until it stood up as proudly as before. Amanda laughed and together they knelt down in front of the lucky lad, taking turns to lick his shaft and then Amanda gobbled the knob hungrily into her mouth and began to suck noisily upon it whilst Susie kissed and licked around his pulsating balls. Then the girls swapped places and Susie lapped at his juicy, bared helmet, savouring to the full the salty sensuality of its taste. He thrust his slippery staff deeper into her mouth and she helped him by sliding her lips as far down his cock as possible until the wiry pubic hair tickled her nose. Charlie groaned as he spent a second time and Susie swallowed his spunk in great gulps, pulling him hard into her mouth as he delivered the spermy contents of his big balls deep in her throat. She sucked on his cock until she had milked the very last drops and his twitching tool started to shrink back to its normal size.

There was a noticeable bulge between Bob's legs as he stood up. 'Well, I'm really glad that you three have enjoyed yourselves! Isn't it ironic though that with two boys and two girls here I've had to play goose-berry!' he complained crossly. 'Don't fret, Bob,' said Amanda as she stepped into her rather crumpled knickers. 'You're dining at Gary Hornby's house in Bedford Square tonight, aren't you? Well, Susie and I have also been invited so we can all walk round there together. But keep your powder dry, Bob, because at the very least you'll be called upon to fuck us both after the meal. Well, don't look so surprised, surely you have been to one of Gary's special suppers before?'

CHAPTER TWO
Country Matters

For a while let us leave Bob, Susie and Amanda snoozing peacefully (and for the time being in separate beds) before Gary Hornby's wild party to which our three fun-loving friends were eagerly looking forward. We will move back the hands of Old Father Time to just after two o'clock that very afternoon. Also, let us take a swift journey in the winged chariot of imagination across the lush grass fields of England to the coast of South Devon and the tiny village of Shaldon which is situated on the bank of the River Teign very close to the popular holiday resort of Teignmouth. There, on the pleasant shelving beach, Bob Goggin's *amorata* Penny and her mama, the formidable Lady Laetitia Arkley, were walking slowly along the promenade.

Spread out on a triangular plateau under the lee of one of the spurs of Haldon, Teignmouth is bounded on the south-east by the English Channel while on the south is the broad estuary of the River Teign. Where the traveller's eye, whilst glancing round the town, does not rest on water there are wooded hills, which so effectually shelter the place from the north that Teignmouth has gained many visitors who are attracted by its warm climate.

Penny had made no objection when her parents

had suggested that she and her elder sister Katie accompany them for a holiday at their Uncle Michael's house which he had rented for the summer season. After all, her beloved Bob was away in London and both Penny and Katie were always kept entertained by their Uncle Michael, her father's younger brother, a jolly silver-haired bachelor who was well known amongst his intimates for his robust and occasionally infamous sexual proclivities.

Michael Arkley's live-in companion during that glorious summer of 1905 was Miss Florence Langley, the cook-housekeeper who he had fucked (and later engaged) after making her acquaintance at Major-General Finchley's Servants' Ball two years before. *[Class barriers were lifted temporarily at these events when – usually around the time of the Christmas festivities – the titled and upper class house guests would melt the hearts of hardworking parlourmaids as the men bowed low before asking for the pleasure of their company at dinner or afterwards for a dance – Editor]* Little did Michael know that Penny's father, Sir Paul, had also enjoyed a passionate night's coupling with the lusty lady in question although, as we shall see shortly, this did not cause too much of a problem for the easy-going dilettante when eventually he discovered that he was sharing Florrie's favours with his equally randy brother.

Be that as it may, back on Teignmouth promenade, Lady Arkley and Penny had decided to walk back to the house. But they had only just reached the main road when one of the few motor cars Penny had seen in the West Country rattled towards them and the driver brought his gleaming new vehicle to a halt as he greeted the two women. He then took off his hat and pulled off his goggles to reveal himself as Cyril Totteridge, an extremely wealthy local landowner and an ardent admirer of Katie Arkley. Penny guessed that he had a favour to beg of her Mama and so she smiled encouragingly at the slim young man as he stepped out of his car.

Her premonition as to the reason for Cyril's accosting them in the street was quite correct for Cyril doffed his hat and said shyly: 'Good afternoon, Lady Arkley. May I offer you and Penelope a ride back to your house?'

'Thank you, but as it is only a very short distance away to Norman Lodge, Mr Totteridge, I would much prefer to walk.' Lady Arkley did not care to encourage the wooing of her pretty eldest daughter by any young man whose family was outside the charmed circle of High Society. Cyril's face fell but Penny came to his rescue, saying: 'Oh, Mama, do let's drive back in Mr Totteridge's motor – it really is a splendid machine, Mama, I saw a photograph of the automobile in the *Tatler* quite recently as Papa's friend Lord Raspis has purchased one. It is a German vehicle, is it not, Mr Totteridge, the Mercedes Simplex if I am not mistaken?'

'I'm afraid that I could not find a British vehicle so well made,' said Cyril apologetically as he hopefully opened the door in an effort to persuade Lady Arkley to take up his invitation. *[Mr Totteridge was an excellent judge of early motor cars – in 1991 a record one and a half million pounds (more than two and a quarter million dollars) was paid for a Mercedes Simplex which was one of the first vehicles which could be recognised as a real car rather than a horseless carriage – Editor]*

Lady Arkley made no move but Penny boldly sat herself down in Cyril Totteridge's car. 'Oh do come in, Mama, the sun is so warm that I'm sure we will become over-heated if we do not accept Mr Totteridge's kind offer.' Her formidable Mama pursed her lips but heaved herself into the back seat alongside her daughter saying: 'Very well, Penelope, although I trust you will not make a habit of jumping into any passing vehicle that takes your fancy.'

Penny suppressed a giggle and turned to their driver who had managed to start his car at the first time of asking and was just adjusting his goggles before starting off. 'Cyril, you will join us for tea, won't you? Katie and I will welcome your company afterwards on the putting green if you would like to accompany us. My Uncle Michael is always keen to play and would be happy to make up a team for a ladies *versus* gentlemen match.'

'Thank you very much, 'said Cyril as he drove carefully to Norman Lodge House. 'I'd love to take tea with you.' When they stopped he swiftly jumped out to open the car door for Lady Arkley. After she had swept by him he whispered to Penny: 'Actually, it so happens that Katie and I have been asked out to dine this evening in London, but if we are to go I need to ask permission from your parents to take Katie. We would stay the night at my Aunt Julia's house which, coincidentally, is two minutes' walk away from where we have been invited.'

'Good luck to you, Cyril, although to be honest, I cannot see Mama agreeing to such a request. Your best bet is to approach my father and even he might not approve,' said Penny doubtfully.

'I should really ask him as soon as possible. Would it be possible to speak with him before tea?' asked Cyril anxiously, for he knew that Sir Paul, a senior financial advisor to the Treasury, spent his afternoons in the library with strict instructions that he was not to be disturbed. Now for many years Lady Arkley has laboured under the impression that her husband spends this portion of his day poring over sets of dry Government statistics. But those of us familiar with the lusty baronet *[see* 'Cremorne Gardens' *and* 'The Temptations of Cremorne' – *Editor]* will rightly assume that the only statistics pored over by Sir Paul are those concerning the figure of the serving girls at home or at his club whom he was fucking at the time or whom he hoped to fuck in the near future! Penny too was under this misapprehension so when she suggested in all innocence that Cyril intrude upon Sir Paul's studies, she genuinely had no idea of what exactly would be interrupted.

As fate would have it, that very afternoon – after several attempts – Sir Paul had inveigled Florrie Langley into his lair and had plied his troth which, in this case, had been a luncheon of roast beef sandwiches, fresh fruit and the consumption of a bottle of his brother's best claret along with the promise of a generous gift on the housekeeper's thirty-third birthday which was due the very next week. The couple had exchanged rapturous kisses and engaged in cuddles of rising passion for some time, the culmination of which was fast approaching. Florrie lay on the leather sofa, naked except for a pair of pink knickers and her silky brown hair was spread out on the cushion as she spread her thighs wide and held her ample ripe breasts in her hands.

Sir Paul licked his lips as he slid his braces from off his shoulders, shaking with desire as Florrie reached forward to unbutton his flies and pull down his trousers. The randy baronet could feel his balls growing tight and heavy as he slid down his underpants and eased his body between the housekeeper's firm thighs. He cupped his hands around each of her large white breasts and playfully nipped each engorged red nipple in turn as her hands slithered up and down the length of his swollen stiffstander. 'Play with my pussey,' she said in a low voice and nothing loath, he rolled down her brief pink knickers, exposing her trimmed brown bush which aroused him even more.

He moved his head down from her titties to her cunney and after licking around her pouting pussey lips, he opened her cunt with his tongue. Unlike many Englishmen, Sir Paul was a skilful pussey eater and he lovingly lapped at her moistening love channel, inhaling and ingesting her savoury juices as he slurped happily on her clitty. This made the buxom Florrie turn and twist herself under this delicious stimulation and her nails raked the back of his neck as she held his face even more tightly against her now sopping cunney. 'Aaaah! Aaaah!' she exhaled with undisguised joy as she achieved her climax, the love juices cascading out of her cunt and running down Sir Paul's nose and into his mouth. 'Now I'm good and ready for you, slide your shaft into my juicy little love box,' she whispered lewdly. 'With pleasure, m'dear,' he gasped and propelled his body upwards to stretch out on top of her, his chest pressing upon her hard nipples. He groaned with delight as his throbbing tool sank gratefully into Florrie's pulpy pussey. Never a man to rush a good fuck, Sir Paul slowly withdrew all but the very tip of his knob out of her clinging quim before plunging his cock in again to the full. This had the expected effect upon Florrie whose bottom began to roll around as she arched her back, working her cunt back and forth against the velvet smooth rammer which was pleasuring her pussey so wonderfully.

Florrie Langley loved to fuck and was thoroughly enjoying her first taste of Sir Paul's experienced prick. 'Oh that's lovely, really lovely! Oooh, Oooh, fuck away, sir, ram your big dick up my cunt! I want it all!'

Sir Paul smiled wolfishly as he worked his hips backwards and forwards to establish a steady rhythm and the lecherous cocksman was building nicely towards his climax when suddenly, like a bolt from the blue, his concentration was broken by a knock on the door! Who the hell had the effrontery to disobey his strict order that at this time he should never be disturbed!

'Sir Paul, are you there?' floated an anxious young voice from the landing. 'It's Cyril Totteridge here, sir. I have something to ask you and as it is a matter of urgency Penny told me to come upstairs and knock on your door. I do hope I am not interrupting anything of great importance.' Oh no, only a fine fuck which I had been looking forward to since we arrived here, thought Sir Paul furiously, but there was nothing to be gained by venting his anger upon the helpless young man, especially as he was not completely sure as to whether he had locked the door! Exhaling deeply, he gritted his teeth and shouted back: 'Well, I am rather busy just now, young Totteridge. Can't your problem wait an hour or so?'

'I'm afraid not, sir. You see, my cousin Gary Hornby has invited Katie and I to a dinner party in London tonight. Many people from the world of the arts will be there including the famous Scottish balletomane, John Gibson, who is travelling down all the way from Edinburgh. I know how much Katie would like to meet him! We could catch the three-twenty train and change at my aunt's house, which is just across the road to the house Gary has rented in Bedford Square and my aunt would be very pleased if we would stay the night with her if we went up to town.'

Now normally it is doubtful if Sir Paul would have entertained such a proposition for more than an instant but his sinewy staff was twitching violently and Florrie Langley was not helping matters by squeezing his hairy ballsack! He had to spend or he would surely burst! 'Katie would love to come with me, sir, but of course we need your permision,' added Cyril timidly just as Sir Paul began the final stroke to glory. The hot sperm bubbled up through the stem of his pulsating prick and shot out of his knob into Florrie's yearning cunney. 'Yes, yes, yes!' he cried out and to be fair to Cyril, the young man could hardly have been expected to know that Sir Paul's clearly enunciated words of affirmation related not to his somewhat audacious request but to announce the soaking of Florrie Langley's cunt by a surging stream of spunk from the lusty baronet's jerking penis! So Cyril called out: 'Thank you, sir, thank you very much – I promise that I'll take good care of Katie,' before bounding back downstairs to convey the glad tidings to Katie and Penny who were sitting outside on the patio with Lady Arkley and their genial host Uncle Michael, Lady Arkley's brother-in-law, whose lady friend was at that very same moment being fucked by her husband!

'Marvellous news, Katie, your father has given us permission to leave for London,' announced Cyril happily after Lady Arkley had retired to the drawing room to catch up on her correspondence. 'It is just as well that you asked Mutkin to pack an overnight bag for you before luncheon. But we'll still have to get a move on, darling, if we're going to catch the afternoon express train.'

'Oh how splendid, Cyril, you must have spoken so persuasively to make Papa agree. Frankly, I never really imagined that you would succeed,' said Katie, her clear blue eyes sparkling with delight for at heart she was easily bored by country pursuits and much preferred the heady whirl of life in London. Katie had many good friends in London and she had become very adept at making the most ingenious excuses to leave the imposing family seat of Arkley Manor in Sussex to stay at her parents' equally magnificent town residence in Hyde Park Gardens, Kensington.

'Well done young fellow, I must say that I also thought your chances of getting my brother to approve were slim,' chortled Uncle Michael. 'But I'd pop off as quickly as you can in case he changes his mind. You are sure he agreed?'

Cyril nodded vigorously, 'Oh yes, sir, there can be

no mistake. I only spoke to him through the door but we heard each other well enough and when I asked him if he would let Katie go he clearly cried out: "Yes, yes, yes." To be honest, I think he was very wrapped up in his work and was glad to get rid of me.'

'Good luck to you,' said Penny with a rueful smile. 'Enjoy yourselves and when you have a moment think of me having to face Mama's rage when she finds out you've skipped away.'

'Don't worry about mother, I'll sweeten the pill for all of you,' promised Uncle Michael. 'Katie, would you care to have Mutkin drive you to the railway station in the phaeton? *[a light horse-drawn carriage with two seats – Editor]*

'No, it's unnecessary, Uncle, as I'll go back with Cyril immediately to his home to pick up his case. His chauffeur can drive us down to the station.'

'Yes, but not in my new Mercedes, I don't let anyone drive it, even you, love!' laughed Cyril as he shook hands with Penny and Michael Arkley. Katie kissed her sister and uncle and the young lovers hurried out before Lady Arkley returned.

'I'd better tell Mrs Langley *[even if unmarried like Florrie Langley, cooks were always accorded the honorary title of "Mrs" and, unlike many other servants, were never addressed simply by their surname – Editor]* that there will only be four for dinner,' said Uncle Michael, stroking his chin. 'Wait a mo', I'll tell you what, Penny, I'll first telephone Reverend Bailey and invite him to dine with us. I know his wife and children are away this week visiting his mother-in-law in Wales so he's almost certain to be free. He's a great bridge player, you know, and even more keen on the game than your dear Mama. Yes, two or three rubbers with Reverend Bailey will keep her occupied, Penny, never you fear, especially as I'll insist on partnering my brother. We're bound to lose and that's bound to put your mother in a good humour.'

Penny's face brightened considerably. 'You are kind, Uncle, though I still think Mama will be dreadfully angry when she finds out about Katie leaving without even saying goodbye. I'm going to retire after dinner and read the book I bought the other day and if I'm not feeling too lazy I'll also write to my boyfriend. It's a shame Katie can only stay overnight or she could have paid Bob a visit. Still, what's more important now is to keep out of Mama's way – I just hope that she won't accuse me of aiding and abetting the perpetration of the great crime!'

'Yes, your Mama can be a bit of a Tartar,' agreed Uncle Michael. 'But as I say, leave her to me and I'll speak to your father and fill him in on our plan after I've called Reverend Bailey.'

As Michael had correctly forecast, the bridge-playing cleric was more than delighted to accept the invitation to dine *chez* Arkley that evening and so, feeling satisfied that he had tied-up all the loose ends to prevent any problems for either Katie or Penny (for he was very fond of his two nieces), Michael decided to speak to his brother there and then. 'Paul really shouldn't lock himself away in the library whilst he's on holiday,' he exclaimed. 'He's been in there long enough already and I'll drag him outside or he will have wasted a glorious afternoon stuck in a stuffy room full of books.' He made his way upstairs. He knocked on the library door and without waiting made his entrance to find his brother sprawled naked upon the sofa with the equally nude Florrie Langley on her knees lustily sucking Sir Paul's stiff penis!

Neither Sir Paul nor the lusty lady who only that morning had slipped from Michael's bed heard the master of the house knock on the door, so totally engaged had they been in their pursuit of oral gratification that Michael stood still for some seconds, dumbstruck by the sight of his brother being tongue-fucked by the curvaceous cook. He closed the door behind him and swiftly locked it before noisily clearing his throat. 'Well Paul, when you said you worked for the government on important domestic affairs, I must say I didn't quite realise how wide a field this labour encompassed. And Florrie, my dear, what can I say? Perhaps I should have explained to you when you joined my household that it was never a condition of your employment that you should gobble any gentleman staying here, however close his relationship may be to me.'

Her mouth still filled with Sir Paul's bulging staff, Florrie Langley looked up at her master with a horrified expression. She unclamped her lips from around Sir Paul's cock as the baronet bit his lip, for neither of the guilty pair could at first think of any fitting response to Michael's ironic comment. 'It's my fault, Michael, I fancied Florrie from the moment I clapped eyes on her and though she told me that you two were already involved, since we arrived here I have never stopped trying to work my way into her drawers.

'So please don't blame Florrie too much for what has happened. I take full responsibility and offer my humble apology,' he added nobly, an act which whilst mitigating his offence was performed (it must be stated) in the context that Sir Paul knew full well Michael would never peach on him to his wife if only for the sakes of Katie and Penny.

'The trouble with you, Paul, is that when you unbutton your trousers your brains fall out,' sighed Michael, 'but I am surprised and disappointed with you, Florrie, weren't you getting enough satisfaction from me?'

'Oh yes, yes, of course I was,' cried Florrie, scrambling up to her feet and padding over to where Michael stood. 'I was just being greedy because my scullery maid Mary's cousin Clare works at Sir Paul's home in Sussex and she wrote several letters to Mary about what went on at Arkley Manor. She said that Sir Paul had one of the biggest cocks any of the girls in the servants' quarters had ever seen and that he knew how to use it. Also, she said that he was very generous to any girl who would consent to be fucked so I was tempted when he began to ask me to sport with him.'

The two brothers thought carefully about this apparantly heartfelt confession which in fact was not entirely true, though few readers will blame Florrie for her slight embellishment of the facts. Although Clare had indeed written about Sir Paul's desire to fuck every girl working at Arkley Manor, she had not penned a word about the size of the baronet's cock. But the clever Florrie had rightly surmised that like most men, Sir Paul was inordinately proud of the dimensions of his love trunk and any reference as to its girth, length and abilities would in Sir Paul's mind swing the scales of any judgment in her favour. Her strategy was immediately confirmed when Sir Paul repeated his earlier willingness to shoulder the blame for the embarrassing situation.

'This really is all my fault, Michael, please don't be too hard on poor Florrie,' he said pleadingly. Michael stroked his chin and then suddenly grinned. 'Well, let's not quarrel over the matter. After all, Florrie is free to grant her favours whenever she wishes and at least she did keep it in the family!'

'Oh you are a kind gentleman, sir,' Florrie breathed with undisguised relief for, despite Sir Paul's intervention, she had thought it likely that not only was she in grave danger of losing her easy well-paid job but that she would be dismissed without any references. 'How can I show you both how grateful I am?' she asked at length.

Michael considered this question for a moment before replying: 'How about sucking our pricks together? That would be exciting for us all. I'll wager you a sovereign, Paul, that you come before me.' 'Done!' said his brother happily and Florrie was very pleased to take both of the Arkleys in hand. Michael quickly undressed and Florrie caressed his fast stiffening prick with one hand, rubbing it up and down before pulling it towards her and opening her mouth wide to ease his rounded red helmet between her lips from a side angle. Then as she gently massaged Michael's balls as she sucked firmly on his throbbing tool, she reached out with her other hand to close her fist round Sir Paul's rigid rod, propelling him slightly to her right so that he was able to ease his mushroomed knob into Florrie's mouth from the right. Somehow she managed to curl her tongue around both cocks as she gripped them both, one in each hand as she knelt on the carpet though naturally she could only suck one at a time in long, noisy slurps. She varied her technique by giving each prick in turn a butterfly stroke of a quick erratic flick from her wet tongue on the underside of the shaft just below the knob which sent both men into raptures.

'Hold on, I've a better idea,' said Michael, laying himself down on his back. 'Suck my cock back up again and ride on my prick whilst Paul prods your tight little rear dimple at the same time. This will allow you to enjoy a double dose of cock and I promise you that it will be great fun.'

The idea appealed greatly to Florrie who, if nothing else, was as game a girl as any man could wish, and without demur she leaned down to take Michael's cock in her mouth, running her tongue down the full length of his shaft and then back up again to the crown to catch a sticky drip of spend which had formed round the 'eye'. The exquisite tonguing soon caused his cock to swell up again as she poked her bum cheeks up in the air in anticipation of Sir Paul's attack. First though, once Michael's veiny truncheon was sticking up in the air ready for action, she climbed over his cock and, opening her cunney lips with her fingers, slid down his greasy pole, exhaling a grateful 'A-a-a-h!' as his thick prick filled her love channel to the limit. She bounced up and down on his cock, thrusting back her large, rounded buttocks as far as possible.

Michael then grasped the two fleshy mounds and parted the globes to aid the passage of Sir Paul's prick towards Florrie's tiny wrinkled bum-hole. When she

felt Sir Paul's cock jamming itself between her buttocks, Florrie let her body go still to let Sir Paul wiggle
his knob whilst Michael's cock was embedded in her
cunt. 'Oooh!' she gasped as Sir Paul's helmet entered
her puckered little tradesman's entrance but once in
she urged him on as he managed to insert three inches
of his long shaft inside her arse as he reached around
to twiddle her titties with his hands. Florrie moved
herself up and down on Michael's cock, gingerly at
first, and she could feel the two pricks fucking her,
squeezed as they were inside her two orifices and with
only the thin divisional membrane separating them.

This lusty three-way fuck brought the trio soaring
to new heights of sensuality until with hoarse cries
of excitement, the Arkley brothers simultaneously
squirted their jets of creamy white foam inside Florrie's cunney and arsehole and the exhausted lovers
flopped back, utterly exhausted from this unusual
experience. Sir Paul was now completely *hors de
combat* but Florrie managed to suck Michael up to
one further cockstand. She gently kissed his twitching
purple dome as she eased his foreskin up and down
until his sinewy weapon again stood smartly to attention. Florrie adored sucking cocks and she greedily
gobbled Michael's pulsating prick as she looked up
with a twinkle in her eye. She gave him a series of
sharp little licks on his swollen shaft followed by a
number of swift kisses up and down the stem, not
stopping at the root but taking in his hairy ballsack
and running even deeper to the amazing sensitive
zone between his balls and arsehole. This sent him
into paroxyms of pleasure and Florrie brought him off
magnificently, thrusting his cock in and out of her

succulent mouth and deep into her throat in a quickening rhythm with her pink tongue lapping at the tip of his cock with every stroke, licking up the drops of milky white fluid which were beginning to ooze out of the tiny 'eye' at the top of his hot, uncapped helmet.

As soon as she felt Michael was on the verge of spending (for by now even the voracious Florrie's appetite was now sated), she made ready to swallow his spunk. Michael thrust upwards and his prick shuddered violently between her full lips. Then in one long spasm he released his sperm, first a couple of early shoots and then with a woosh Florrie's mouth was filled to the brim with his copious emission. She gulped down his jism as his cock bucked uncontrollably as she held his staff lightly between her teeth and she let the rivulet of frothy spunk flow down her throat as she teased the now spongy deflating crown of his cock until his shaft lay limply in her tongue. She let his wet cock slide free and Sir Paul, still lying prone on the carpet, said: 'You have the stamina of a nineteen-year-old, Michael, I wish I had your staying power.'

'Oh, don't be jealous, you can hardly complain – why, there can hardly be room for any further notches on your gun,' retorted his brother.

'I'm not complaining,' sighed Sir Paul. 'Jealousy is a green-eyed monster which can easily devour you if you let it enter your system.'

Florrie picked up her knickers and wriggled into them. 'Only insecure people suffer from the pangs of jealousy. I think as far as you men are concerned, much of it is to do with your need for possession and power. I once knew a gentleman who wanted to own a woman in the same way he owned a house. Anyhow, I am glad we are still all friends though I think it only right, Sir Paul, that in future you look elsewhere for a good fuck.'

'Fair enough, Florrie,' said Sir Paul gloomily. 'I might even have to offer my wife her conjugal rights more often, God help me.'

Michael could not stop himself smiling. 'Come on, it won't kill you, old boy. Let's face it, you would never have married Laetitia if she had not come with a dowry of £100,000 which has kept you in idle luxury since your wedding day. And that reminds me, I have to warn you that she will be in a fearsome paddy this evening and is likely to be gunning for you.'

'Oh no,' groaned the unhappy husband. 'What the deuce is troubling her now?'

Michael looked rather puzzled and decided to recount the story Cyril Totteridge had given the company earlier on. 'And he said that when he asked you whether he could take Katie to London tonight you shouted back, "yes, yes, yes" and the young man understood that to mean you agreed which would not be an unreasonable assumption.'

'I never agreed to anything at all, the boy is fabricating a total falsehood,' spluttered Sir Paul angrily, but Florrie gently took hold of his arm and said: 'Excuse me, sir, I don't wish to contradict you but I do recall when you first had your cock in my cunt we were interrupted by a knock at the door and someone asked you about something or other. I didn't hear the exact words myself as I was engaged in squeezing your balls at the time but you did cry out, "yes, yes,

yes" as you spent. I thought you were replying to whoever it was shouting at you from behind the door but perhaps you were just letting out your emotions as you spunked into my pussey and like me, the questioner, who we now know was Mr Totteridge, thought you were replying to him, which was a reasonable assumption for which he can hardly be blamed.'

Michael Arkley burst out laughing. 'Florrie, you should have taken service with Sherlock Holmes! I'm sure that's exactly what happened – Paul, don't fret, Cyril Totteridge is a nice lad and Katie will enjoy herself in London. She's always loved meeting new people and Cyril's cousin Gary Hornby is a noted socialite. I'm sure Katie will be in good hands – and don't worry about Laetitia, I've asked Reverend Bailey to dine with us tonight and we'll play bridge afterwards which will keep her in a good mood. She won't even have time to work herself up into a paddy because Katie will be back here tomorrow afternoon.'

'Well, thanks for trying to soften the blow,' grunted Sir Paul as he searched amongst the heap of clothes for his drawers. 'Just stay with me at all times, Michael, there's safety in numbers!'

This ancient folk-saying may contain elements of truth but as we shall see the eventual presence of two other girls in the luxurious first class carriage did nothing to prevent and indeed was the prime cause of Katie losing her knickers on a surprisingly lewd journey to London. Katie was not a complete stranger to the joys of railway fucking *[see* 'Cremorne

Gardens' *for a detailed account of her journey with her old boyfriend Walter Stanton – Editor]* but neither Cyril nor Katie had planned to indulge in sensual sports at least until after they were safely tucked up in bed together after Gary Hornby's party.

The young couple had reached Bristol where they were set to join the London express which would thunder through the country non-stop to Paddington. There was a fifteen-minute stop there where an apologetic announcement was made that due to an earlier derailment, the only first class carriages on the express train would be of the old-fashioned variety which were without the benefit of corridors. This did not at first trouble Cyril and Katie unduly as they alighted and made full use of the spotlessly clean facilities. Then they treated themselves to cake and iced lemonade in the first-class refreshment room, where Cyril also purchased a small hamper containing sandwiches and bottles of mineral water. Katie watched the porters manhandling trunks and valises as the crowds of passengers mingled and jostled on the busy platform.

'Time to board the train if you please, ladies and gentlemen,' called out the guard, resplendent in his liveried uniform. As he ushered out the passengers towards the train, Cyril said: 'I doubt if we will have the luxury of being alone for the rest of the journey, Katie. I just hope we won't have any disagreeable companions in the compartment because we won't be able to escape except by pretending to sleep.'

'Don't be such a misanthrope,' chided Katie, wagging a reproving finger as she took hold of his arm. 'If the other seats are all taken, we'll read our newspapers and have a little sleep just the same. We may strike up a conversation which will pass away the time very pleasantly.'

'I very much doubt it, for I can hardly make mad passionate love to you whilst other people are present!'

'Not unless they all join in!' she giggled and Cyril pretended to be shocked. 'You naughty girl, I should put you over my knee, pull down your drawers and spank your bare bottom,' he muttered as he held open the door to their compartment. 'Promises, promises . . .' sighed Katie wickedly as she climbed into the coach.

Now Cyril Totteridge might well have preferred to have enjoyed the rest of the journey making love in all kinds of erotic ways to the lovely Katie in the privacy of a sumptuously furnished compartment of a first-class Great Western Railway coach. But if these dreams were not to be fulfilled, he would surely have settled for the two passengers who had chosen to sit with Katie and Cyril for the rest of the journey until they reached Paddington Station. For sitting opposite each other in the far corner were two extremely pretty girls, both dark complexioned and well dressed, who were speaking quietly to each other in French and who were obviously foreign tourists coming back to London after spending some time in the nearby city of Bath.

To Katie's amusement (for like her father she was not a jealous person) within ten minutes of the train leaving Bristol, Cyril struck up a conversation with the two girls and offered them some refreshment from the hamper. The two girls had politely declined and asked Cyril and Katie to speak to them *seulement en anglais, s'il vous plait* as they wished to better their English which in fact was already quite excellent and needed little improvement.

The girls' names were Mimi and Yvette Gallimond and it turned out that they were not from France at all but from a small village very near to Geneva in Switzerland. 'We are so near the French border, however, that we could spend an hour shopping in both countries,' explained Mimi whose slender figure and languid hazel eyes must have made many mountaineers reach for their alpenstocks! She was twenty years old and spent her time working in the large drapery and fashion store owned by her family alongside the other girl, her cousin Yvette who also industriously spent her days as a *midinette* in the Gallimond emporium in Geneva.

Yvette was only nineteen and was a truly lovely rosy-cheeked girl with a pretty face and a merry twinkle in her brown eyes. Her full red lips were most attractive, and even more so, thought Katie, when she giggled at an amusing remark which caused her to display pearl-white teeth which sparkled in the sunlight that poured through the windows of the compartment. Her pink dress was nipped in at the waist which further accentuated her large, rounded breasts which were covered by an exquisite cream coloured silk blouse which, as Katie was later to learn, had been purchased for her in Paris by an ardent admirer.

'Did you enjoy your stay in Bath?' enquired Cyril to the girls. 'Very much so,' replied Mimi. 'It is such a beautiful place with so many lovely buildings. Is it a very old city?'

'Oh yes, the Celts settled there but it was the Romans who built a magnificent town with baths and a temple to the goddess Minerva around the hot springs. Edgar, the first king of all England, was crowned at Bath Abbey and people have been coming to Bath to take the waters for more than a thousand years. Modern Bath was constructed during the early eighteenth century when the stone quarries were opened up and a brilliant architect named John Wood was patronised by wealthy gentlemen. He was responsible for many of the fine buildings in the city.'

As the conversation became more animated the two girls moved across the compartment to sit closer to Katie and Cyril. Perhaps it was all the excitement of leaving Teignmouth so rapidly coupled with the fact that the sun was shining so brightly that Cyril was forced to cover the window with the blind, that after a while Katie felt quite drowsy and slowly but surely her eyes fluttered to a close and she slumped against Yvette with her head resting against the Swiss girl's generous bosoms. She was soon gathered in the arms of Morpheus, yet slumbering lightly enough to feel her feet being gently lifted from the floor so that she was lying full on the seat with her head now cushioned by Yvette's soft body although she was now using her tummy rather than her breasts as a pillow.

Katie was partially woken from her doze when the train rounded a sharp bend and she felt herself being caressed by tender feminine hands. 'Aren't you too warm in all those clothes, Katie?' she heard Yvette murmur and she nodded sleepily in agreement. She made no effort to resist the eager groping that led to her dress being unfastened and she lifted her body so that the garment could be slipped completely off, leaving her clad in just a bodice and knickers. She opened her eyes to find Yvette caressing her face and across on the other seat Cyril and Mimi were exchanging the most intimate of embraces. 'What a handsome young chap you are, I hope you are not one of these Englishmen who prefer *le cricket* to *l'amour* or are you like your nice old King Edward who comes to the Continent every year to fuck all the girls on the French Riviera?' breathed Mimi softly.

Carried away by her boldness, Cyril worked his hands inside the top of Mimi's dress and the naughty girl eased his passage by unbuttoning herself and sliding down the straps of her chemise to allow Cyril's hands to roam across her bare breasts. Her ruby nipples were sticking out like two hard little corks as Cyril ran his palms over them and pressed her perky white globes in his hands. With a gasp Cyril disengaged Mimi's mouth from his own and said with heartfelt feeling in his voice: 'Believe me, I really do prefer fucking to any other sport, Mimi, but Katie is my special girl friend and it would not be proper for me to be unfaithful even if she were not sitting just three feet away from us.'

Katie was deeply touched by these noble words and she determined that not only would she allow Cyril to make love to her tonight (so far their amatory affair had only progressed to Cyril being allowed to squeeze her covered breasts whilst they french-kissed) but that she would encourage Cyril to fuck Mimi if he wished for, as aforesaid, Katie was not a jealous girl and although she enjoyed Cyril's company she was not so involved with him that she would not herself refuse to be fucked by another man should she meet some other young fellow who might take her fancy. Also, Katie's blood had always been fired when she had watched erotic entertainments ever since her previous lover Walter Stanton (who was now living permanently in Buenos Aires where he had amassed a fortune from the export of cheap ready-made clothes to the United States) had taken her to a secret spicy cabaret at the exclusive Beesknees Club in New York.

So she said brightly: 'Go ahead, Cyril, do fuck Mimi if she would like you to, I don't mind at all, really I don't.'

'Are you absolutely sure?' asked Cyril, his hands still cupping Mimi's naked breasts. Katie nodded and Mimi, after murmuring a hasty *merci* began to divest herself of her clothes until she was completely nude. All the others in the compartment admired her slender, lithe body as she stroked her small but proudly uptilted breasts, before moving her hands to the base of her flat tummy where between her legs lay a mass of glossy dark hair which extended to all over her mount and curled down between her thighs. Cyril now replaced her hands with his own as he smoothed his palm over this inviting moist bush of cunney hair. They sat down and kissed while Cyril moved one hand up to tweak her titties and with the other started to frig Mimi gently with his forefinger, making the pretty girl wriggle madly under this two-fold sensual stimulation. Her hand now wandered between Cyril's legs to feel the huge bulge which had appeared in his lap. One by one she delicately undid his fly buttons and then her soft tapering fingers took possession of his bursting prick and she pulled out his stiff naked shaft which under her gentle touch was visibly palpitating with unslaked desire.

Yvette and Katie reached across and helped pull off his trousers and Mimi slid down his underpants so Cyril was now naked from the waist down, his big cock standing upright from between his legs. Mimi decided she would like to ride upon his blue veined boner so she climbed up upon him and taking hold of his throbbing tadger, guided his bell-end into her already wet love channel. She wiggled on his tool delightedly until she was fully speared and then with a little cry she began to fling herself up and down on his vibrating shaft, squealing happily as her breasts jiggled merrily as she clamped her knees around Cyril's thighs.

'*Alors, j'arrive, j'arrive,*' she screamed and from the rather smug smile on Cyril's face it seemed that he too was going to spend very quickly. He bucked his hips in time with hers until with one enormous thrust he rammed his thick cock up her cunney to its fullest extent. Mimi shrieked with delight as Cyril spunked inside her, filling her cunt with a delicious flow of hot sticky froth and she cleverly contracted her cunney muscles to empty his balls of all their jism as she too spent copiously as the shameless pair swam in a sea of lubricity.

The exhilerating sight of Mimi's pussey being so gratified sent shivers throughout Katie's body and she could feel her own pussey beginning to dampen. How she would love to suck in Cyril's tool into her own hungry cunney! Ah, there is nothing to be compared to a stiff cock for satisfying a girl like herself who knew and understood the supreme delights of *l'arte de faire l'amour*. Lost in this lewd reverie, Katie had not noticed that Yvette had now divested herself of her clothes and that her hands were now sliding Katie's knickers down her legs. Then she grasped Katie's chemise and Katie lifted her arms back over her head so that Yvette could pull it off. Now Katie too was nude and Yvette smiled lasciviously as she knelt between Katie's knees which she parted to make room for herself.

'What a gorgeous little notch, I must, how you say, pay homage to it,' breathed Yvette as she placed her hand upon the fine covering of blonde hair which partially hid Katie's pouting pink pussey lips. Katie lay back and let the tingling waves of pleasure which were rising between her legs sweep through her entire body. Yvette teased her quivering pussey, pulling open the cunney lips and rubbing her knuckles back and forth across the entrance to her now very damp slit. Then she eased a finger into Katie's juicy crack which made the English girl tremble all over. She raised her bottom and the exquisite sensations were heightened as Yvette's finger was joined by one and then two others as she frigged Katie's cunney at an ever quickening pace.

Yvette moved up over her, still keeping her busy fingers working inside Katie's oozing pussey as the girls exchanged a passionate kiss. A velvet tongue slithered through Katie's lips to make contact with her own as Yvette relentlessly continued plunging her fingers in and out of Katie's cunt which sent her into paroxyms of ecstasy. Her buttocks tensed as Yvette's fingers toyed with her erect, pulsating clitoris.

'Aaaah!' cried Katie in a blissful agony as she was brought to the very brink of a spend by Yvette's finger-fucking. Then she felt herself swept up over the peak in a welcome release and she groaned and twisted around as her love juices gushed down all over Yvette's fingers and her saturated clitty sent out tremulous spasms of excitement throughout her entire body as she achieved a wonderful climax.

'Let's change seats,' suggested Cyril and he moved across to take Yvette's place whilst she sat down next to Mimi. *'Ma pauvre*, you have not spent yet,' exclaimed Mimi, running her hands across Yvette's delectable dark nipples. 'Lie back and I will bring you off.' Yvette was happy to lie flat as Mimi cupped her firm little bottom cheeks, bending forward to suck the younger girl's engorged titties. She tweaked and rubbed them up until they were as erect as Cyril's cock which was now stirring again as Mimi slowly kissed her way down Yvette's marble white belly to the black cushion of glossy cunney hair which guarded the entrance to her honeypot. Mimi licked all the way up and down the long cleft of Yvette's pussey and then extended her pink tongue to delve between the puffy cunney lips, subtly parting them with the tip of her wicked pink tongue. Now the joyful fluttering tongue sought the moist crack where already the clitty was swelling with passion.

'Mais oui, c'est ça!' cried Yvette, cradling Mimi's head in her hands and her lovely cousin responded at once, clutching those magnificently rounded bum cheeks as she thrust her face even deeper between Yvette's legs, sucking and slurping with great ardour, rolling her tongue round and round, nipping and

biting the rubbery clitty and lapping up the sweet love juices which were now pouring from Yvette's sopping cunt.

Cyril and Katie were spellbound by the sight of the two voluptuously endowed creatures engaged in their uninhibited intimate pursuit of the delights of Lesbos and Cyril whispered in Katie's ear: 'Just look at those tribades – why, it seems that Mimi uses her tongue like a miniature cock to fuck Yvette's cunney.'

For answer, Katie took hold of his rock-hard prick and began to manipulate it in her hands as they leaned forward to see at close quarters how Mimi was passing her tongue so expertly around the other girl's pussey. By now the serrated red lips of Yvette's pussey parted and her erect fleshy clitty, as big as a thumb, could be seen projecting at least a couple of inches between them. Mimi took that sizeable clitty in her mouth, playfully biting it with her teeth. Then after receiving one last rasping lick from Mimi's tongue, Yvette began to spend. Her hips jerked wildly and then from her cunney was flooded by a fine, milky emission which cascaded between Mimi's lips and which was greedily swallowed by her. Yvette ground her pussey again and again against Mimi's open mouth until finally she shuddered into a state of limp exhaustion, heaving and panting as the delicious crisis ebbed slowly away.

Cyril's cock was now twitching violently away as Katie gently pulled on his shaft, which was gleaming wet from Mimi's spendings. Then she was opening her mouth wide and taking in the uncapped purple crown, making Cyril groan hoarsely with delight. She pushed downwards until his helmet was at the back of her mouth and she sucked and slurped on her giant lollipop until she felt his whole body go rigid and she swallowed in anticipation as she waited for the creamy white spunk to come rushing through the shaft. Almost immediately her mouth was filled with his powerful globs of foaming jism and she gulped down every last salty drop of sperm, tonguing his smooth knob until his cock began to soften under her tongue.

Suddenly a piercing whistle came from the engine as the train reached the furthest outskirts of the great railway town of Swindon. As the train slowed sharply before grinding to a complete halt, Cyril let up the blind which had shielded them from the glare of the sun which was now shielded by layers of puffy white clouds and peering out of the window Cyril could see a West Country bound train also drawing to a halt on the opposite track.

'*Ma foi,*' gasped Mimi, 'look out of the window!' The others craned forward to see what had caught Mimi's attention. Perhaps a disgruntled employee of the catering establishment that supplied the railway refreshment rooms had mixed an aphrodisiac potion in the coffee but a randy couple in the compartment directly opposite Cyril and the girls, oblivious to the fact that they could be seen, were a couple in the blissful throes of a frenzied fuck. The girl was leaning up against the window, her dress pulled down so that her well-formed naked breasts were clearly visible to one and all, whilst from behind her skirt had been lifted by her gentleman friend, a tall man wearing mutton chop whiskers and a huge moustache, who was fondling the cheeks of her bum as he jerked his cock in and out between her bare buttocks.

At first, the girl was so taken up by the exquisite sensations emanating from her pussey – for as both Penny and Katie Arkley would always tell their less experienced girl friends, a cock entering a cunney from behind will more often than not tickle the clitty better than when inserted in the usual 'missionary' position – that at first she did not realise there were spectators on the stalled London-bound train gawping at her. Then she realised her situation and immediately covered her breasts with her arm. But then, no doubt thinking that she was being overlooked by complete strangers who she would in all probability never ever see again, she decided that the occasion was best suited to a saucy display rather than one of maidenly modesty. A teasing smile lit up her face and she cupped her large creamy breasts in her hands as if to offer them to her avid audience across the track as the tall man behind her continued to slew what must have been a prick of godly length between her bum cheeks.

'Perhaps she is trying to signal to us, Cyril,' said Katie brightly. 'Waggle your cock at her as our answer to the putting on show of those luscious titties.'

Alas, they were never to find out whether the lecherous lady ever noticed Cyril's stiffstander or indeed whether she had received similar answering flourishes from other gentlemen on the London train. But she seemed to respond by holding her nut brown nipples so close to the window that her titties brushed and stiffened against it. She traced little circles across the pane with her breasts as she rolled them against the glass. From the other compartments on the

London-bound train, cheers of encouragement could be heard along with an occasional cry of outrage from the carriage occupied by Dame Hortensia Harcourt-Everleigh and other members of the Devon and Dorset branches of the Society to Promote Chastity Amongst Young People who were *en route* to their annual conference at the Albert Hall.

There was just time for the hirsute fellow to complete the exhibition of rudery by ejaculating his spermy essence inside his beloved's pussey when, with a jolt, the London express lurched into motion and as the train drew slowly away from the splendidly staged scene which had whiled away the few minutes. The unknown young lady turned round and displayed her bare bottom, pulling her plump cheeks apart in a final flamboyant gesture of farewell.

'I wonder what it is that makes fucking on a train so enjoyable?' mused Yvette and Cyril answered by her recounting the tales of his Uncle Lionel who had expounded at length upon the joys of what he termed 'railway rogering'. 'Yes, Uncle Lionel always maintained that the best fucks of his life had been on trains – in addition to the never-to-be forgotten time in India when the eighteen-year-old daughter of Mustapha Pharte, a maharajah near the Afghan frontier, sucked him off whilst bobbing about in a *howdah* on the back of an elephant during a tiger shoot.

'Uncle Lionel always use to say it was the thrill of speeding along at seventy miles an hour which made women feel randy – all that sort of business about brightness of eye, a flushed complexion and a slight breathlessness as they squeeze their thighs together under their skirts.

'"Play your cards right, Cyril," he would say with great solemnity. "First always make sure the door is locked, for the sake of modesty, and with any luck you'll have an eager, grateful girl impaling herself on your John Thomas with a happy squeal of *joie de vivre*. There are always openings for amorous adventures when you're safely locked into your compartment and the train is speeding merrily along." Mind, I must confess that this is the first time I've ever had my wedding tackle out on a train, although Uncle Lionel was always keen on the idea. He used to take Auntie Dorothy up to Scotland regularly and managed to come at least four times between King's Cross and Newcastle. After their silver wedding, however, he could only manage to fuck her twice at the very best by the time they reached Edinburgh. He still reckons now to raise a stand between London and the Highlands which isn't bad going for an old boy of seventy-nine.'

'Hurrah for Uncle Lionel,' said Katie warmly. 'Fucking should not be reserved for those under sixty.'

After they arrived at Paddington Cyril told the girls to wait whilst he found the services of a porter on the platform. 'Where are you staying in London? I have arranged for Godfrey, my Aunt Julia's chauffeur, to meet us here and he can take you to your hotel,' he told Yvette and Mimi.

'How kind of you, Cyril. We have rooms at the Hotel Splendide in Kensington High Street but tonight we have been asked to a party somewhere in Bloomsbury by a friend of Mimi's mother and we shall spend the night at the house of this gentleman,' said Yvette, opening her bag to look for the address on the invitation.

The English couple exchanged glances and Katie swept back a lock of her beautiful blonde hair from her face. 'No, surely not, Cyril, the coincidence is simply too great! Still let's find out,' she said and turning to the Swiss girls, Katie asked them the name of their host. Yvette passed over the invitation to Katie who laughed out loud. 'I can hardly believe it! We're all going to Gary Hornby's party this evening!'

Yvette and Mimi looked puzzled and Katie explained the extraordinary circumstances. 'How lovely! Are you also staying with Mr Hornby?' asked Mimi. 'No, but we won't be far away – just across the square in fact at my aunt's so things couldn't be easier,' said Cyril, hailing an ancient porter just as Harold the chauffeur spied the group and hurried over to help with their bags.

The Totteridge family were all keen motorists and Cyril's Aunt Julia had also purchased a new Mercedes Simplex which stood waiting for them. Of course, Harold had not expected four passengers and there was no room for all the luggage but Cyril insisted that the chauffeur drove the ladies to Bedford Square whilst he followed in a taxi-cab. 'I wouldn't mind driving myself but I'm not too sure of the way and this heavy London traffic is bloody beastly and takes all the fun out of motoring,' he explained.

As it turned out, he arrived in Bedford Square a minute or two before the Mercedes and with a great flourish he opened the doors for his lady friends. 'Would you like to come in for a moment?' he asked the Swiss misses but Yvette and Mimi said they preferred to go straight to Mr Hornby's house which was literally across the other side of the well-kept park square. 'We'll see you at half past seven!' cried Katie as Harold engaged the clutch and the superbly engineered automobile moved away smartly from the curb, causing a passing hansom cabbie to pull in the reins of his horse with a well-chosen oath – there was no love between the drivers using traditional conveyances of equine transportation and those who opted for the modern new mechanised motor vehicles.

So let us recapitulate the scene, dear reader, as the hour approached for the start of Gary Hornby's *soirée*. You will remember that Bob, Susie and Amanda spent the afternoon resting and were now busying themselves getting ready for the party as were Cyril, Katie, Mimi and Yvette whilst John Gibson, the writer and lover of the ballet, was at this time engaged in handing a generous tip to Chester, the head porter at the Hotel Excelsior in Piccadily where he was planning to spend the next few days in his favourite indulgences of choreography and copulation. 'Thank you very much, sir,' said the porter. 'Now is there anything else I can do for you? I mean, I see you are by yourself on this trip, Mr Gibson, so might you be interested in any female company this evening? We've a lovely new waitress in the residents' restaurant whose attentions were very warmly welcomed by your old friend Captain Northbridge of Cambridge last month.'

'No thank you, Chester, I'm dining with friends tonight.'

'But it's only just six o'clock, sir, why don't I ask Linda to come and visit you in ten minutes?' urged Chester. 'She may be working as a waitress at the moment but she really wants a career as a professional dancer and, knowing of your love of ballet, I'm certain you would find her conversation of interest.

'And more importantly, Captain Northbridge told me as he left for home that in his opinion Linda's the best cocksucker south of Birmingham,' added the porter with a conspiratorial wink.

John Gibson carefully considered the matter. 'I suppose there would be time to make the young lady's acquaintance briefly. Ask her to come up here with half a bottle of chilled white wine as soon as possible.'

'Very good, sir,' said the porter, whose smug expression typified of a man who knew that, barring accidents, a further generous gratuity would be winging its way towards him. John Gibson, the Laird of North Musselburgh, was but one of the many Scottish gentlemen whose natures give lie to the ridiculous canard about the so-called miserliness of our Caledonian cousins, and who invariably showed tangible appreciation for services rendered.

Within ten minutes there was a knock on his door and he called out for the person to enter – and when the door opened, it revealed a feminine presence which made the heart of even such a seasoned cocksman as the wealthy Edinburgh landowner beat faster. His visitor was, of course, the beautiful Linda who turned out to be a slim young girl of no more than eighteen years of age. The Scot's eyes roved over her wavy brown hair, her pretty face blessed with large blue eyes and a pair of delicious dimples, her slim figure with firm, well-rounded breasts and long shapely legs. She was carrying a tray on which rested not only the expected bottle swathed in a cool white towel and two wine glasses but also an open folder which appeared to contain a number of hand-tinted coloured photographs.

'May I put this down on the table?' she asked and as John Gibson nodded his approval he stared unashamedly at her cream coloured blouse which was made of such a fine transparent material that the outline of her dark, swollen nipples could be seen pressing against their thin covering.

The introductions over, John Gibson poured out two glasses of '98 Moet et Chandon as Linda settled herself on the sofa. 'So you want to be a professional dancer?' he said, sitting down next to her. 'Yes, for though I could never aspire to be a prima ballerina I know I have talent enough to work in the popular theatre. But I need to take a year's course at a dancing school and it is such an expensive business. My family cannot afford to pay the fees but I am determined to further my career.

'So I have taken employment here at the Excelsior as a waitress and to further supplement my income I also sell products from Madame Titchfield's Dildorium in Stoke Newington. Many guests of both sexes find these hand-made comforters make perfect presents, expecially when a gentleman is forced to leave his beloved for any lengths of time on matters of business or whatever.'

John Gibson grinned as he took the photograph folder Linda passed to him. 'Yes indeed, and is this the manufacturer's slogan – *The Gift to Leave*

Behind? Very apt if I may say so.' He flicked through the first photographs, which showed a wide array of finely modelled members nestling on a small, plump velvet cushion. Most had been glazed with lifelike flesh but others had painted decorations of all kinds, from simple colouring to the famous Chinese willow-pattern which had been produced for the noted Sinologist, Lord Benjamin Dunn.

'All these are commissioned dildoes fashioned from the dimensions of the donors' penises,' explained Linda. 'The method of manufacture may be of interest to you. I was fascinated when Madame Titchfield took me round the establishment.'

'Do tell me more,' murmured the lusty son of Hibernia, putting his arm around the attractive girl who smiled and snuggled herself into a comfortable position besides him.

'Well, to begin with, the donor's prick is oiled all over from the base to the tip. Naturally this can be properly executed when the shaft is erect and often the clients have to be helped to maintain a stiffstander. This presents few problems as the factory is staffed by only female labour and employees take turns to bring customers' cocks up to the mark. Usually one touch of a soft feminine hand is all it takes to stiffen up their pricks and then the member is plunged into a container of liquid plaster. A few days later, when the plaster is completely hardened, the mould is filled with liquid wax and when that is set the cast is broken open and hey presto, we have a perfect replica of the prick! Then the mould is filled with clay and fired in a gas fired kiln which means that a precise control over the temperature can be maintained.

Then the dildoes are glazed and painted and after a second firing at a far higher temperature the finished obect is ready for display and use.' *[Interestingly enough, plaster-casting of this kind became very popular during the wild swinging sixties and groupies vied to produce plaster casts of their favourite pop stars – Editor]*

She turned the page and added: 'You may enjoy looking through some photographs of our dildoes in action especially as I was chosen to model the 1904 range. They were hand-tinted by no less an artist than George Lucas, the famed miniaturist.' She handed the folder across to John Gibson whose eyebrows rose sharply as he gazed at a coloured photograph of Linda sprawled on her back, her long legs wide apart. At the base of her belly a mass of brown hair formed a perfect veil over a pouting little cunney at the side of which, grasped in hand, was a prime dark specimen of Madame Titchfield's craft. 'That's rather an outsize model, isn't it?' said John Gibson with a slight air of envy in his voice as he turned to the next photograph which showed Linda teasing her cunney lips with the rounded tip of the black monster. 'Yes, it was modelled on the organ of a Negro pugilist Riley Matthews,' *[a British and European welterweight champion – Editor]* she replied, laying her hand on his thigh which caused his own well-proportioned member to jump to attention inside his trousers. The next photograph showed Linda writhing in ecstacy as with one hand she held the base of the giant dildo which was now firmly ensheathed inside her cunney, whilst the other was across her breasts as she rubbed a red nipple up between her fingers.

'Well, what do you think of the merchandise?' Linda demanded on her prospective customer who had certainly been impressed by what he had seen. 'A superbly executed range of goods displayed to their best advantage,' he pronounced, 'and next time in London I will certainly visit Madame Titchfield's to have my own personal cast made. I shall be visiting Canada shortly and a gift such as shown here would undoubtedly make a perfect momento for the lady with whom I shall be staying. The dildo could be painted in the colours of my clan, I presume?'

'That can be easily arranged,' she said, giving him a quick kiss on the cheek. 'Now although I do enjoy using Madame Titchfield's dildoes I do prefer the real article. I understand from Chester that you have no time to fuck but I'd very much like to suck your cock if you have no objection.'

'None whatsoever,' said the delighted Scotsman politely as she rose up and said: 'I'll be back with you in a minute. Perhaps you'd like to start changing for your party tonight whilst I run your bath?' He obeyed her with alacrity, tearing off his clothes as she rose quickly to the bathroom. He heard the bathtaps being loosened and moments later she returned with her dress unbuttoned and standing just in front of the gallant and partially unclothed Mr Gibson, asked him to tug at the sash of her frock. He pulled it and the sash fell to the ground, the gown opened and she stepped out in all her naked glory for she had taken off her underclothes in the bathroom. Her beautiful full breasts swung gracefully as she pirouetted lightly on the balls of her feet and John Gibson's cock sprung out of his drawers at the luscious sight. She knelt down and pulled down his pants before taking hold of his veiny truncheon. She passed her tongue over her lips before taking the pulsating shaft in her hand. Then she gave a quick moistening lick to the purple knob and proceeded to suck in at least three inches of his twitching tool into her mouth.

Chester had not exaggerated the skills of this pretty *fellatrix* and John Gibson was soon in the seventh heaven of delight as her moist mouth worked up and down, licking and lapping at ever last inch of his length, her hand holding the base of his cock as she pumped her head up and down, keeping her lips taut, kissing and sucking until she suddenly pulled her lips away. The pre-come juices were already oozing out of the tip of his knob and were lapped up instantly by her darting, pink tongue. One hand now gently massaged his hairy ballsack and the other clamped itself around his shaft as she jammed her mouth back over the smooth domed helmet. 'A-h-r-e!' he croaked as with a convulsive jerking of his hips he spunked a tremendous jet of gushy foam into her throat. She sucked and swallowed his copious emission of milky sperm until at last his prick stopped twitching and slowly began to shrink down to its normal size. He lay panting as Linda looked up at him and said: 'Oooh, that was grand, what a pity we had to rush it. I'll go and turn your bath off. Would you like me to soap your back for you?'

He regretfully declined this kind offer as Gary Hornby had left a note at the hotel asking him to come round early to Bedford Square before the other guests arrived to meet Hal Freedman, an American art dealer who was selling a picture which Gary believed John Gibson might well want for his prized collection.

In the drawing room at 47 Bedford Square, Gary Hornby and Hal Freedman, the aforesaid gentlemen from across the Atlantic, were talking about the short visit the American had just made to France where he had purchased several paintings. 'I had a really good time in Paris, Gary. You must come with me on my next trip,' chuckled the art dealer. 'You'd really have a ball at the *café concerts*.'

'*Café concerts*?' echoed his host. 'What might these be?'

'Oh, a kind of cabaret but usually with a stage, footlights and a curtain – much like our vaudeville or your music-hall. The audience joins in the choruses of the songs and we all have a jolly time. Mind you, something extraordinary happened on my last visit to a "*Caf Conc*", the Ambassadeurs to which I was taken by Monsieur Robert, my gallery's French representative. The dancers were particularly pretty and I remarked to Monsieur Robert that I would love one to take to bed with me that night. "But *monsieur*, I wish I had known beforehand – I could have made arrangements," he said. "But if you would like some entertainment, come home with me after the show. Do you remember meeting my wife, Laura, at Count Gewirtz's party the other night? She told me how delighted she would be if I could persuade you to fuck her." I could hardly believe my ears and must have looked so dumbfounded that Monsieur Robert said: "Don't be shocked, my wife and I have been married for eight wonderful years. But we have an understanding which allows us to enjoy ourselves as we will so long as the other partner freely consents."

' "A happy arrangement," I commented, thinking of Monsieur Robert's shapely young wife who could only be in her late twenties at most and who was a most attractive woman. "*Mais oui*," he smiled. "And I assure you that I very much enjoy seeing my wife fucked by another man whilst I watch. Come, I have a cab waiting outside, let us leave now."

'In the *fiacre* Monsieur Robert told me how recently he and Laura had first practised this unusual pursuit of erotic pleasure. "I have a seventeen-year-old assistant, Maurice, who anyone could see was obviously very excited by Laura who would make a point of visiting the gallery whenever she could, dressed in clothes which accentuated the swell of her breasts and which left her free to show her leg through the slit of her skirt. So one day I told Maurice to deliver a letter to my wife and I waited about ten minutes before walking back to our apartment. I let myself in as quietly as I could and then walked into the bedroom. *Mon Dieu!* My cock stood up as hard as a rock! They were both naked on the bed and my lovely wife had her head between the young man's legs, sucking his thick prick like she wanted to devour it. I watched in awe as she rolled over on her back, exposing her hot pussey to him, her legs spread wide as she fingered her clitty to get herself wet enough to take in his big cock."

' "He raised himself up and crawled on top of her, positioning himself so that he could nudge the knob of his cock between her cunney lips. Once he was in place he plunged forward with a cry and rammed it in all the way deep inside Laura's cunt. I watched as it slid in and out of her wet cunney and I noticed that she was thoroughly enjoying it. I stripped off my clothes and joined in and Laura sucked my cock whilst Maurice fucked her. We then changed places and would have continued all afternoon, Monsieur Hal, but I had to be at the *Gare du Nord* to meet your train!"

'We laughed at this coincidence and I must say that I was feeling very randy by the time we arrived at his apartment. At first, I was rather timid at the thought of what might be on offer when we entered his home but as soon as we entered Laura made me very welcome and insisted that her husband open a bottle of champagne which was already standing in the ice-box. Laura was walking around barefoot and was wearing only a light green, wrap-around robe. She sat perched on a high chair and opened her robe just enough to show her knees and a glimpse of her upper legs. "There's no need to be shy, darling," said Robert and he leaned over to uncover some more of her creamy thighs. "Go and see yourself what beautiful breasts she has, *mon ami*."

'I had never fucked any man's wife before let alone in front of him and with his encouragement – but what the heck? – If that was what they wanted it was sure okay with me! So I finished my drink and stood up and boldly pulled away Laura's robe from her shoulders. I now saw two pretty pert pointed breasts each topped with a strawberry coloured nipple surrounded by large pink circled aureoles. My cock was now throbbing violently against its confinement as Laura slipped off the robe and stood naked in front of me. She knelt down and unbuttoned my flies and pulled out my pulsating prick. She ran her talented tongue over its head before her lips closed over it and slid down my eight inch shaft down her throat in one fluid gulp. Then she eased back, licking along the underside of my shaft until she reached my balls which she sucked into her mouth and swished around before licking up to my knob again before taking all of my cock back between her lips until I could feel her nose nuzzling my bush at the root. I love being sucked off and always try to make it last but Laura was just too much. I came quickly, exploding in hot sticky jets which filled her mouth as she continued sucking, milking every last drop from my cock, until she felt me begin to soften.

'When I took my prick out of her mouth I saw Robert had undressed and was playing with himself as Laura wrapped her hand around my shaft and stroked it up back again to a fine stiffness. "Take your trousers off and lie down," she whispered and in a trice I was flat on my back on the plush red carpet. She told me later she had intended to take her time but her pussey was tingling so much that she straddled herself over me and impaled herself upon my cock. "*Alors*, Hal, fuck me hard!" she panted and I did my best to oblige as she rode me like a bucking bronco, pounding the delicious round cheeks of her arse against my thighs as I hammered her from below. For at least two minutes we fucked like that without a pause as her gorgeous breasts jiggled up and down. "I can't hold back any longer!" I moaned and I came in a thunderous orgasm which nearly bucked her off with each huge squirt of spunk. The gush of hot jism made Laura come instantly and she shuddered to a grand climax as if her cunt had been wired to an electric shock machine. She clenched her thighs for one long, delicious moment as she nurtured every last throb of current. Her love juices trickled down over my pubic hair and – well, as you can imagine, Gary, I didn't go back to my hotel that night!'

Gary Hornby stood up and said: 'I hope you are not too tired after all that exertion, Hal, because I have some lovely girls joining us tonight who won't want to be disappointed.'

'Don't worry, I'm fully recovered and raring to go,' advised the American. 'As we say in New York City, just bring on the girls!'

CHAPTER THREE
A Night To Remember

John Gibson was the first guest to be ushered in by the butler whom Gary Hornby had hired from Aspiso's Staff Agency in Clerkenwell for his party. Although Mr Edwards, of Aspiso's, charged the highest rates in London, his domestics were unsurpassed not only in their work but also in their discretion. Woe betide any Aspiso employee who blurted out any juicy details of what he or she had seen! This was just as well on this particular occasion, for the butler who showed Mr Gibson into the drawing room was none other than George Formbey, who at one time headed the staff at Sir Paul Arkley's country establishment and who could, if he had been basely designed, made life somewhat uncomfortable for Katie Arkley. She was as surprised as Mr Formbey when at the end of the evening they came face to face at the door. *[See 'Cremorne Gardens' which chronicles the doings of Mr Formbey and other former servants of the Arkley household – Editor]*

But as asked, John Gibson came early to talk over the possible purchase of a Toulouse-Lautrec picture with Hal Freedman. 'You know what André Suares said of the wee man,' said John Gibson thoughtfully. 'Toulouse-Lautrec is a Baron who has taken root in a brothel. Not that this bothers me, but my fellow citizens up in Edinburgh can be a terribly sanctimonious crew. I don't want to cause any controversy when I show pictures from my collection at the Assembly Rooms later this year. I put on the whole damn thing for charity and want as many people as possible to come along.' Hal Freedman shook his head. 'It's up to you, John. I'm simply giving you first refusal on *The Morning After*. You are familiar with the painting – it's of his mistress Valadon sitting at a table in front of a bottle of red wine and a glass, propped on her elbows, her head resting in one hand as she stares into space.'

'We'll talk about it later,' promised John Gibson as they heard the chimes of the front door bell. *[Unfortunately, Mr Gibson's name does not appear in the provenance of this famous masterpiece – such a disappointment for his heirs and the city of Edinburgh's art gallery! – Editor]* Bob Goggin was the next arrival and, as he had promised, he had squired Susie and Amanda, the two tribades he had seen performing in the open air earlier that afternoon. The girls made their entrance a few minutes later and a footman offered the guests champagne or the fashionable new drink of Buck's Fizz – champagne and fresh orange juice which was a particular favourite of the host.

Shortly afterwards, the two Swiss girls, Katie and Cyril met on the doorstep and were ushered in together by Mr Formbey who gave no indication that he had recognised Katie from his previous employment. Perhaps fortunately (for she may have felt embarrassed by being seen at a fast party by a former employee of her family) Katie was too busy conversing with Yvette and Mimi to notice that it was George Formbey who took her velvet evening cape in the hallway. The guests all chatted away with animation, for Gary Hornby was a hardworking host and made sure that everyone was introduced properly as the company formed itself into little groups.

Of course, far more embarrassing for Katie than seeing George Formbey was the sight of Bob Goggin, the former under-gardener at Arkley Manor and the youth she knew was enjoying a romantic liaison with her sister Penny. And of course, Bob too was shocked at the sight of Katie. He had understood from Penny's last letter that she was spending the summer in Teignmouth!

As soon as possible Katie and Bob manoeuvred themselves into a corner and Katie whispered: 'Bob, what on earth are you doing here?' 'I could ask the same question, Katie,' he retorted. Katie half-suppressed a little giggle. 'I suppose that both of us are being naughty tonight so let's make a pact. I won't tell on you if you promise not to peach on me.'

'Done!' said Bob promptly and with a wink went over to join the group around Hal Freedman. He was telling John, Susie and Amanda of his previous trip to England earlier in the year when Lord Breslaw had taken him to Liverpool to see the Grand National. 'I'm not a great sportsman,' confessed the American, 'but the race sure is an endurance test. Of course I had a small bet which made the race more exciting.'

'Don't tell me you backed the winner, you lucky bastard,' said Gary Hornby as he passed by. 'As I recall, it came in at twenty-five to one and the bookies had a field day!'

'What was the name of the horse that won, Hal?'
asked Susie. 'I remember my father, who is a keen if
inexpert punter, telling me about how this giant horse
came from New Zealand but was shipwrecked off the
Irish coast. To everyone's surprise, he galloped home
eight lengths in front to become the first colonial
winner of the great race.'

'The horse was called Moifaa and you're right,
Gary, he came in at twenty-five to one. I didn't back
him but just by closing my eyes and sticking a pencil in
the list of runners I managed to pick out The Gunner
which came in third so I won about fifteen pounds.
Lord Breslaw wasn't too pleased as, being a patriot,
he had laid a hundred guineas on the King's horse,
Ambush II, which fell early on. But that's what
gambling's all about – you can't tell a horse how to
win a race. Anyway, as my Uncle Mark always told
me: "Hal, my boy, the best way to throw a dice is
away."'

'Sound advice,' commented Gary Hornby as
George Formbey threw open the doors to the dining
room and announced that dinner was served. The
company trooped into the lavishly furnished *salle à
manger* to partake of a magnificent meal.

The food and wines served were of the highest
quality, as one would expect as the repast had been
prepared under the direction of Mrs Hetty Beaconsfield, another former member of the Arkley family's
staff, who was now earning a very good living preparing lunches and dinners for wealthy young gentlemen like Gary Hornby. Her old friend Mr Formbey,
who often worked with her on such engagements,
strolled into the kitchen whilst the guests were

tucking into the succulent *boeuf wellington* to tell Mrs Beaconsfield of Katie's presence in the dining room. 'She's just as lovely as when we worked at Arkley Manor,' said Mr Formbey. 'And the young fellow sitting next to her has had his hand on her thigh every time I've passed by with the wine. If those two aren't having an affair, I'll eat my hat.'

'Good luck to her, though I just hope her Ma never finds out. Can you imagine what the old dragon would say?' said the cook who, like Mr Formbey, did not have happy memories of the formidable mistress of Arkley Manor. Mr Formbey grinned as his eyes followed the progress of the red-haired Lottie, Mrs Beaconsfield's buxom young assistant, as she struggled to lift a heavy cut-glass bowl of fresh fruit from the kitchen table onto a serving trolley.

'Here, let me help you with that,' said the butler as Lottie beamed her thanks. But his face fell when Mrs Beaconsfield muttered: 'Forget it, George, you'd be third in line there after the two footmen you've left in the dining room!'

Meanwhile the party was going with a swing. After Mr Formbey had supervised the clearing away of the desserts, the ladies retired to allow the gentlemen to enjoy cigars and port. In fact only Hal Freedman chose to smoke as Gary Hornby preferred the port to Bob Goggin. 'Hal had a remarkable experience in Montmartre last week,' remarked the genial host. 'I am sure you will find his story most entertaining.' At first the American demurred but, after being assured that neither Bob, Cyril nor John would take offence, Hal launched into his tale about Monsieur Robert who liked nothing better than to see his wife being fucked by another man.

'So that's it – a most astonishing experience, don't you agree?' finished Hal. 'Aye, but anybody who still thinks the sky is the limit is short of imagination,' said John Gibson as he downed his glass of port. 'I have a girl named Carolyn up in Aberdeen who enjoys parading herself nude in front of other men and having sex with them whilst we are out having a good time. For example, last month she came down to Edinburgh and we had dinner in her hotel before making our way to the lounge. Here we struck up a conversation with three Americans who were spending their vacation touring Britain. Walter and Harold Godfrey were brothers and Janie, a cute little blonde, had slipped away from her parents who were spending the evening with friends, to be with these two strapping lads. We joined them in the Godfrey's suite and after a few drinks I noticed that in a certain light I could see Jane's nipples through her dress!

'I must be seeing things, I thought to myself, but Harold had seen me staring at the front of Janie's dress for he chuckled and said: "Yeah, she really has great nips, hasn't she? Janie, why don't you show us those beautiful titties naked as nature intended?" The pretty girl laughed and pretended to be shocked. "My, what a thing to say, you naughty boy. Still, if you really would like to see them, why not unbutton my dress and see for yourself?" Harold's eyes gleamed as he accepted this naughty challenge and he swiftly unbuttoned the front of Janie's dress. Her delicious creamy breasts spilled out in all their naked glory. She cupped the two full rounded globes in her hands and asked who would like to suck them. "First come, first served," she smiled and, being nearest, I nuzzled my lips around her left tittie whilst Walter managed to beat Harold to the draw and began sucking her right raspberry coloured nipple. The flicking of our tongues on her titties raised her nips up to stand like stiff little rubber soldiers whilst Carolyn entered into the spirit of things by unbuttoning our flies and taking out our stiffstanders. I glanced round to see her clasp Walter's prick which was immense and knowing how Carolyn liked big cocks I guessed that he would fuck her before the evening was out. At the same time Harold was busily engaged in undressing himself and after he had divested himself of all his clothes he came round to assist Janie and Carolyn take off their dresses. Walter and I tore off our own clothes though neither of us disengaged our mouths from Janie's succulent nipples.

'Then Carolyn, who was now totally nude, still with Walter's cock in one hand mine in the other, found her pussey being fingered by Harold. "Let's all fuck," she gasped and this sentiment found us all in total agreement. Janie led me to a sofa and laid herself down upon it invitingly her thighs spread and her hand between her legs, fondling her fluffy pussey hair with her fingers. I glanced back and saw Carolyn sucking Walter's cock as both he and Harold caressed her breasts and diddled her cunney. But I had more important work to hand and I started fucking Janie. She proved to be really talented at *l'arte de faire l'amour* and the sound and feel of my cock squelching its way through her juicy love channel soon sent the spunk boiling up from my balls and shooting through my staff. Janie squirmed around wildly as she squeezed and milked my cock of its milky essence and her wickedly clever pussey.

'After I came Janie called over Harold to watch us. She heaved herself up to suck my cock up to stiffness as I watched Walter fuck Carolyn from behind, sliding his thick prick in between her pert bum cheeks and rubbing her small uptilted titties with his hands as he threw his arms around her. She stood with her bum thrust out and her hands spread flat against the wall. Harold proceeded to kneel down and lick out Janie's sperm-filled cunt and she twitched and bucked as a series of sharp little orgasms racked through her body. Over the next hour or so we all switched around and took turns with the two eager girls. Carolyn spent so much that her juices dribbled down her legs and stained the carpet, especially when she lay down on the rich shag pile (how aptly named!) and let Harold and Walter lap at her cunney whilst she sucked my cock.

'Then Carolyn and I returned to her room for one final slow but extremely satisfying fuck in bed. She inserted my knob directly into her sopping crack and as it slipped in I sucked on her erect little red titties, moving my head from one to another until I brought her up to a real frenzy of excitement. I fucked her quite powerfully, plunging my prick in and out of her cunt, letting my balls bang against her bottom as my shaft crashed in and out between her cunney lips. She squealed with delight as she reached her peak and just moments later I felt my own climax approaching. I let out a great gasp as the frothy white foam jetted out of my cock to flood her pussey hole as we writhed together in paroxyms of pleasure until, like long-distance runners who have breached the white finishing tape, we gently slowed down to a standstill.

'We've often enjoyed fucking with other people. To date, Carolyn and I have swopped around with two couples, and seven men in threesomes and two women in a whoresome foursome but the encounter with these sturdy young Americans was perhaps the most arousing of all.'

There was silence for a few moments until Cyril Totteridge murmured: 'If the young lady prefers to spread her favours and you have no objections, John, I would be grateful for her address as I plan to visit Scotland in September for a weekend's shoot on the Duke of Glasgow's estate in West Lothian. It would be my pleasure to journey up to Aberdeen to meet this delightful creature, if you think she would deign to receive me.'

'I'm sure she would if I write to her and tell her to expect a letter from you,' said John Gibson cheerfully. 'I don't want to give the impression that she fucks with any old Tom, Dick or Harry. But a nice, clean young man like you – who I presume is well-endowed enough to satisfy her – would interest Carolyn very much.

'I believe that Society treats women too daintily – but not in terms of politeness nor of chivalrous behaviour, heaven forbid! Any man worth his salt must accept that when a girl says "no" she means it and her wishes must be respected. But I often think of the poem written by Sir Lionel Trapes [*a bon viveur of the notoriously fast South Hampstead set that included Aubrey Beardsley, Henry Spencer Ashbee, alias*

107

"Pisanus Fraxi", and the most famous of nineteenth-century collectors of erotic literature, Sir Andrew Stuck and many Cremornites. Sir Lionel's verses deserve a wider readership than that of 'The Oyster', *one of the rudest of late Victorian underground magazines in which they originally appeared – Editor]*

> Let those who never tried, believe
> In women's chastity!
> Let her who ne'er was asked, receive
> The praise of modesty!
>
> Tho' woman's virtue's true as steel
> Before you touch her soul;
> Still let it once the magnet feel
> 'Twill flutter towards the Pole!'

'Well said, John,' said Gary Hornby, passing the port to Cyril Totteridge. 'I do so thoroughly agree with you that when a girl says "no" she means what she says. Only a cad would attempt to force her to do anything to which she did not freely consent. However, one can often get lucky, as you Americans put it, Hal.

'For example, earlier this summer I accepted an invitation from an old friend of mine, Dr Sinclair, to spend a week with down in his summer home near Bournemouth in Dorset. The weather was exceptionally glorious but alas, he contracted one of those beastly summer colds and for two days was confined to his bedroom. So one day I trudged down to a secluded part of the beach by myself with a deck-chair and a copy of *The Oyster*. I set up my chair and just before I settled down I noticed behind me one of the two extremely pretty girls who had rented a bungalow for the summer across the road from Dr Sinclair's house. I had been introduced to them at a party a few evenings before and I remembered that her name was Rosie and that her friend's name was Judy. Rosie was lying down on her tummy and as I watched, she slid down the straps of her swimsuit and wriggled her breasts out of it so she could expose more of her figure to the gentle summer breeze.

'I moved my chair round, stealing a glance at her as often as possible to see if I could obtain a good look at those magnificent titties. Well, at first I had no luck but then after about ten minutes or so her girlfriend Judy came walking towards us. She was carrying a glass of water and, with a little giggle, she poured the water on Rosie's back. Naturally, Rosie was so shocked that she screamed and leaped up, giving me and anyone else who might have been around full view of her superb naked breasts, two full rounded fleshy orbs topped by nut-brown nipples which look- ed as though they were aching to be rolled around in my hand.

'I stood there as the two girls giggled and then Rosie saw me staring at her. Making no attempt to cover her bare breasts, she asked me if I liked the look of her melons, as she called them. My cock was hardening fast as I said they looked ripe enough to eat. "Goodbye, I must leave you two as I promised Leonard that I'd meet him for a swim round by the pier," Judy called out as she skipped away. At last Rosie slipped the swimsuit back on and as we talked I thought I detected her looking at the bulge in my swimsuit as my cock was now almost fully erect.

'Anyhow, to cut the story short, she accepted my invitation to come back to the house for a glass of iced lemonade. I set up two comfortable chairs on the verandah and I could swear that she was looking more than once at my cock which was still in a semi-swollen state. After we drank the lemonade I took the glasses and tray to the kitchen but when I returned to the verandah Rosie had disappeared – but she had left a clue, for her swimsuit was draped over the chair. With my heart beating twenty to the dozen I looked in the lounge and there sprawled totally naked on the sofa was Rosie, joyfully playing with herself. She had one hand on an erect rosy nipple whilst the other was busy rubbing up and down her hairy brown bush, her fingers tracing her crack from top to bottom.

'My cock now sprang to its full length as she looked up and asked me if I liked what I saw or did I wish to return the goods to the manufacturer? For answer I pulled off my trunks and joined her on the sofa where I discovered that she had peeled a banana and had inserted it inside her cunney. "How about some fruit for your mid-morning snack?" she asked lewdly as I nibbled on the banana, withdrew it slightly and then shoved it back in. This drove her wild and she told me to eat the banana as she wanted to be fucked properly. "I'm going to sit on your lovely thick cock, Gary," she whispered in my ear. "And you'll feel it gliding juicily into my moist little cunt."

'Rosie was as good as her word – she positioned herself on top of me leaving the lips of her pussey just inches away from the tip of my straining tadger. She took my hands and placed them on her stiff little titties and I moved my palms over them which seemed to excite her even more. Then she moved up and over my cock which she took lovingly in her hand and guided it firmly into her lubricated love-channel. She sat down on it, trapping the entire length in her engorged cunney. How she wriggled with pleasure as she bounced up and down, leaning forward to let those heavy fleshy breasts dangle in front of my face. I was mere putty in her hands as my raging prick impaled her sopping cunt and automatically my hips pushed up to meet her downward thrusts.

'She increased the speed of her fucking rhythm and my cock began to throb uncontrollably. I knew that a spend was near. With one last push upwards I gushed out a fierce jet of hot foam inside her and this finished Rosie off nicely and we whimpered with joy at every spasm as our love juices mingled together in a veritable flood of mutual jism.

'Although the sun shone brightly we decided to stay the rest of the day in bed. As soon as my penis regained its stiffness we began kissing and cuddling again and soon we found ourselves in a comfortable *soixante neuf* position. Rosie's thighs were clasped around my head and her spunk-coated pussey lips were pressed firmly against my mouth. As I lapped up the morsels of our previous repast, she sucked my cock up to its fullest height and then, to my great delight, began to lick around that sensitive area between my arsehole and my balls. I don't know about you gentlemen, but a tonguing down there simply drives me insane! Well, after giving that area a thorough going-over, Rosie transferred her wicked pink tongue to my knob, flicking at it with the very tip of her tongue so expertly that I could feel my balls tightening. My prick was now rocklike and yearning to be placed in her squishy honeypot.

'She too was ready for a further bout of fucking but this time Rosie lay on her back, her legs open and her pink pussey lips jutting through her silky mound. I sank my rigid rod deep into the wet warm softness and I felt the walls of her cunt clamp round my cock: this made me start pumping madly in and out of her, sliding deeper and deeper, grinding my trusty tool against her clitty. On this second fuck, Rosie was the first to spend, shivering and trembling as she reached the apex. Her cunney gripped my cock even more firmly as she entered the delicious throes of orgasm. I pressed my finger against her clitty as spasm after spasm shook her lovely body. "Come on Gary, I want more of that spunky fuck juice inside me," she groaned and with her hands now gripping my bum I found myself thrusting in and out of her sopping cunt at an even speedier rate. The spunk soon boiled up in my balls and I exploded into her, filling her delighted pussey with copious gushes of spunk as we screamed loudly in the frenzy of emission until I slumped exhausted upon her.

'We then rested and I lay my head down on her beautiful big breasts whilst she gently played with my limp shaft, purring like a kitten as she let her fingers wander all over it. I told her what a wonderful lover she was and she replied: "Thank you for the compliment. I know that many girls say that sex is not the most important factor in a relationship but for me it is perhaps the most important. I am not too difficult to please. I do love fucking and having a stiff penis deep inside me is what I like best of all. There is nothing in the world to compare with that feeling – I love it!"'

Here Gary Hornby drew breath. After listening so intently to this stirring tale which he had so graphically recounted, the guests slumped back in their chairs, feeling as though they had been well fucked themselves!

After a minute or two Hal Freedman stood up and said: 'Shall we join the ladies? His story has made me dreadfully randy but if what our host told me earlier on was true, gentlemen, we might all be in for a night to remember!'

As it so happened, the girls were feeling equally fruity! Amanda and Susie had just regaled them with the story of how their expedition to Lesbos that afternoon had been interrupted by Bob Goggin. 'Do you not enjoy cock?' Mimi had enquired curiously, for she was a girl who enjoyed fucking above all other pleasures.

'Certainly we do, why, I've even been seduced by the very highest in the land!' said Susie. Just then the door opened and the male guests filed in. 'Take a seat, gentlemen, you're just in time to hear how I was fucked by no less a personage than His Majesty The King, Edward VII, God bless him!

'Ah, now this sounds like a good rude story,' said John Gibson, settling himself down next to Amanda whose mane of blonde hair had been catching his eye throughout the meal.

Susie giggled and continued: 'Well, it was just four summers ago – only a few months before the old Queen died, so actually he was the Prince of Wales when we met. I was only eighteen and I was living with my family near Windsor. One fine morning I took our dog for a walk in the park and when I reached a bench I let him run free and sat down for a while, meaning to read the book I had brought with me. I was so engrossed in my book that I did not even hear anyone approach me so when I looked up and saw this large man looming over me I jumped up in surprise. "Oh my dear, I am so sorry to have startled you, please accept my apologies," he said in a slightly accented voice. I stared at him and at first did not recognise the broad figure and handsome bearded face of the Prince of Wales. I saw my dog in the distance and whistled for him to come back to me but to my surprise two dogs answered my call, my own mongrel and a corgi which obviously belonged to the Prince.

'Dogs are marvellous animals for breaking the ice when one first meets a stranger. The Prince told me that he walked round Windsor Great Park as often as he could when he was staying at the Palace, as his doctor had told him that he needed to make more exercise. "You are a lovely creature," he said to me. "What is your name?" "Susie de Vere Forrester, Your Royal Highness," I replied shyly. Though I was a mere commoner we talked away ten to the dozen whilst our dogs played happily on the grass.

'Then I stood up to leave and the Prince took my hand and said softly: "Ah, Susie, this has been such a pleasant conversation – must you really go?" I told him that I had to leave but then he asked if we could meet here at the same time tomorrow morning. Well, the temptation was too great and though I guessed that it would lead to some rumpty – well, we all know what the Prince is like! – I agreed to see him there the next day. When I arrived home I sat in the garden and tried to concentrate on my book, a splendid romantic novel by Miss Boote, but I could not get the Prince out of my mind and I began fantasising about how his body would look with no clothes on. I pictured his powerful frame with a lovely furry chest, a huge stiff cock and a nice, bunchy bum. These thoughts made my mouth water and idly I let my fingers stir between my legs as I imagined what it would be like to be fucked by the next King of England!

'The morrow dawned and the weather was even warmer. I left the dog at home and made my way to our meeting place. Although I was five minutes early, the Prince was already there and I quickened my pace to run towards him. As I reached him I stumbled and he caught me athletically in his arms, moving surprisingly quickly for a big man in the prime of life. He pressed me tightly against him and I felt his prick instantly harden against my belly. It *was* big, even bigger than I had imagined. He drew me into the privacy of an overhanging tree and we exchanged an impassioned kiss. We licked each other's lips and our tongues tangled juicily as we sank down to the ground. His hands felt for my breasts and a hiss of excitement escaped from his lips when his fingers found my stiff nipples. He swiftly unbuttoned my blouse as I shrugged off my jacket and he grunted with satisfaction when he saw that I was naked underneath. He brought his head down to suck on my engorged red cherries and the sheer pleasure of his tonguing of my nipples caused an anguished throbbing between my legs and made my pussey start to moisten.

'By now I was shaking with desire so I simply grabbed the royal hand and shoved it between my legs. He smoothed his hand up and down my thighs and he gave a second appreciative gurgle of surprise when he discovered that I had already discarded my knickers which were safely tucked away in my handbag. I helped him tear off his own clothes and soon we were both naked. I looked down upon his body and to my delight his cock was as mighty a weapon as I had speculated. The shaft was rigid, thick and long, slightly curving to the right and the plum coloured cap winked up so naughtily at me that I immediately took hold of this majestic prick, stroking it gently along its massive length before cradling his heavy balls. It just had to go into my mouth, there and then and the Prince let out a sharp intake of breath as I juiced his knob with my saliva before forcing this smooth skinned helmet between my lips. His hands played with my hair and when I felt him start to tremble he pulled away slightly and reluctantly I let it slip from my mouth. He indicated that I should climb higher up his body, higher and higher until I was kneeling across his face with my bum practically touching his nose. His tongue leaped out to lick my pouting cunney lips and I eased myself gently down so that he work his tongue in between them. He worked hard and strong with his lips and tongue as his fingers made little circles around the tip of my tiny clitty. It's only weeny but it gets as hard as a little rock when I get really steamed up. I found my pussey was soon disgorging its love liquid onto the royal hand.

'What a magical *soixante neuf* we enjoyed as he sucked on my cunt and I gobbled his cock but we both wanted desperately to fuck so I wriggled round on top of him until I was fully astride. I sat firmly down upon his big, fat prick, clamping my thighs together and placing my legs inside his spread-out ones, levering myself up and down with my arms and feet. I know that some men don't appreciate the woman-on-top position as, for some silly reason, they feel it takes away from their masculine pride, but for the Prince and myself the position was ideal for a truly grand fuck. He jerked his hips to drive his wonderful penis right up me and I had maximum pressure from it against my clitty. I was now so juicy that as I rode the royal rod, we could hear the wet, sucking sounds made by the rhythm of my love channel sliding up and down over his tool.

'In almost no time I felt myself coming and my cunney muscles spasmodically gripped his prick anew and began to ripple in the first warm waves of a delicious spend. I eased back until my swollen, parted cunt lips gave up their prize but then I sank back slowly until our hairs crunched together. I bounced and shook and leaned right back as he lay there with his eyes closed as I thrashed around on his pulsating pole. I threw my head back and moaned as my orgasm began in earnest and the delicious spasms of pure ecstasy shot through me. Each spasm tightened my cunney muscles and then he growled as he jerked and twisted underneath me. Thrusting his hips upward he let loose three or four tremendous thrusts which released a torrent of hot jism that drenched every nook of my already sopping slit.

'He may be a mature gentleman but the Prince's prick stayed hard after I had milked his cock and I was able to let my own orgasms flow and gradually subside until, exhausted, I slipped off him and sank content beside him. But he was raring to go for another joust so this time I lay back and let him do all the work as he inserted that majestic love trunk inside my still juicy crack and rhythmically fucked me again, his shaft sliding easily in and out of my slick cunney. He kept his cock in motion for close to five minutes before sending a frothy gusher of creamy spunk spurting past my excited clitty.

'Only then did the noble penis finally start to shrink and frankly I was so well-fucked that I did not mind at all! "We'll meet again, I hope, sir," I said as we dressed for neither of us could afford to stay any longer. "I sincerely hope so, Susie, write to me care of Count Gewirtz at 66 Green Street, Mayfair – can you remember that? Yes? Good, and so for now farewell, *mein liebchen*."'

'Gosh, how marvellous – and were you ever in contact again?' asked Katie. 'Alas no,' she replied, 'although I did write and he sent me a beautiful piece of jewellery, a lovely diamond brooch from Smolask's in Hatton Garden which I will always treasure. He did ask me to a party at Green Street a year or so ago but unfortunately I was unable to go.'

Gary Hornby grinned and said: 'You would probably have enjoyed yourself there, because this is where his old friend Johnny Gewirtz arranges very select orgies for His Royal Highness.'

'Really?' said Yvette with interest. 'And what sort of games do they play at such gatherings? We have heard naughty rumours about King Edward in Switzerland but I have always wondered whether they were true.' *[Interested readers should see* 'Cremorne Gardens' *for a detailed account of one of Count Gewirtz's infamous orgies – Editor]*

Gary chuckled and said: 'Well, for example, I happen to know that one of the Prince's favourite party pastimes is a game not dissimilar to Blind Man's Buff.'

'Ah, we have a similar game in Geneva,' chimed in Mimi. 'This is where a person is blindfolded and when he catches somebody he has to guess who he has caught. If he is right that person takes his place and if he is wrong he has to pay a forfeit.'

'Y-e-s-s,' said Gary slowly. 'Only the Prince's version is sometimes described as Blind Man's Bell End or better still as Blind Girl's Cock. The rules are simple – a girl is blindfolded and she has to guess which prick she has hold of. If she is correct the gentleman must pay a forfeit and if she is wrong she must suck off the cock concerned.'

'Sounds like a great game to me,' said Hal Freedman, his eyes gleaming with anticipation. 'Are any of you ladies game to have a go?'

The girls retreated into a huddle in the corner of the room and after some frantic whispering, Mimi emerged to say: 'I will gladly play but all you men must promise that you will pay your dues if I guess correctly.'

'That's more than fair,' said Cyril Totteridge, whose prick had been at bursting point as he mulled over Susie's erotic experience with the Prince of Wales. 'Count me in,' said Hal Freedman whilst Bob

Goggin and John Gibson nodded their assent, with Bob hoping that his bargain made earlier in the evening with Katie would hold good no matter what! 'I accept the terms too,' said Gary Hornby, tossing over a linen antimacasser to Amanda who bound it round Mimi's face so that her eyes were well and truly covered. The men then stood in a line, their trousers round their ankles, none of their pricks completely erect as they were slightly shy about exhibiting their wares – except for the brash Yankee, Hal Freedman, whose bone-hard circumcized cock stood up solidly like a flagpole almost flat against his paunch. With a nervous titter, Yvette led her friend to the line and informed her that the gentlemen's pricks were on parade in front of her.

Mimi gingerly stretched out her right arm until she felt her fingers brush against the stiffening shaft of Bob Goggin and she sighed with pleasure at finding such a sizeable specimen with which to begin the sport. 'This is a very nice cock,' she said admiringly, rubbing Bob's stalk as she fell to her knees and opened her sweet lips to slip the red uncapped knob between her lips. 'H'mm, and it tastes good too!' she added indistinctly which caused Amanda to call out: 'Now, now, Mimi you must never talk with your mouth full!' As the company roared with laughter, Mimi began sucking Bob's prick in earnest, enclosing her lips around his helmet as firmly as she could, working on the sensitive cap with her clever little tongue. She eased her lips and took in a little more of his bulging shaft as her hands now circled the base of his cock. She worked the loose skin up and down his pole at the same time as she began to bob her head up and down. Bob's hands went automatically to the back of her head, pushing her mouth further and further down his swollen organ. Somehow she managed to swallow almost all his nine-inch staff and Mimi was obviously enjoying herself as were all the other guests, the men showing their arousal by the fact that all their pricks were now fully erect and standing up in the air as high and hard as they could manage.

Mimi sucked vigorously on Bob's large cock, tonguing it without inhibition so that her efforts were accompanied by a stimulating erotic squelch as she slurped with undisguised relish on this glistening mysterious penis. 'Do you know whose prick you are sucking?' asked Susie but Amanda interrupted and said: 'Oh, do let him finish first, it would be awfully unfair if he were denied being finished off.' This kind sentiment found favour though the pretty Swiss miss was so well-schooled in cocksucking that Bob could contain himself no longer as he thrust his hips forward and the sperm spurted into Mimi's mouth in an outpouring of white milky foam. She tried as hard as she could to swallow his creamy emission but some of the precious fluid dripped from her lips onto the carpet.

'Those spunky stains won't please Gary's landlord,' whispered Katie to Amanda who let out a little giggle before replying that a few months ago after a strenuous night's fucking which had left wet patches all over a valuable Chinese rug, Susie had discovered Professor Bucknell's Magic Elixir, a marvellous cleaning fluid which would remove all evidence of erotic activity. 'This was just as well as Gary's girl friend was due back from the country later that very evening,' commented Amanda as Yvette poised the question to her friend. '*Alors*, Mimi, whose cock have you been sucking so enthusiastically?'

Mimi pondered for a moment before replying slowly: 'You know, I can truthfully only guess because, except for a brief interlude this afternoon with Cyril, I have not handled any of the pricks on display before. Really I can do little more than to guess. But I don't think the cock belongs to Gary because I heard my mother's best friend, Madame Dereta, who has been fucked several times by him, that Gary's instrument is somewhat lacking in length although it does have a thickness which made it most pleasant to lodge in her pussey.

'Now from my experience earlier with Cyril I am almost certain that the cock I have just sucked was not his and I will also rule out John Gibson because most European girls say that Scottish spunk is usually less tangy because of the soft water – and this sperm was exceptionally salty. This leaves just Bob and Hal and at this point I can only speculate . . .'

Mimi thought hard for a moment and said: 'I am going to choose Bob Goggin!' and from the great cheer that went up the pretty girl knew that she had made the right choice. Yvette and Susie untied her blindfold as the company toasted the clever young lady with a fresh bottle of champagne. Gary Hornby asked her what forfeit she would like Bob to perform. 'Within reason you can ask him to do anything at all,' he promised and Bob thought, Oh God, I hope she doesn't ask me to do anything with Katie or the fat will truly be in the fire all round. Penny would never forgive either her boy friend or her sister if she ever found out that they had been seen canoodling together! Fortunately for Bob, however, Mimi did not choose such a problematical chore for him to perform. 'Well, come on, Mimi what devilish little task have you set for Bob?' urged Hal Freedman, whose own stiffstander looked ready to burst as Amanda, whose penchant for circumcized cocks began after being impaled upon the enormous prick of the philanthropist Sir Bernard Rubin, lovingly caressed his throbbing shaft.

After further hurried discussion Mimi finally decreed: 'Very well, I have decided upon Bob's chore – he must tell us exactly how and when he lost his virginity, though he may change the name of the girl in question if he believes that she may be known to us.'

A chorus of approval greeted this announcement though Bob blushed furiously. 'I'm not very good at recounting stories,' he protested. 'Perhaps you're still a virgin,' laughed John Gibson as the guests paired off to listen to Bob's confession. Katie Arkley was sitting on Cyril's lap, her hand idly sliding up and down his twitching tool whilst Yvette curled herself into the arms of John Gibson who was busy unbuttoning her blouse to slip his hand inside to fondle her lovely large breasts. Gary Hornby and Mimi were sitting close together with the host proving himself dextrous at the art of removing her skirt and knickers whilst Hal Freedman had Susie and Amanda on his knees, the two girls kissing each other whilst they both kept their hands clutching the American's sinewy staff.

Bob cleared his throat and began: 'Virginity can be a truly bothersome state after the age of sixteen. I had

to wait until my seventeenth birthday to be introduced fully into the mysteries of love-making but I
was fortunate to have as my tutor an experienced,
kind girl who ensured that my rite of passage was
made easy and enjoyable for me.

'So let me begin on the very day that the great event
occurred. Indeed, I always raise a glass to Melanie
Marley on June 23rd and will do so until my prick can
no longer rise and pay tribute to her! Like many a first
fuck it all started at work – not that I was an early
starter for, at the time, I was already seventeen years
old and was working as an apprentice gardener at
Miss Stevenage's School For Young Ladies in Muswell Hill, North London. Well, one afternoon my
friend Colin and I heard sounds coming from the
school's indoor swimming pool. It was a warm day,
near the end of term, so we guessed that the Sixth
Form girls had been given use of the pool instead of
spending the afternoon studying. Now Colin and I
also knew that the sports mistress, Miss Coote, often
left the girls to shower and dress by themselves so we
decided to sneak up to the door and see if we could
enjoy a free exhibition. We managed to reach the
door without being seen and Colin opened the door
slightly and we peered in.

'My God! I thought I had died and gone to heaven!
For there, before my very eyes, were some twenty
young, mostly naked girls chatting away amongst
themselves as they were taking off their swimming
costumes before going in to shower and dress before
returning to the school. Instantly my cock sprang up
to attention at the sight of these lithe nude bodies,
particularly when the Honourable *['Honourable' is a*

courtesy title for the children of viscounts and barons and the younger sons of earls – Editor] Melanie Marley, a truly stunning blonde girl who was captain of the school, came into the changing room and, with her back to me, pulled off her scanty bathing costume. The sight of her tight, chubby bum cheeks almost made me spend then and there and when she turned round and I saw her firm young breasts and the fluffy golden hair covering her pussey, my stiffstander threatened to burst through my trousers. Just then, however, our erotic reverie was broken by a shout from Godfrey, the head gardener, who was calling for Colin to help him weed the lawn in front of the headmistress's study. Poor Colin! He ground his teeth in frustration and let rip some choice oaths under his breath but he had no alternative but to heed his master's voice. So I was left alone, panting with excitement as, one by one, the girls filed out to the showers from where they would go through to the changing rooms at the back of the building. Melanie had been one of the last girls to leave the pool and most of the others had gone through by the time she had arrived. As the last group went through the showers, one of the girls called out: "Hurry up, Melanie, you'll be late for the next lesson!"

' "Oh, I'm in no rush – I have free time for the rest of the afternoon," replied the blonde bombshell, stroking her thighs carelessly as, totally naked, she walked around the room, flexing her muscles in a series of exercises. She looked right at the door behind which I stood, fairly trembling with excitement, and she ran her fingers lightly over her proud, uptilted breasts, tweaking up her cherry red nipples until they were as stiff as my sore cock! Then I nearly toppled over with shock as she suddenly said: "All right, Bob Goggin, you can come in now."

'I stood stock still, unable to move but Melanie was made of sterner stuff. She moved forward towards me, her breasts swinging like pendulums, until she reached the door and she opened it and pulled me inside. "Come on in! Don't be so shy, you silly boy! We all knew that you and Colin were out there watching us. Such a shame that he was called away by old Godfrey but there were at least four of us who wanted to be fucked by you. As captain of the school, though, I pulled rank and so here we are." She took my arm and steered us both towards the centre of the room.

'I had definitely passed away, I decided, and this surely was heaven as Melanie stood smiling just a few inches away from me. She shook her head and her long tousled blonde hair shimmered in the sunlight which poured in through the skylight. Obviously she was enjoying my discomfiture but like most girls, although she was almost exactly the same age as me (our birthdays were only seven weeks apart), she was far more mature in these matters than me and, I suspect, than most boys of my age. She gave me a wicked little smile and whispered quietly: "You would like to fuck me, wouldn't you? Well, take off your clothes and put your cock in my cunney. Come on, Bob, we haven't got all day, worse luck."

'I looked up and our eyes met. Still, I was transfixed and this gorgeous creature stepped forward three paces and began unbuttoning my shirt. This broke the spell and I literally tore off my clothes and before you could say Jack Robinson we were locked into a passionate embrace. Her tongue instantly darted into my mouth and we french kissed for what seemed like an eternity before she broke away and said with that commendable directness of expression which marks the true aristocrat: "I think it's time we fucked, Bob, but I'd like you to begin by kissing my pussey." What a delightful command as fortunately – and here you must forgive my immodesty – unlike many other lads, I had experience of the joys of eating pussey even if I had yet to taste the delights of an actual fuck. So her request did not worry me in the slightest. I kissed each of her thrusting breasts, lovingly sucking each firm nipple into my mouth before sliding to my knees and running my tongue lower, across her flat, white belly into the silky strands of her golden bush. My hands circled her glorious buttocks as I buried my head between her thighs and drew her against me. The tip of my tongue flicked along her slippery snatch which was already nice and moist and she gasped and shivered as I found her clitty and began to roll my tongue around the erectile piece of flesh.

'Melanie moaned in ecstasy as I chewed and nipped at her clitty and she clasped my head in her hands as I brought off her off there and then, her pussey flooding with her love juice as she writhed in excitement. "Now, it's your turn!" she exclaimed and she pushed me down on the floor saying: "I'm going to sit on your lovely big prick, Bob, and I want to feel it glide juicily up into my wet little cunt." With those lewd words she positioned herself above my straining prick and let out a cry of sheer delight as she slowly impaled herself upon it. She leaned forwards and my mouth again met those delicious red nipples and sucked each in turn as she moved herself even faster up and down my rigid cock.

'What exquisite pleasure! I thrilled to the feel of her clinging cunney walls as she rode up and down my cock, moving her hips so sinuously as she pumped up and down and I jerked upwards, meeting her every thrust with one of my own, my hands now clasped around her tight round bum cheeks as I felt the spunk boiling up inside my ballsack. Then I felt a fresh electric stab of desire as she took my balls in her hand and her soft, warm touch of Melanie's fingers sent me over the top and I came straightaway, shooting my frothy white juice inside her love channel, flooding her cunney with a real torrent of sperm as the sticky love juice poured out of my prick just as she too achieved her climax with my jism already dribbling down her thighs.

'When she had recovered she lifted herself off me and buried her face in my groin, kissing and sucking my semi-erect cock as her busy hands drew back my foreskin and rubbed my fast stiffening shaft up to its fullest height and thickness. Then once my prick was ready she teased my knob against the roof of her mouth with her tongue and in no time at all I felt the surge of a powerful spend coursing through my throbbing tool. Melanie sensed this and sensibly took her sweet lips away for a moment. Then she returned to the attack, stroking her tongue along the underside of my cock, making it ache with anticipation as it throbbed even more urgently. She squeezed her hand around the base of my shaft, sucking me harder. The sight of her pretty face, her mouth filled with my hard, pulsating prick and her blonde tresses intermingling with my own dark pubic hair was simply too much and I could no longer contain myself. With a hoarse cry I arched my back and my lusty young cock gave one final pulse before I jetted spurt after spurt of creamy spunk full into her adorable mouth. She did not cease to draw upon my prick until the very last drops of milky white essence had been swallowed.

'She purred with satisfaction as I lay gasping, exhausted both physically and mentally from my crossing of the Rubicon. As she raised her head, the sweet girl kissed my glistening cock which now hung limply over my thigh. Alas, the bell for the next study session rang and we were unable to begin a third encounter. Indeed, we never managed to get together again for Melanie was in her last term at the school and we have never met again since.

'I have read about her fast social life in *The Tatler* and the other society papers and I still hope that one day our paths might cross again.' Bob sighed as he raised his glass and drank a silent toast to the health of this wonderful girl whose needs were matched so exactly by those of the lusty young gardener.

After the spontaneous round of applause for the clear and frank way Bob had related how he had lost his virginity, Susie suddenly gripped Hal Freedman's prick which she and Amanda had taken turns to suck and called out: 'Bob! I've just remembered that I'm going to meet this very girl next weekend! Amanda and I have been invited across to Ireland to stay for a few days with Sir Harold Brown at his villa near Killarney. In his letter he mentioned that amongst the guests would be Melanie Marley! What a coincidence! Oh Bob, you must come with us and meet her again! I'll telegraph Sir Harold, he won't mind at all, I'm sure as he is the most hospitable of men.'

'Oh, you just can't ask someone if they'd mind bringing an extra person to a party,' Bob protested. 'And anyhow, I don't think I can afford either the time or the money to go.'

'Nonsense!' said Gary Hornby firmly. 'If I know Sir Harold he'll be only too happy to have an extra prick on hand. There's always so much fucking going on at his place that I don't know how he manages to find time to look after his estate. Anyhow, he always sends first-class tickets to any guest making the journey over from England so it will cost very little to go. He's a very informal host too, isn't he, Susie?'

'Oh yes,' said Susie eagerly, still gripping Hal Freedman's cock so tightly that the American visibly winced. 'Oh dear,' said Susie, suddenly remembering just what she was holding so tightly. 'I'm afraid I've squeezed you too hard,' and she relaxed her grip and began caressing his prick with regular but featherlight strokes. All the pain was quickly smoothed away and Amanda suggested that Hal might now like to fuck her. 'I sure would, young lady,' he declared and without further ado, lowered himself on top of her. His fat prick slipped immediately through the already damp thickets of her pussey hair and found the equally moist entrance to her cave of lewd delights. At his touch she wriggled her bottom into a more comfortable position and Hal slid the entire length of his chopper in up to the hilt until their pubic hairs tangled together. 'Ah, this is just what I need,' said

Amanda as the Yankee slowly began to slide his cock easily in and out of her warmly clinging cunney. She in turn rose to meet his pumping as, like any gentleman, Hal Freedman endeavoured to keep his weight on his elbows to allow Amanda to enjoy her fucking even more.

Now the pace of their efforts increased and they soon established a fine rhythm which showed Hal's wide experience in *l'arte de faire l'amour*. Even though this was their first fuck together it was as though they had performed the act many times before. Their breathing was in unison, deeper now as a slight sheen of perspiration oiled their bodies. 'A-h-r-e . . .' groaned the American as his cock tingled deliciously as her cunney walls pressured the sensitive skin of his shaft. Amanda then lifted her legs still further and crossed them behind his waist, pressing him down into her, yet she did not grasp him too tightly for she had no desire to inhibit his pacey rhythm. Hal speeded up and then with admirable control relaxed his efforts a little. Again his efforts increased and again slowed down and Amanda too enjoyed an excellent sense of timing, understanding by a natural instinct when to lower the tension so that the joint pleasure might be prolonged.

So they fucked together for a considerable time, locked together as one. Each renewed level in tempo took the pair one step further to the inevitable final climax as from an easy canter the pace was raised to a full yet sustainable gallop as Hal's cock squelched in and out of Amanda's juicy honeypot until the tidal wave of spunk roared through his staff and jetted into her welcoming cunt. Hal panted and shuddered as she milked his prick but Amanda did not cry out. Instead she moaned softly as he discharged his copious emission matching him surge for surge as she spent too and tide met tide and blended together in a whirlpool of love juice. Smoothly they slowed, both breathing deeply, relaxing gently, still responding to the other's needs until Hal withdrew his softening shaft which glistened wetly from their spending. Amanda turned her head to one side, a look of complete satisfaction and fulfilment spreading over her face.

Although Mimi was keen to try her luck again at guessing which cock she was sucking whilst blind-folded, the company decided to play another some-what *recherché* parlour game. As they debated as the suitability of the sports suggested, Cyril Totteridge sat down at the piano and played two popular waltzes. He played with dash and style and Katie said admir-ingly: 'Cyril, I never knew you possessed any musical talent.' 'I don't know whether I do, but any skill I have was brought out by the lady who taught me,' said Cyril modestly. 'Here is a little composition she wrote for me, *The Hound That Caught The Pubic Hair.*'

If music be the food of love, says the old maxim and its truth was shown by the fact that Cyril's music encouraged the party to throw off all inhibitions. By the time he had finished his tune, the whole company, except for himself, was stark naked. He jumped up from the piano and after flinging off the remainder of his clothes, joined the rest of the guests who were ranged up in a semi-circle after Gary Hornby and John Gibson had pulled a couch into the middle of the room. Yvette sat down on the sofa and took hold of

John Gibson's thick prick in her right hand and Cyril Totteridge's longer yet thinner instrument in the other. She gave them a good rub until they stood up against their bellies like two staunch flagpoles. Then, squatting on her knees on the plump cushions of the sofa, she pulled them gently together and took both the gleaming uncapped helmets into her mouth, washing them both over with her tongue, causing both gentlemen to groan loudly with genuine ecstasy. Yvette leaned forward and Mimi stepped forward to part the cheeks of her friend's glorious backside. 'M'm, tools rush in where angels fear to tread,' said Gary with a flourish as he climbed behind the girl and positioned the knob of his rubicund tadger between her luscious buttocks. He slid his knob into her cunney from behind but unfortunately he was unable to restrain himself and spent almost immediately, washing Yvette's crack and bottom with frothy white spurts of sperm. Susie kindly wiped off as much spunk as possible from Yvette's wriggling bum and inserted two of her fingers into Yvette's arse as the Swiss girl continued to lick and lap at the two rock-hard cocks which filled her mouth so nicely.

'Bad luck, Gary old fellow! It could happen to any one of us,' said Bob Goggin sympathetically as he took the host's place behind Yvette. Amanda took hold of his prick and ensured that his cock slipped in immediately into Yvette's dripping pussey which had been further moistened by Susie's manipulation. Bob's tool entered her cunney with a lovely squelch and Yvette pushed out her bum to receive as much of Bob's ramrod-stiff staff as possible. Meanwhile the two boners of John and Cyril were bounding and swelling in her mouth as she continued to jerk her hands up and down their swollen shafts as she palated the two pulsating pricks. Both the men found this conjunction so stimulating that together they spurted great globs of spunk into Yvette's mouth and she swallowed as much as she could although their emissions were so copious that the creamy white liquid ran out between her lips and dribbled down her chin.

But Bob was still happily pushing his prick in and out of her juicy cunney from behind. Yvette's entire body quivered as he rammed home again and again, sheathing his cock so fully inside her love channel that his hairy ballsack banged against her bottom. 'A-a-r-g-g-h!' gurgled Bob as Susie stepped forward to squeeze his balls and he leaned over to fondle Yvette's lush breasts. The girl waggled her bottom from side to side and this artful monoeuvering soon led to Bob sending spout after spout of spunk flowing into her pussey as the pair shuddered to a flawless mutual climax before rolling off the sofa onto the carpet, where they stayed, oblivious to anything and anybody else.

Now it was Cyril and Katie who took the stage. The young man's blood was up and, despite his sucking off by Yvette, his prick soon stood up again ready for action. He took hold of Katie and kissed her large nipples with tremendous passion until they stood out like twin rosebuds. They sank onto the sofa with Cyril still sucking on Katie's delicious titties. Susie scrambled up between them to slip one hand around Cyril's blue veined champion and the other into the soft blonde hair that decorated Katie's pouting pussey.

She immediately parted these serrated cunney lips with her tapering fingers and began rubbing and pinching Katie's projecting clitty with her thumb and forefinger. 'Oooh, that's nice!' gasped Katie as she imprisoned Susie's hand between her legs, wrapping it tightly between her jerking thighs as she built up to her climax. Susie's left hand was far from idle, meanwhile, as she kept it frigging Cyril's thick prick which by now had been teased up into a fine state of erection. She brought her head nearer the uncapped pink crown and licked her way round the sensitive rim. Then she opened her mouth wide, enclosing her lips around it as tightly as she could, working the loose skin up and down the shaft whilst sucking on the mushroom helmet with unbridled gusto. Somehow she managed to take in almost all of Cyril's cock inside her mouth as John Gibson grabbed two cushions and lay them behind her so she could play with Katie's cunney and suck Cyril's cock in comfort.

This also enabled Gary Hornby (who had now recovered from his previous over-eagerness) to make the threesome a quartet as he pulled Susie's legs apart to give the company sight of the pretty chestnut fringe of hair that covered her cunney. Susie took her hand away momentarily from Cyril's cock which she was munching on so frenziedly to take Gary Hornby's iron-hard rammer into her quim and she worked her lips up and down until his throbbing tool had sunk all the way into her juicy crack.

'I wonder how many more people can join in the fun,' muttered Hal Freedman as he clambered up behind Katie and presented his stiff circumcized cock to her which she popped between her lips without any hesitation. Mimi was next to join in the fun by lying on her back and sucking Hal's balls whilst opening her legs for John Gibson who placed his head between her legs and ran his tongue lightly all along her slit before licking and lapping at her dark curly bush in earnest. He sucked at the Swiss girl's hairy pussey before repositioning himself and lowering his muscular frame gently on top of her and the tip of his Caledonian cock nudged itself between her cunney lips. With a smile Mimi threw her arms around his buttocks and pushed him forward so that his prick was totally ensheathed inside her. He began fucking her in a steady rhythm and she rose to meet his ardour as every jab struck home.

'Slower please, John, if you don't mind,' she begged for she wanted to ensure that on each stroke the whole of his superb Scottish sausage tickled every inch of her cunney. Her legs were now wrapped around his waist as he continued to piston his hips up and down as Mimi took Hal's ballsack from her mouth a second time to goad the Edinburgh cocksman to even further heights.

'Aaah! What a big, fat prick! Aaah, push in harder, I must have more of it please, John, fill my cunney with your cock!' she shrieked and he made every effort to comply with her demand, burying his substantial shaft to the hilt as his balls flopped against her heaving bottom. His movements became faster and faster until, with a loud cry, he exploded into her, filling her cunt with huge squirts of spunk which set off a chain reaction as Hal Freedman shot his load into Katie's waiting throat and she in turn climaxed sending a flood of female love juice streaming into

Susie's face. As she frantically tried to swallow the tangy nectar, Gary Hornby emptied his balls into her cunt. The sperm from Cyril Totteridge's cock fizzed out all over her hand and the group sank back sated upon the couch. Unfortunately their combined weight overturned the overloaded settee and it toppled over, sending the interlocked group of naked bodies crashing to the floor. Luckily no damage was done to life and limb, though Susie's flailing hand grabbed at Hal Freedman's balls, an act which brought tears to that gentleman's eyes but he was thoroughly restored by the speedy infusion of a large glass of Gary Hornby's best cognac.

To a man, the male guests now required an interval from these hectic fun and games but Susie de Vere Forrester was an insatiable girl and her sucking of Katie's blonde pussey had only heightened her appetite for a further tribadic encounter. Yvette was now sitting upright on the carpet with her back against the now righted sofa. Susie guessed correctly that the sparkling eyes of the gorgeous Swiss girl promised further sultry pleasures. So Susie moved across to sit next to her and immediately cupped one of Yvette's lovely rounded breasts in her hand. *'Quelle bonne fille,'* murmured Susie as she ran her other hand along Yvette's shoulders. Indeed, what a beautiful girl she was, with such well proportioned limbs and such a glorious profusion of light brown hair which now hung loose down her back in a dense mass almost down to her plump bum cheeks. Susie caressed her thighs and let her hand stray between Yvette's legs into the mossy brown bush which guarded her warm, wet crack.

This lesbian dalliance continued as Susie continued to flick Yvette's nut-brown nipples into hardness with her palm. Then, without a word, Yvette moved across to kneel in front of the English girl. Their eyes locked and Yvette gave a knowing smile before her head dived down and her lips were nuzzling against Susie's thighs.

Susie lay perfectly still, enjoying the sensation as the busy little tongue twirled around inside her, delighting in the ripples of pleasure as Yvette reamed out her dripping crack, teasing the labia that sat exposed through the net of fine hair, gently licking and sucking until both were in a perfect frenzy of lust.

'Oooh, that's the way to do it!' gasped Susie as Yvette wrenched her mouth from her sopping muff and replaced it with her long, tapering fingers. Immediately she found the swollen clitty she tugged at it vigorously and before long Susie's body was threshing around wildly as Yvette cunningly slipped a finger inside her bottom-hole. Susie's back arched upwards as spasms of excitement coursed through her body before exploding into a gigantic peak of orgasmic lust.

When she had finished her spend, Yvette hauled herself up into Susie's arms and the two girls embraced, crushing their soft breasts together, their tawney titties rubbing against each other as they kissed deeply and feverishly. Yvette now lay back, no doubt expecting Susie to perform a similar service for her. Indeed, Susie would have willingly done so, had not their tribadic love-making so excited Cyril Totteridge that, before either could move, he plunged his naked body between them. Then he gathered Yvette into his arms, an act which did not displease her – for as she was later to say, a thick stiff cock simply cannot be beaten – and she reached down for his bursting prick as their mouths met and their tongues waggled against each other as they kissed with the utmost passion. She rubbed his stiffstander up to its peak, gently pulling his shaft up and down and marvelling at the beauty of his sinewy staff and large pink hairy ballsack.

Yvette pulled her mouth away and kissed Cyril's chest, moving swiftly downwards with a series of butterfly kisses until she opened her mouth wide and, wetting her lips, took in the rounded bulbous knob of his cock in her mouth as he moaned with pleasure. She pushed downwards until this massive fleshy lollipop was at the back of her mouth and she sucked and slurped on her sweetmeat, jamming her mouth over the mushroomed red helmet until his prick started to twitch and she felt the creamy sperm rush up the shaft. 'M'mmm,' she gurgled appreciatively as the gushing white foam filled her mouth. His cock bucked wildly as she held it lightly between her lips, gulping down all the tasty essence, sucking up every last drain of juice.

But Yvette still needed a cock in her aching cunt so she squeezed Cyril's balls and looked around to see that Bob Goggin had managed another stand. With the light of pure lust in her eyes, she beckoned the young man over to her. Grabbing him by his cock, she planted a warm wet kiss on his uncapped helmet. Bob needed no further urging as Yvette lay back and opened her legs. She eagerly lifted her hips to welcome his thrusting prick which slid in without hindrance between the waiting pussey lips. Yvette squirmed with joy as Bob played with her large breasts as he fucked her cunney. Her rubbery titties jiggled around as Bob pumped his prick again and again in and out of her juicy honeypot, fucking the sweet girl in a series of long, sweeping strokes as his trusty truncheon squelched noisily in and out of Yvette's sopping cunt. Bob's cock felt wonderful inside the panting girl as he used his tool expertly, varying his angle and speed which stretched her pussey deliciously. They fucked merrily away for a full five minutes until Bob shot his spunk into her. Yvette spent instantaneously the first jet of sperm drenched the walls of her womb. At her request, Bob stayed in her cunney for a little while before he slowly withdrew his still rigid rod which was coated with the juices of their marvellous fuck. 'Such staying power,' sighed Hal Freedman to Katie Arkley. 'Even when I was his age I don't think I could have fucked so much and for so long a period of time.'

'Yes, youth is wasted on the young,' commented Gary Hornby though John Gibson would have none of it. 'Och, it's no good to be worrying about all that,' he said robustly. 'I'm sure the girls will all agree that there's many a good tune played on an old fiddle!'

'Quite right, John,' said Amanda. 'Some of my best lovers have been aged forty or more. They may not be able to fuck all night as they did when they were twenty but an experienced man often knows how to pleasure a girl better than a headstrong young lad.'

This comforting thought brightened up the older gentlemen though none felt able to take up Susie's suggestion of forming one final fucking chain. 'The party's over,' said Gary Hornby sadly, 'and it's time to call it a day.' 'Not quite,' joked Bob, 'because although it's well past midnight, dawn won't break until five o'clock!'

The guests started to dress themselves and when everyone was in at least a semi-respectable state, Gary Hornby rang the bell for the butler. 'Do have some coffee before you go,' he urged his guests. 'It won't take long to make.'

In the kitchen the sound of the bell woke up Mrs Beaconsfield, who had been dozing in an easy chair. It also disturbed both Lottie the buxom kitchenmaid, who was bending over a chair in the scullery with her skirts thrown up and her knickers pulled down, and Andrew, one of the two strapping footmen who, after liberally annointing his love trunk with butter, was engaged in slewing his strong young cock in and out of Lottie's tight little bum-hole. Jonathan, his fellow footman, and Mr Formbey were watching the randy pair with a mixture of envy and admiration when the bell rang. 'Damn, they'll probably want coffee,' grumbled the butler, correctly guessing the reason for the late summons. 'Hetty, put the kettle on and get out the sponge cake and biscuits,' he called as he marched out of the kitchen.

Afterwards, whilst they sipped Mrs Beaconsfield's superb coffee and sampled her featherlight cake, Susie and Amanda made Bob Goggin promise that he would go with them to Ireland the next weekend if, as they confidently expected, Sir Harold Brown extended an invitation. And on that happy note the party broke up, with Bob escorting Susie and Amanda back home to Mrs Trenton's boarding house. A motor car from Prestoncrest, the discreet private hire company used – it was widely rumoured – by none other than King Edward VII himself when he wished to slip away for a secret assignation, stood ready to transport Hal Freedman and John Gibson back to their hotels. Yvette and Mimi were staying the night with Gary Hornby whilst of course Cyril and Katie had only to walk through the square back to their rooms.

In fact, although like several others, Cyril and Katie had thought they would spend the time after the party engaged in suitable nocturnal romps, they were all too tired from their exhausting erotic exploits after dinner. Without exception they all fell into bed and were asleep in no time. Indeed, the only torrid love-making occurred in the attic of 47 Bedford Square where Mr Formbey and Lottie were finally enjoying a salacious session of fucking with the butler's cock-shaft being occasionally substituted by the top of a bottle of champagne Mr Formbey had filched from the cellar.

CHAPTER FOUR
In The Emerald Isle

In summer Bob Goggin usually woke with the dawn, but it was almost half past eight the next morning before he stirred. As he yawned and stretched his arms, a wide grin spread over his face. He recalled the wanton erotic excesses of the previous evening – and then he gnawed on his lip as he suddenly thought of the consequences if Katie Arkley reneged on her promise to keep silent about his presence at the party. But surely she wouldn't want to incriminate herself, he reasoned, as he threw back the covers as a prelude to heaving his naked body (for Bob only wore a nightshirt in winter) out of bed.

But to his discomforture, just at this very moment there was a knock on his door and before he could utter a word in walked his landlady Mrs Trenton with a cup of tea in her hand. 'Good morning, Bob, I thought I'd wake you up with a cup of . . .' Her voice trailed off as her eyes whisked up and down Bob's naked body. He blushed and quickly snatched up a towel from a chair and knotted it round his waist. 'Er, yes, thanks Mrs Trenton, that's very good of you. Just put it down there and I'll drink it after I've washed.'

The landlady set the tea down on his bedside table but made no move to leave. In fact, to Bob's surprise, she sat on the bed and said: 'It's no trouble, Bob. But do tell me all about the party. You and the girls must have got home very late as I didn't hear you come in, though I was reading till past midnight. It's lucky that you don't have to be at St Dominic's till twelve on Thursdays!'

'I'm glad we didn't disturb you,' said Bob, reluctantly sitting down beside her after she motioned him to join her on the bed. 'There really isn't much to tell about last night. We had a splendid dinner and later we played a few parlour games.'

'Parlour games!' snorted the landlady scornfully. 'Now don't give me all that nonsense – I know all about the kind of games you must have got up to! Go on, Bob, be a sport, and tell me the truth. I'll hear something anyway this afternoon from my sister Mrs Shawn with whom old George Formbey lodges, but George always keeps mum about any goings-on and anyhow, he'll have probably been too busy trying to get his hand up the kitchenmaid's skirts to have noticed anything else!'

Bob laughed and said: 'Yes, I know Mr Formbey from when he was the butler in the Arkley household, but honestly Mrs Trenton – ' 'Call me Jennifer, it's much more friendly,' she prompted. 'Don't be shy, Bob. Your friend Mr Hornby has quite a reputation, you know, and as far as I'm concerned if those two young trollops Amanda and Susie were at the party, there must have been some fun and games as those two girls have had more cocks between them than I've had hot dinners! So come and sit down and tell me all about it.' And the landlady sat down on the bed to wait for Bob to respond to her request.

He thought for a moment and then decided that he had best quench Jennifer Trenton's curiosity. After extracting what he speculated would be an empty promise from her that she would not repeat anything untoward to her sister, he started to recount some of the scandalous escapades that took place after dinner, though he scrupulously avoided giving any hint of the surnames of any of the guests. But when he told about how after Mimi had sucked him off he had been forced to give an account of how he had lost his virginity, she clucked her tongue against the roof of her mouth and said: 'Oooh, that was a bit naughty wasn't it?' 'I didn't really mind,' Bob admitted, 'especially as it turned out that I might very soon see the girl who took his cherry for the first time since she let me thread her.'

'I bet you'll give her a good seeing-to if you do meet up again,' said the landlady roguishly. 'And good luck to you too! I wouldn't mind being in her shoes, as it's been some time since I've had a good fuck. After all, it's been more than four years since Mr Trenton passed away.'

Bob was about to mutter a word of consolation but she placed her hand on his arm and continued: 'Oh no, Bob, there's no need to be sorry, it was good riddance to bad rubbish, as I said at the time. Harry used to booze his wages away by Saturday night and I'd be lucky if he could manage one cockstand a week. Not that he was any great shakes in bed, mind you. No, I couldn't say I was bowled over with grief when one night, coming home pissed as usual no doubt, he fell into one of those big holes near Russell Square they've dug for the new underground railway.

The company gave me enough compensation money to buy this house and put a little by in the Post Office.

'Still, a good man's hard to find, and it's been almost three months since I've had a good fuck,' she said, looking pointedly at Bob's lap which was covered only by the towel he had hastily draped round his waist when she had first entered the room. 'After all, I'm only just thirty-six,' she continued, 'and I've kept my figure, haven't I?' But before Bob could answer her question she suddenly stood up and began unbuttoning her dress. She slipped off the garment to reveal an almost transparent chemise, sloped at the waist and tied with coloured bows at the shoulders through which Bob could see the gorgeous swell of her full, rounded bosoms. Then, looking steadily at him with a crafty smile on her lips, she slowly slid the straps of the chemise down and exposed her beautiful naked breasts to Bob's gaze.

The sight of these white globes topped with perhaps the largest ruby nipples Bob had ever seen made his cock stir noticeably under the towel. Mrs Trenton licked her lips and sat down again to kick off her shoes and peel off her stockings. Then she stood up again and very deliberately pulled down her knickers directly in front of him so that the thick curly hair of her pussey thatch was just inches away from his face. She took Bob under his chin and helped him to stand up next to her. As he did so the towel slipped down to his feet and Jennifer Trenton grabbed his stiff prick greedily in her hand, rubbing its swollen head and moving her fingers gently up and down the hot, quivering shaft. She pulled his head to her with her other hand and they kissed, their tongues meshing together as Bob let his hands drop onto the fleshy *rondeurs* of her soft bum cheeks as he pressed her eager body against his rock hard cock.

They reeled back onto the bed and crashed down together upon the mattress. Bob grabbed a pillow and inserted under Jennifer Trenton's back so that her thighs and cunney were positioned at an excellent angle for his bursting cock which he held in his hand as he moved between her legs, nudging her knees a little further apart as he squeezed his shaft, capping and uncapping the red helmet. She now took hold of his cock as his hands moved to her huge breasts and covered her large nipples, whilst she guided his knob between the folds of her pussey into her dripping crack. Immediately he began to slide his cock in and out of her yearning love channel at a slow yet steady pace and the landlady sighed with pleasure as she relished the feel of his veiny shaft easing its way to and fro inside her juicy wetness, moaning with delight as Bob pumped away, pressing up to meet his thrusts to make certain that she had every last inch of his cock inside her. He continued to fuck her slowly until she gasped: 'Oh Bob, I've come twice already. Now fuck me hard, you big-cocked boy!'

Nothing loath, he increased the tempo until he was pistoning in and out of her squelchy pussey at a great rate of knots, his balls slapping against her thighs as she wrapped her legs around him at each stroke as he cupped her ample breasts, pinching the erect nipples between his thumb and forefinger. His cock sluiced in and out, causing her to experience the most divine raptures as with one final effort they moved into the last lap. Her body writhed out of control as Bob's cock drove in and out of her cunt at an ever-increasing speed until he exploded into her and sent a fierce stream of frothy spunk shooting into her vitals whilst he shuddered into an explosive spend, her saturated cunt radiating out delicious convolutions of supreme ecstasy all over her body.

As soon as he felt his cock begin to soften, Bob rolled off the landlady who gave him a big cuddle and said: 'Oh thank you, Bob, you're every bit as good at fucking as Susie told me.'

Bob looked at her in astonishment. 'Susie told you *what*?' he said incredulously.

'She said you had the most beautiful penis and that you knew how to use it,' she confessed meekly. 'It was only about half an hour ago. I was quite surprised to see her up and about so early but she said she had to go out first thing to send a telegraph to somebody in Ireland. She also told me that there had been some high jinks last night but that you had acquitted yourself very well. That's why I was so keen to hear all about what had happened at Mr Hornby's house.'

'Well, I'm glad I haven't disappointed you, Jennifer,' laughed Bob, who like any man was hardly displeased to hear good things said about his ability to make love. 'Now if you really want to show me you're grateful, how about popping downstairs and cooking me a nice kipper for breakfast. I don't really understand why I'm so jolly hungry because we had a big dinner last night.'

The landlady smiled gaily. 'It's all that fucking,' she

said knowingly. 'I always say that you need a stoke up for a good bang between the sheets.'

Although he would very much have liked to accept Jennifer Trenton's warm invitation to come to her room after breakfast, Bob resisted the temptation and spent the rest of the morning in his room, studying his notes of Dr Radley-Thatcher's last lecture. Time was running out, he thought, and he really should at least begin some preliminary sketches for the picture he and the other students had been asked to produce for his final examination at the art school. At lunchtime he decided to go for a walk down to the local public-house for a pint and a sandwich but Mrs Trenton was waiting for him in the hall. 'Bob, I've taken the liberty of preparing a little snack for us in my private dining room,' she said. 'I didn't want to interrupt you whilst you were working but Charlie brought in some lovely fresh salad this morning from the market and there's plenty of cold roast beef to go with it.'

'Oh, that's very kind of you, Mrs Trent – I mean, Jennifer, but you shouldn't have gone to all that trouble,' Bob protested.

'It's no trouble at all,' she replied quietly as she led him back up the stairs. 'It's nice to have someone to eat with but there's something I want to tell you when we're alone.' After she had set the table she said: 'Bob, I don't want you to think that you have to fuck me every day – or even every week for that matter. I don't expect anything more than a good friendship from our relationship, no more, no less. It's important that neither of us feels obliged to each other in any way.

'I know I'm a horny girl – I just love to feel a long hard cock sliding in and out of my mouth or plunging deep inside my pussey. Why, just talking about fucking makes my cunney wet and willing like it makes your prick stand up. But so long as we understand each other at the beginning, no-one will get hurt.

'Well, now that's off my chest, let's see what we have to eat,' she added brightly as Bob squeezed her arm in silent appreciation for her wise words. But by the time the happy couple had polished off the beef and a bottle of a very good claret, they were sitting together on the landlady's chesterfield *[a large tightly stuffed sofa usually upholstered in leather – Editor]* and Jennifer Trenton was idly caressing Bob's semi-erect cock through the material of his trousers whilst he stroked her large breasts through the open buttons of her dress.

'You told me all about last night, Bob, so would you like me to entertain you with a story about Joe, my last boy friend? You would? Yes, I thought so,' she said, snuggling up even closer to him. 'Joe was a very nice man who kept a greengrocer's shop just round the corner. He's about my age and has never been married though he's had his moments with the girls. He's a decent sort but not exactly a bundle of laughs and so although I enjoyed going out with him and sharing his bed, I could never feel totally wild and uninhibited. That's important to me, Bob, because for me it's the spontaneity of the moment which counts for so much. I love it when a man follows his impulses recklessly, like pulling the dog-cart over to the side of the road and fucking behind a bush or even

150

doing it in a very public place where you might get caught . . .

'If I'm really honest about it, I'll admit now that the idea of such dangerous fucking has always appealed to me. So one night I turned round to Joe and suggested that we went for a walk. He was agreeable enough and we walked through to the park where you saw Susie and Amanda playing with themselves. I'm sure Joe thought I was just aimlessly wandering but what he didn't know was that I'd taken off my knickers and that I was going to make sure that we would end up having some nookie. The poor man had no idea that I had any such thing in mind until we passed one of the bigger trees by the tennis courts. Then I suddenly turned round, stuck my hand between his legs and said: "Joe, I want to suck your lovely cock right now!"

'He was shocked, as you can imagine, but he made no objection as I unbuttoned his trousers and pulled out his already stiffening truncheon. I started sucking and within seconds his shaft was rock-hard and he was moaning and groaning as he clutched at my head as I washed his knob with my tongue. But then I stopped, stood up, and lifted my skirt and started to stroke my bared pussey whilst Joe frantically looked around to see if anybody else was watching me.

'I made him move back and lean against another tree as I continued to play with myself, stroking my crack and fingering my clitty, feeling myself get all wet. My cunney was juicing up beautifully as I closed my eyes and pretended that a stranger was watching me wank. Then I opened my eyes for an instant and saw that Joe had disappeared but that another dark figure in blue was staring at me – it was none other than little Mr Dawson, our local butcher and he had taken out his cock from his trousers and was frantically jerking himself off. He might have been short of stature (only an inch at best taller than me) but you know what they say about little jockeys having big whips! His prick looked enormous as he rubbed his shaft up to what looked an enormous size.

'I continued to stroke myself faster and faster, feeling my pussey getting wetter and wetter, all the while staring back at Mr Dawson who suddenly walked over to me, grabbed me and buried his big cock deep into my clinging cunt, squashing me between the tree trunk and his body. "Oh yes," he gasped. "Oh, what a lovely juicy cunt, I'm right up it!" Then he began to fuck me like a madman, pumping his prick powerfully in and out of my squishy cunney as I jerked my hips backwards and forwards to keep up with him. How I enjoyed the tingling sensation in my cunt as he slewed his shaft in and out as I continued to play with my clitty and soon I felt a tremendous spend well up inside me. "Oh God, I'm coming – I'm going to spunk up your cunt!" he wailed and when I felt his thick prick tremble and the first shoot of sperm jet out from his knob I clung on to him for dear life as my pussey creamed up and we spent together so deliciously that we were left weak-kneed and exhausted. He told me later that I had screamed so loud that he was sure that someone would hear me but we were lucky and remained undisturbed. As his cock slackened, still in my soaking wet hole, he slowly withdrew it and it hung down, still quite big and coated with my love juices. "I think we both needed that, don't you?" he said as he stuffed his cock back inside his trousers.

'I went home by myself and Joe was waiting for me outside the house. He just couldn't understand why I acted the way I did so we agreed to finish seeing each other. He sold his shop soon afterwards and moved to Colchester and, though we promised we'd keep in touch, we've never even exchanged a postcard since he left London, which is rather sad really, I suppose. As for Mr Dawson, well, somehow we've never had the opportunity to fuck again – but since that wild night, I've always had the very best cuts of meat whenever I go into the butcher's!'

As Jennifer Trenton had expected, Bob's engorged prick was now threatening to burst out from his trousers and so she reached out and unbuttoned his flies, letting his veiny love trunk spring up to salute her. She gently took hold of it and briskly pulled her hand up and down from his balls to the tip of his helmet. She paused to pull her dress over her head and Bob saw that she was wearing only a pair of frilly knickers underneath. "I'll tell you what else I really like, Bob,' said the lewd landlady. 'I love having my titties splattered with spunk – will you come over them for me?'

Bob nodded his approval and she took hold of his prick again and this time as she frigged him, with her other hand she took her erect nipples between her fingers and coaxed them up further between her fingers so that they began to resemble two reddish brown stalks. "Come on, Bob, shoot your spunk over my nips!' she urged as she wrapped her fist around his hot cockshaft and bent forwards to give an encouraging little lick around his knob. This soon finished Bob off and he panted with pleasure as he sprayed a great fountain of frothy white spunk over Jennifer Trenton's creamy soft globes. She took hold of his prick and aimed his jerking staff between the valley of her enormous breasts, stuffing his twitching tool between her cleavage as he spurted out the last drops of spunk. He fell back onto the chesterfield, quite worn out from this hurried little tit-fuck as she smeared his spunk all around her saucer-shaped aureoles.

She tugged once more at his limp cock but Bob said wistfully: 'I'm sorry, Jennifer – the spirit is willing but the flesh is weak. Can we perhaps postpone matters until tea-time?' 'Certainly we may,' she replied soothingly. 'Come up to my room at five o'clock and we'll have a good fuck to set us up for the evening.'

Bob buttoned up his trousers and gave her a quick farewell kiss on the cheek. He went back to his room and picked up a notebook and pencil, for he had decided that there were too many distractions here at home and that he would be better off trying to work in the Reading Room of the British Museum which was only a short walk away in Great Russell Street. He rummaged around until he found the valuable entrance ticket which the St Dominic's School of Art authorities provided for all of their students. But as he opened the front door he almost collided with the lithe figure of Amanda Crombleigh, who was standing on the doorstep.

'Bob Goggin! Just the person I wanted to see,' she cried excitedly, waving a piece of paper at him. 'Look, we've already had a reply from Sir Harold Brown and he would be delighted if you would join the party at Killarney this weekend. Read his telegram for yourself, Bob.'

She pushed the telegram into his hands and he read it out loud. '"*Very pleased indeed to accommodate Mr Goggin. Will send Johnstone of Prestoncrest Carriages round with tickets at 4.00 PM on Friday. – Harold.*" Well, that's very decent of him. You are sure that I won't be in the way?'

'Of course not, silly! Harold's a very dear old friend and I promise you that if he didn't want you to come he'd say so. We'll have a fine time, don't you worry, Sir Harold is a lively old bloke and we always have a good time in Killarney. It's very pretty country, you know, and if you're keen on fishing you're in for a real treat.

'And won't it be jolly seeing your very first love again?' she teased as Bob spread his hands out in surrender. 'Well then, I'll be ready and waiting on Friday afternoon. I'd like to buy something for Sir Harold, though, as I've never visited his house before. Is there something I can get him from London?'

'That's a sweet thought, Bob, but bless you, Sir Harold only lives for about a month or so every summer in Ireland. He has far grander homes in London, Scotland and the South of France. For the rest of the year he lets out the villa at a peppercorn rent to the Guild of Master Tailors who send sick members and their families there to recuperate after illness. Still, if you wish to buy him a gift, pop down to Holywell Street and see if any of the print shops there have any good new books about fucking.'

'I beg your pardon, Amanda, did you say about fucking?' repeated Bob, clutching the stair-rail as he reeled back in astonishment.

'Yes, that's right,' Amanda continued coolly. 'Sir Harold has the greatest collection of gallant literature in Europe with the possible exception of the famous library of erotica which Count Gewirtz keeps in his castle in Prague. I know he would like to extend his collection of French postcards so you won't go wrong with any of those, especially if you can find any produced by the German photographer Hans Falda, as I know that he is very keen to buy anything by him. *[Hans Falda (1871–1957) was a noted Berlin portrait photographer whose studio on Unter den Linden was patronised by Kaiser Wilhelm's family – and who also supplied the Kaiser and his friends with uncensored photographs and films, many of which were unfortunately destroyed during an Allied bombing raid on Berlin during World War Two. – Editor]* You'll probably do best by going to Stanley Goldhill's at number fourteen. Mr Goldhill's always got a good selection of stuff for selected customers. Just mention Sir Harold Brown's name and he'll show you what he keeps under the counter.'

In for a penny, in for a pound, thought Bob, who decided to take Amanda's advice then and there, making his way to Holywell Street *[A Bloomsbury Street noted during late Victorian and Edwardian times for the risqué reputation of its picture and print shops – Editor]* to see if he could find anything that might be of interest to Sir Harold Brown. On Amanda's recommendation he went to Stanley Goldhill's shop where he asked the owner if there were any new Hans Falda photographs that he could buy as a present for Sir Harold Brown. 'I think Sir Harold has every Falda photograph available in this country,' mused Mr Goldhill. 'But I tell you what, though, I've just got in some lovely stuff from Colin Ramsay, a young British photographer who the trade thinks very highly of. Come through to the back room, sir, and I'll show you some shots from his latest portfolio.

'Make yourself comfortable and I'll find his latest album for you,' urged Mr Goldhill as he waved Bob to sit down at a small side table. 'Here it is,' added the shopkeeper, passing him a large sized leather book. 'Oh dear, that's the front bell, I'll leave you here to browse through this selection and you can tell me later which ones you'd like.'

Bob settled down and quietly whistled his appreciation of the beautiful photographs in the book. He looked long and hard at a set of voluptuous colour tinted photographs of a beautiful naked dark-skinned couple who Mr Ramsay must have photographed in India and indeed when Bob looked on the back of the photograph he noticed it was dated Madras, 1903. The young man was pressing the soft bum cheeks of his partner who was holding his enormous cock in a tender, loving grasp. In the next plate the buxom beauty was shown lying on a bed, her legs spread wide apart with her splendid pussey lips protruding from the crimson crack which could be seen through the silky black hair of her pudenda. The slim lad stood beside her, holding his huge stiff prick just an inch from her open cunney and the next photograph showed his uncapped knob pushing its way through her pussey lips. In all there were twelve plates in the set which showed the lewd pair engaged in frigging, fucking and sucking in a variety of positions.

'You won't go wrong with those,' declared Mr Goldhill who had come in from the shop whilst Bob was gazing spellbound by Colin Ramsay's lascivious photographs. 'I've a bound set over from a cancelled order from Portugal, I'll let you have them cheap, especially if they're for Sir Harold Brown who's one of my best customers.'

A bargain was soon struck and Bob made his way to the Reading Room of the British Museum. At his desk, however, he slipped the photographs he had purchased out of the discreet folder provided by Mr Goldhill and looked again at the dark-skinned couple performing so heroically for Colin Ramsay's camera. As he studied the photograph he suddenly became aware of the shadow looming over his desk and he looked up to see a white moustached military looking gentleman, who must have been passing by him, standing beside him. Bob's face coloured crimson as the gentleman patted his shoulder and beckoned him to come outside into the corridor. I'll be drummed out of the Reading Room, thought Bob miserably, as he followed the man out, but to his relief the stranger introduced himself as Colonel Piers Rankin of the Buffs and continued: 'I must apologise for interrupting your studies, sir, but I couldn't help noticing that fine set of photographs you were studying so intently.

You see the girl bears an almost uncanny resemblance to a young lady I knew when I was posted on the North West Frontier, and I wondered whether you were behind the camera and so might have been acquainted with her.'

'An extraordinary coincidence, sir, but I'm afraid I simply purchased these photographs today,' stammered Bob.

'Ah, I thought it was too good to be true,' said Colonel Rankin genially. 'Still, it reminded me of the last time I fucked her. I'd come back to camp in a hurry disguised as a native woman – well, I didn't want to be captured in uniform by the Baluchi tribesmen. They'd cut off your balls without a second thought but they'd only bugger any women they suspected of passing on information to the British. Better buggered than lose your wedding tackle, eh? Anyhow, I made it back to the fort, safe and sound but had the devil of a row with the Adjutant.'

'Why was that?' asked Bob.

'Women were never allowed in the Mess – not even officers' ladies, let alone wives and other women. So the stupid young pup didn't want to let me in and I had to untangle my sari to convince this dolt that I was a man. He was new to the regiment and didn't recognise me, you see. I don't mind telling you that I felt a complete fool standing there in my sari waving my prick in his face. "What the hell do you think this is?" I said. "Can't you recognise a British officer's prick when you see one?" That took the wind out of his sails by Jove! Took my revenge though later that evening by fucking the fellah's fiancée. Then I went

159

back to my quarters to see if Gita – the girl of whom I was reminded by looking at your splendid photographs – was waiting up for me. The dear girl was there, fast asleep, warming my bed with her sweet body. I climbed in and leaned forward to kiss the pink pouting lips of her slit which beckoned so invitingly from the dark forest of silky black hair. I worked my mouth all around her moistening crack, inhaling her fragrant scent as I licked all around her muff, rubbing my mouth against her cunney lips which woke Gita from her slumber. "Put your fingers in me, Piers," she begged as she put her hands on her inner thighs and pulled her legs further apart. Her pussey was now so wet that I could easily slip three fingers into her snatch. I worked up a good rhythm, sliding them in and out of her juicy quim as at the same time she started to frig herself, rubbing her little clitty between her thumb and forefinger.

'Being an officer and a gentleman I naturally replaced her hand with my own whilst I lapped away inside her juicy honeypot. She let out little yelps of pleasure as she reached a climax and her love juices filled my mouth as I tongued her crack from top to bottom, licking and lapping the tangy juices that now overflowed onto her thighs.

'"Please fuck me now," she asked plaintively and so I heaved myself up across her so that we could kiss passionately as my knob eased its way inside her cunt. As my cock slipped in I sucked on her firm little brown titties which made her writhe in delight. Gita liked to be fucked strongly so I plunged my prick in and out of her sopping cunney at a good rate of knots, thrusting downwards so powerfully on each downwards stroke that my balls fairly slapped against her bottom as I buried my length fully inside her welcoming sheath.

'Ah, how we revelled in these voluptuous delights. Gita had loaned me a copy of *The Eastern Art Of Fucking* by Mustapha Pharte and I can now keep going for a good half hour without spunking. But Gita's cunney was so soft, warm and wet that all too soon I felt myself fast approaching the ultimate pleasure, and though I tried to delay the final release as I was enjoying fucking this dusky beauty so much, my body was being wound up tighter and tigher until I could hold back no longer. With a cry, I exploded into one climactic release, shooting wads of hot sperm deep into the girl who was writhing beneath me, her hips rotating wildly, her cunney throbbing as my prick spurted jets of love juice, lubricating her love box as we went off together, soaking the sheets with our juices as we rolled around in a delicious frenzy.

'But this story has a sad end, my friend. Gita was called home the next day and from that day to this I have not clapped eyes upon her, which explains why I was so curious about your photographs.'

Bob explained how the photographs came to be in his possession and Colonel Rankin's eyes widened. 'But my dear sir, what an extraordinary coincidence. I have also been invited to Sir Harold Brown's weekend gathering, so we'll see each other again in just a few days time. Now what did you say your name was, young fella?' After a formal introduction and a handshake the Colonel insisted on buying Bob coffee and cakes in the Museum cafeteria. 'How are you getting across?' enquired Colonel Rankin. When Bob told him that Sir Harold had made all their travel plans he nodded and said: 'Ah yes, you'll go from Paddington via Fishguard in Pembrokeshire to Rosslare. It's the most direct route and you'll travel overnight of course, but as I have some business in Dublin I'm going the previous day from Holyhead. It's a lovely voyage and at this time of year if the weather's clear one can usually see Snowdon from one side of the boat and the hills of the Irish coast from the other. Beautiful bay, Dublin, especially if you approach it from Killiney Hill or Howth. You know Lady Dufferin's verse:

Oh, Bay of Dublin! My heart you're troublin',
Your beauty haunts me like a fever'd dream;
Like frozen fountains that the sun sets bubblin',
My heart's blood warms when I hear your name.

So I look forward to seeing you, my boy, at Sir Harold's – we should be in for a weekend of fun!'

For Bob Goggin the rest of the week seemed to fly by and Friday afternoon saw him pack his suitcase ready for the fray. When he was ready he went to Amanda and Susie's room and helped bring their cases down into the hall. The promised Prestoncrest vehicle arrived punctually and the three travellers reached the railway station in good time for their train. The journey down to Fishguard was uneventful though they enjoyed a well-cooked supper on the train. At Fishguard they transferred themselves to a waiting ship and Bob admired the clean, well-appointed facilities in the first-class cabins of the steamer which would take them across the Irish Sea. It was just before midnight when they sailed out of Fishguard but despite the long journey Bob was not yet sleepy. He looked round in vain for the copy of the *Evening News* he had bought in London. 'Damn,' he muttered as he realised that on the train he had given the newspaper to one of the girls who were sharing the next door cabin. They won't be asleep yet, he reasoned, so he quietly went out into the corridor and gently knocked on their door. 'Who's that?' called out Susie. 'It's only me,' he replied. 'Come on in, then and shut the door behind you,' she instructed as Bob entered the well-appointed room.

Susie was already tucked up in bed but she was sitting up wearing only a frilly low cut nightdress which accentuated the swell of her breasts. 'Hello, Bob, what do you want?' she said brightly, but her face fell when Bob explained the purpose of his visit. 'Oh dear, you gave it to me but I'm afraid I left the newspaper on one of the seats in our carriage. I am so sorry, Bob, I thought you'd finished with it.'

At this point Amanda came in from the bathroom dressed in a pink towelling robe. 'Did you really want the paper, Bob, or just something to read until you get to sleep?' she asked.

'Oh, anything will do,' he replied. 'Why, have you brought a good book with you?'

'Well, it's not exactly a good book but you're welcome to read it just the same,' said the blonde girl with a giggle, passing a copy of a small leather bound book across to him. 'It's Sir Harold's copy of the first volume of his autobiography which he leant me on his last visit to London and which now I'm returning to him. It was printed in France, of course, and I think you'll enjoy it. Why not sit down in that armchair and dip into it?'

That sounded like a good idea, thought Bob. He wanted to know something about his host, of whom he had never heard until he had told all about losing his virginity to Melanie Marley. Heavens, he had forgotten all about Melanie – what would it be like meeting her again after all this time? He opened a page at random and settled down to read, but what he read did nothing to make him sleepy. His eyes opened wide as he read of Sir Harold Brown's own crossing of the Rubicon which had occurred when, as a young undergraduate at Oxford University, he had offered to deliver a note to his English tutor's wife. Let us peer over Bob's shoulder as he read Sir Harold's shameless memoir . . .

'One's first fuck can be rapturous and idyllic – though equally, alas, it can often turn out to be a complete disaster. Which way the coin falls will depend on the circumstances and to a very great extent upon the participants themselves. In my humble opinion, every young man would benefit (as did I) from the experience of being tutored by a more mature partner to tutor him in the paths of love.

'The exact circumstances of my initiation are as follows: now believe it or not, whilst I was at Brasenose College I rapidly acquired the reputation of being somewhat of a swot and spent much of my time reading in my room instead of having a roistering good time with the chaps down on the river or in the many taverns of the town. Well, one afternoon my mathematics tutor, Dr Rickmansworth, came up to my room and asked me if I would be kind enough to deliver a note to his wife about a matter of some urgency. They were not yet connected to the telephone exchange and so the only way he could communicate with her was by a messenger as he had a class to take in twenty minutes time. Naturally, I said I would be happy to oblige and set off straightaway on my bicycle for his home which was in Botley village some two miles away.

'It took only fifteen minutes to ride there and I wheeled my bike up to the front door and rang the bell. There was no answer however even after I had pressed the bell twice more. I wondered whether I should simply drop the envelope through the letter-box and go home or whether I should investigate further. I took the latter course when I saw a side gate leading to the garden and I decided to see if perhaps Mrs Rickmansworth was outside enjoying the warm Autumn day. And indeed my supposition was proved right as I made my way into the garden, for there she was, and what a stunningly beautiful woman was the wife of my tutor! As I later discovered, Mrs Katherine Rickmansworth was only thirty-four (at the age of eighteen this classed her as being positively middle-aged in my reckoning!) but Gad, what a lovely lady! She had long, dark hair and large dark eyes that brimmed with mischief with a sweet little nose and rich, red lips. She was lusciously proportioned with full, rounded breasts which were only scantily covered by a low cut white blouse, a narrow waist and slender, shapely legs.

'I introduced myself and gave her the note. "Thank you very much, Mr Brown. Do stay and have a glass of lemonade before you go back to college. I've just made a fresh jug." I thanked her and we sat down and chatted about life in Oxford. She told me that her name was Kathie and that whilst she enjoyed living amongst the dreaming spires, life could occasionally be rather dull. "It's all very well for Edwin, he has his books and his students but I'm rather shy and truthfully I haven't made many friends in Botley." I confessed that I too had so far made few friends in Oxford. "Well, you be my friend, Harold," she said with a smile, "and I'll be yours." Gosh, if only she would be mine, I thought as I tried desperately to keep my eyes away from her jiggling breasts which quivered with each breath she took.

'Kathie asked me to take the tray with the half empty jug of lemonade and the glasses back into the kitchen. I did so but when I returned my heart began to beat madly for there in front of my eyes was Kathie lying face down on the *chaise lounge* stark naked, the luscious bare cheeks of her backside staring up at me.

'Frankly, reader, I was flabbergasted. I had never seen a woman totally naked before. Oh, I'd had my moments at parties and in Sally the parlourmaid's bedroom at home and a never-to-be-forgotten dark night in Regents Park when Sally took out my prick and tossed me off. But the girls with whom I had enjoyed a kiss and cuddle had always remained partially clothed even if I'd managed to slip down a chemise or raise up a skirt. So I stared dumbstruck at Kathie's sun dappled nudity as she turned her head and said softly: "Harold, I hope I haven't shocked you but I've been suffering from a skin ailment lately and my physician, Doctor Zane, suggests that I allow the sun to reach every part of my body."

'Now without realising it, I already had a terrific rock-hard boner which was very noticeable since I wasn't wearing anything under my cycling shorts. Kathie looked amused at my predicament as I tried to pull my shorts across this tremendous erection. "Here, let me help you," she said kindly and simply pulled down my shorts to let my bare cock spring free up against my belly. Lazily she flicked the long red nail on her index finger over my knob, scooping up a drop of liquid which had already oozed out of it. Well, as you can imagine, her touch was simply electrifying, especially when she brought the finger to her lips and flicked her tongue onto the nail.

'So there I stood, my shorts round my ankles and my throbbing cock just inches from her mouth. I could still only utter a hoarse little croak as her warm hand encircled my shaft as she turned over onto her back and said to me: "Tell me, Harold dear, have you ever fucked a woman?" The direct question came as a shock and I stared down at the grass in order to hide my red face. "Not really," I mumbled. "Oh, well have you seen a woman with all her clothes off before?" "No," I muttered and she smiled knowingly at me. "Dear boy, there is no need to be embarrassed – tell the truth and shame the devil is an old proverb which will always hold good in my opinion. Now, you may be a fine scholar but I think we should complete your education."

'Then she told me to stroke her. My trembling

hands glided over her smooth skin, lightly brushing her big red nipples and then down over her tummy. When I reached the crisp thatch of pussey hair she opened her legs for me and her hand tightened its grip around my prick when my fingers slipped over the wet lips of her cunney. "What a lovely hard cock," she breathed. "No, do not feel shamed in any way. When a man's penis rises in the presence of a woman it is but a compliment to her beauty. Indeed, creating such a fine stiffstander as you now sport is a proud function of feminine charm." These words made me grow bolder and I rubbed my hand all along her damp slit. Ecstatic tremors shot through me as she leaned across and planted a delicate little kiss on my cock. Never, not even in the throes of vigorous masturbation, had I even fantasized on such boldness on the part of a pretty lady! She opened her mouth and for a moment let her tongue play all around my pulsating prick. Then she took her head away and whispered in a low voice: "Shall I teach you how to perform a *soixante neuf* Harold? Wouldn't that be nice?"

'Truthfully, I had only a vague notion of the practice known by this magical number. But I was more than ready to find out! So I answered: "Yes, please, that would be really lovely."

'"Very well, then," she replied. "First, you must take off the rest of your clothes." I obeyed as fast as I could and when I too was stark naked she said: "There's a good boy. Now you lie down with your head toward my feet so that we can taste each other. I take it that you've never licked out a pussey before?" "No, ma'am." I admitted though by now I guessed what she had in mind. "Well, I'm sure you'll like it, Harold. Just lick me," she instructed. "Slide your tongue over my pussey lips slowly. Once you've done it a few times you'll see how naturally it will all seem."

'And how right she was! Once my lips found their succulent target, I inhaled deeply, savouring the piquant frangrance. The bouquet of sweet perfume (for she bathed her pussey daily in *eau de cologne*) blended with the natural spicy aroma of female prurience. I grasped her chubby bum cheeks in my hands and buried my face in that delicious nest of love. My tongue now seemed to enjoy a life of its own, whipping back and forth, up and down, boring deep into her tender spongelike cunney. Drawing her labia into my mouth I sucked on it as if it were treacle toffee as her quim unfolded like the petals of a flower.

'At the same time Kathie's tongue was committed to a similar joyful tour, flicking over my bell end, down the shaft, over my balls and then back again to my knob. Then, with a passionate little squeal, she opened her mouth wide and slid her lips over my cock, slipping down the shaft until it was fully engulfed in the wet warmth of her mouth. She sucked on my prick with undisguised relish and when her hand stole round and probed for the cleft of my arse, I almost swooned with ecstasy. My prick quivered and twitched violently before releasing a torrent of sperm which Kathie swallowed with great enjoyment and her own love juices were suddenly released into my face as she shuddered into a long, sensuous orgasm that burst from deep within her, grinding her sopping cunt against my mouth as I lapped up her tangy spend.

'My cock was still heavy though it had lost some of its stiffness when Kathie released it from between her lips. She wriggled round so that she was lying on her back and with my cockshaft now firmly in her fist she said: "Harold, it's time for your first lesson in *l'arte de faire l'amour*. I'm going to rub your cock until it's nice and stiff again and then I want you to guide it inside my cunney and fuck me. You would like to fuck me, wouldn't you?" Again I found myself tongue-tied but a nod of the head sufficed to show my approval and Kathie's warm hand began to travel up and down my shaft which was still damp from her magnificent tonguing. "Now I want you to enter me," she whispered huskily. "Climb over and I'll guide your knob onto my cunney lips. Then all you have to do is push home and we can begin our fuck. But do try and take your time, Harold. Remember, there is no rush, we have no train to catch."

'She pulled me by my prick until I was on top of her and carefully placed my knob between the portals of her cunt. "There we are, Harold, push your helmet between my love lips, dear boy." I drew a deep breath and with a hoarse moan pushed my cock forward as instructed and *eureka*! My shaft slid inside the welcoming sanctuary of her honeypot until every inch was firmly ensconced inside her. I lay still for a moment so as to concentrate my mind on this wonderful initial penetration of a juicy pussey by my throbbing young tadger. Truly, I felt as if I had entered paradise. "A-a-h-r-e," breathed Kathie as she revelled in the tingling sensations coming from her engorged cunney. "Now it's time to fuck," she whispered lustfully and began to move her hips up and down, telling me to copy her movements. To begin with, I moved my cock rather tentatively but then gained confidence when Kathie muttered: "Good boy, fuck away now, don't be frightened. Fuck my sweet pussey with your big thick cock!" With her hands now gripping my backside, I soon found myself engaged in a delightful fuck, effortlessly pumping my cock in and out of her pussey. Our movements became faster and faster as we writhed together in our lewd passion with Kathie pressing up to meet my thrusts and it was not too long before I was spurting a second spray of spunk, this time drenching the walls of her cunney as her soft body quaked beneath me.

'"You're a natural fucker, Harold Brown," she said with a wide grin on her pretty face. "My, what a thick, fat prick you've got between your legs and how well you used it. For a first time fuck, you score ten out of ten. What has happened to the shy young student? I think he has gone for good and has been replaced by a fully-fledged man."

'Afterwards we rested and I lay my head down on her beautiful bare breasts whilst she gently played with my limp prick. But five minutes later she had frigged me up to another erection and she asked me if I would like to fuck her again. "Yes please, I'd love to," I said and this time she rolled over on her elbows and knees with her gorgeous bottom raised up in front of my face. "Take me from behind, Harold," she called out and so I mounted her from behind, squeezing my cock between the narrow crevice between her buttocks and squeezing her erect titties in my hands. My prick slid back and forth in and out of her dripping cunney and though I couldn't reach another climax, it wasn't too long before Kathie began gasping and moaning as she reached a final orgasm.

'As I have said, first love can be idyllic or disastrous. I count myself fortunate that my first teacher was so patient and loving and I am convinced that every woman who I have fucked since Kathie Rickmansworth has benefitted from her tutelage. I last heard of Kathie around the turn of the century when her husband was offered a prestigous post at the nascent University in Christchurch, New Zealand. Wherever you are now Kathie, I hope a copy of this book reaches you. Thank you again for everything. I'll always be eternally grateful to you.'

Bob closed the book and breathed heavily. Sir Harold Brown's carnal confession had made him fearfully randy and he tugged at the bulge his swollen member had caused to make in his lap. He looked across at Susie and Amanda but alas, both were sound asleep. To his credit, Bob did not attempt to wake them up, although just then he would have given his right arm for a good fuck! Noiselessly he crept out of their cabin and made his way back to his own. He undressed and clambered into bed. He caressed his still stiff prick but even as he debated whether or not to indulge in what the vulgar multitude know as a five knuckle shuffle, his eyes closed and he too was soon in the arms of Morpheus.

Early the next morning, after a hearty breakfast,

Bob, Susie and Amanda proceeded due west by train to Waterford and then on the Dungarvan and Lismore where the girls pointed out the Duke of Devonshire's fine castle, and on to Mallow, an important centre for horse racing where Sir Harold kept a sizeable stable.

'It is Harold's ambition to win the Derby,' said Susie as the train chugged on towards Rathmore.

'The Blue Riband of the turf,' mused Bob. 'Does he own a horse that has a fighting chance?'

'He's entering Sportsman's Aid next year and we'll all have a flutter on it. But don't put your shirt on it,' chimed in Amanda. *[Let's hope none of them put their shirts on Sportsman's Aid which finished three from last in the 1905 Epsom Derby – Editor]*

They journeyed on past Rathmore, the scene of a shocking disaster at Christmas nine years before in 1896 when some two hundred acres of bog rolled bodily down a hill and swept away houses and caused several fatalities. Then onwards they travelled through some beautiful woods and the finely situated Flesk Castle until they arrived at Killarney Station where Sir Harold Brown himself was waiting to greet them. He had driven from his house in his motor car, one of the few horseless carriages in south-west Ireland at this time.

Sir Harold Brown was a broad-shouldered well-built gentleman in the prime of life, with a friendly craggy face. Susie and Amanda rushed over to him to each plant kisses on his cheek. 'Ah, you must be Bob Goggin,' he said, striding towards Bob who was busy supervising the taking down of their luggage from the train. 'I am so pleased you could come, welcome to

Ireland.' His coachman took hold of the barrow in which the guests' luggage had been deposited and wheeled it away towards the donkey cart which had been brought from Abroch House, Sir Harold's pretty villa which was situated near Killarney House *[destroyed by fire in 1913 – Editor]* at the west end of the town. 'McGinty will bring back your bags in the cart,' explained Sir Harold, shepherding his guests towards his motor car whilst at the same time shooing away a small crowd of interested young boys who had gathered around the vehicle.

Frankly, the town of Killarney was at first a disappointment to Bob Goggin who, like most people, imagined that one only had to descend from the train to see the famed vista of blue hills, lovely lakes, sparkling streams and romantic water-falls. In fact, as he was soon to find out, the nearest lake is a mile away and the market town itself is not particularly attractive. Nevertheless, as he was also to discover it is still the centre of some of the loveliest scenery in Ireland.

At Abroch House they were welcomed by Bob's acquaintance from the British Museum, Colonel Piers Rankin, who had arrived the previous evening from Dublin. Bob introduced him to Susie and Amanda. Melanie Marley had also arrived the previous day but she had gone into town to the Post Office to send a telegram to her parents. She returned shortly after Bob and the girls had unpacked and joined the rest of the party in enjoying a refreshing pre-luncheon sherry on the verandah. 'How nice to see you again, Bob,' said the leggy blonde girl. 'It's been a good few years since we last saw each other at

Miss Stevenage's school in Muswell Hill.' She looked at Bob warmly and when the opportunity arose to speak to him without being noticed, she whispered in his ear: 'I still remember our glorious fuck in the changing rooms, Bob, and I hope you've learned how to use your cock since then.'

'I've had no complaints so far,' he replied quietly, as the guests filed in for luncheon, the centrepiece of which was a superb salmon caught by Sir Harold the previous morning on the River Laune. After luncheon Susie and Amanda decided to catch up with their correspondence and Colonel Rankin decided to join Sir Harold for a round at the Deer Park Golf Club.

This left Bob and Melanie Marley to their own devices and Bob was more than happy to fall in with Melanie's suggestion that they take an afternoon constitutional in the wooded park around Courteene Hall. They walked through the varied and vigorous vegetation and Melanie, who had stayed at Killarney before, assured Bob that the beauty of the countryside was unsurpassed. 'The best view of the lake country is that from the elevated ridges at the southern end of the Upper Lake on the road from Kenmare,' she said thoughtfully. 'Here, at a sudden turn, as at the lifting of a veil, the three lakes flash upon the eye at a glance. I have brought my camera with me for I have been commissioned to take some pictures for a book being written on the beauties of Killarney to be published in America.'

'I didn't know you were a professional photographer,' said Bob admiringly. Melanie laughed and said: 'Hardly professional, Bob, if I had to live on what I earned from my work I'd starve! But I enjoy taking photographs. Though I specialise in portraiture, the author of this travel book, James Everleigh, is an old friend and it would be churlish of me to refuse his request to help illustrate his words, especially as I had already accepted Harold Brown's invitation to spend a few days here. But tell me, Bob, what have you been up to since we last met?'

He began to tell her how he had left the employ of Miss Stevenage shortly after Melanie had left school and had since worked at Arkley Manor in Sussex whilst studying drawing and painting at night school. 'Oh, you must know Penny and Katie Arkley,' said Melanie. 'I haven't seen them for some time but we do keep in touch. They are both very nice girls, rather quiet of course but that's partly because of their Mama, Lady Laetitia who is a bit of a dragon.' Bob resisted the temptation to tell Melanie that he and Penny had been lovers for some time and that only a week before he had been a guest at a wild party in London at which Katie Arkley had been one of the girls who had frigged, sucked and fucked uninhibitedly in front of an appeciative audience. Instead he was about to tell her how he was spending the summer at St Dominic's School of Art when suddenly he felt a splash of rain on his head. The couple had been so engrossed in conversation that neither had noticed how the sky had clouded over. Kerry has a deserved reputation for rain and they ran as fast as they could towards a nearby cottage to shelter from the rain which was now beating down quite fiercely. There was no answer to Bob's knock on the door but

176

Melanie just bent down and extracted a key from under the doormat. 'This cottage belongs to Jeffrey Green, the local magistrate, and he always leaves the key there when he is out.'

'You surprise me, because any housebreaker would look for it there straightaway after ascertaining that no-one was at home. A magistrate should know that better than anybody,' remarked Bob.

'Ah, such an attitude comes from living too long in London and other great cities where you must lock your doors at night. Here, burglary is almost unknown,' Melanie replied as she opened the door. 'Are you sure Mr Green won't mind us coming in like this?' asked Bob anxiously, as he followed her inside. 'Oh no, Jeffrey is a dear friend,' she said as rays of sunshine began to light up the room. In summer the rain clears quickly and, as Melanie added, the views are never so lovely as on these changeable days when the sun breaks through the clouds and the hills are seen through a delicate blue haze.

'Talking of change, it's a pity we can't change out of these wet clothes,' said Bob ruefully. 'Well, why don't you take off your jacket and shirt whilst I put on the kettle and we'll have a nice cup of tea,' suggested Melanie.

Half an hour later, the pair were curled up snugly together on Mr Green's sofa, Bob having divested himself of his shirt and Melanie of her blouse. Melanie had added a liberal amount of Irish whiskey to the tea and this had the effect of making them both relaxed as they lay in each other's arms. Bob stroked the girl's silky blonde hair which she had now let down to tumble freely over her shoulders. She responded by moving her hand across his face and brought it forward until inexorably their lips touched and they sank back, entwined in each other's arms, exchanging the most ardent of kisses as Melanie unbuttoned Bob's trousers, releasing his straining cock which sprang up like a flagpole between his thighs. She then put her hands underneath her dress and pulled off her knickers and then whispered: 'Help me off with my dress, please.'

Bob needed no second bidding and in a trice her skirt was on the floor to be followed by her other clothes until she stood naked in front of him. At first he could only stare with wonder at Melanie's lush, exquisitely proportioned uptilted breasts capped with large red titties and her smooth flat belly below which twinkled the blonde curls of pubic hair and the prettiest pair of pouting cunney lips. Filled with unabashed lust he tore off his trousers and other clothes until he too was naked.

Melanie lay him down on his back and then bent forward over him, rubbing his rigid rod against her breasts, squeezing her luscious globes along its blue-veined length and then moving to straddle across him so that her pert young bottom was in front of his face as she lowered her head and parted her lips to take Bob's bursting knob into her deliciously wet mouth, sucking slowly and deeply as Bob moaned with pleasure. She manoeuvred her mouth until she had slurped down almost all of this throbbing tool into her throat and the cheeks of her bare backside wriggled provocatively in front of Bob's eyes. His groping fingers soon parted the moist lips of her juicy pussey and her buttocks began a lustful dance as Bob forced his head upwards and slipped his tongue inside her wet crack which thrilled the lovely girl as she sucked frantically on his pulsating prick. She wriggled her hips anew and the curled point of his tongue found the wrinkled tiny bum hole which made her shudder as her body exploded into a series of short multiple spends and her clitty squished against his fingers as they slipped in and out of her now dripping cunt with ease, coated with the tangy love juice which now freely trickled down her thighs.

He knew that he could not hold this position without spunking so Bob gently eased the trembling girl off until she lay on her back. He pulled her legs apart and knelt down between them, savouring the distinctive flavour of her juicy cunney as his tongue searched out her stiff clitty. Like nipples like clitty, says the motto on the wall in the officers' mess of the Irish Guards, and Melanie proved the old adage right for her fine little clit projected pink and shiny quite two inches from her pussey lips. Bob sucked on this excited cunney flesh with vigour and this titillated her sensitive pussey so well that she spent profusely as his tongue revelled in her creamy emission till she begged Bob to cease tonguing and insert his fat prick inside her honeypot.

Bob scrambled up to place himself on top of her. Resting on his elbows he looked down upon the thrilling young body which ached for his cock. Melanie was breathing heavily, her eyes closed and her thighs parted as she reached out blindly for his throbbing tool which she grasped with both hands to guide it into her soft, wet cunt. Soon they were locked into a hard, sweeping rhythm and Bob's big cock slid in and out of her clinging cunney. He let himself be enveloped in her frenzy, glorying in the smooth motion of her hips which moved up and down at an ever increasing speed. Bob felt himself swell even further inside her love channel as she kept driving up against the power of his thrusts, bouncing up to meet him, over and over again as she met every fresh onslaught with eager delight, crossing her legs to trap his cock inside her excited cunt.

'Oh, oh, oh! Fuck my cunt, Bob, fill my pussey with your spunk!' she panted. Then she screamed with great passion as a convulsive tremor racked through her body and her cunney was flooded by a copious emission of creamy love juice. She bucked wildly beneath Bob as his shaft throbbed and as he plunged it once more into her juicy cunney, Melanie arched her back to receive the thick squirts of sperm that spurted out of his knob.

This simultaneous climax rocketed through the pair with such force that they whimpered with pleasure as the hot gobs of spunk from Bob's cock mingled with Melanie's own emission as he collapsed on top of her.

Melanie was the first to recover from the post-fuck fatigue. Her fingers traced a pattern on his shoulders as she said softly: 'Well, Bob Goggin, you really have turned out to be quite a man.' She gazed upon his lithe manly torso with admiration. His shoulders were as broad as hers were narrow. His deep, masculine chest covered with a light dusting of hair contrasted well with her own graceful firm breasts whilst his powerfully muscled arms had little of the soft pliancy of Melanie's own body. But what really caught her attention was his magnificent heavy cockshaft which lay on her belly and she reached down beneath him to cup his big hairy ballsack in her hands. She wriggled out from underneath him until she had climbed on top of him and hungrily searching for his lips, she kissed him fervently, their thighs moving together until their pubic muffs rubbed against each other's groins. Bob's prick had now swelled up to its former grand stiffness and his uncapped helmet probed through the blonde bush to the entrance of her exquisite loveslit and remained there, throbbing with intense power until Melanie moved her hips, emitting a little squeal of delight as the swollen knob forced its way up inside her cunney, massaging her clitty beautifully as he arched his back to thrust his prick inside her dripping crack.

Melanie paused, like a rider testing a new mount, and then she clamped her cunney muscles around his shaft as Bob flexed himself, delighting in the clinging silkiness of his cuntal prison. He tried to ram upwards again but the weight of Melanie's thighs left him in no doubt as to who was directing the pace of this wonderful fuck. She pumped her fleshy bum cheeks furiously up and down, digging her fingernails into Bob's shoulders. Each voluptuous shove was accompanied by a wail of ecstatic ululation. Bob lifted his hands to cup her breasts and brought them down to his lips so he could suck the rosy nipples, helping her in her ride, pushing her up and letting her drop down upon his rock-hard shaft. Her body shuddered as she began to spend, shivering and trembling as she neared the pinnacle of pleasure and Bob felt her cunney grip his prick even tighter as she entered the throes of orgasm. She climaxed beautifully and then her movements slowed and they lay entwined in a euphoric peace.

But Bob had not yet spunked so he carefully pulled out his glistening shaft out of her pussey as she lay panting with lustful exhaustion. His hand slid across her flat belly down through the silky blonde pubic thatch till he found the moist crack into which he dipped his finger. Melanie giggled and said: 'Oh Bob, are we going to have a final fling? What a splendid fucker you've turned out to be.' Her hips began to rotate and her hands groped for his erect cock. She touched the hot shaft, rubbed it and kissed it until it pulsated in her grasp and then the sensual girl rolled on to her back, her eyes closed and mouth open.

'Are you ready, Bob?' she asked as her knees came up to her breasts, the rounded thighs opening as he came over upon her, between her legs. He found her soaking cunney immediately and his cock sank slowly inside her, the walls of her cunt closing deliciously around his shaft. They pulled him deeper and deeper until he was totally engulfed as her legs wrapped themselves around his back as her hands clutched at his shoulders. She cried out with joy as Bob thrust his trusty tool to and fro, searching out every little wrinkle as he fucked her with all the strength he had left in his wiry frame. Melanie began to buck from side to side, with her backside rising and falling as she responded to Bob's pistoning thrusts. Her body gyrated faster and faster as, with a tremendous surge, Bob clasped her to him. With a convulsive shudder he poured out a luscious flood of frothy jism in an ecstasy of enjoyment which brought Melanie sobbing and shivering to one last gigantic climax as Bob emptied himself, the white love juice gushing out of his bulbous knob in a miniature fountain.

'Phew, what an exhausting fuck,' said Melanie, wiping the perspiration from her forehead. 'Bob, I hope enjoyed that as much as I did.'

'I should say so, Mel, I just hope we won't lose touch again like last time,' he replied gallantly.

Then they almost jumped out of their skins as a voice cheerfully echoed Bob's words: 'Well, let's hope you don't lose touch, it would be a terrible pity because you fit together like two peas in a pod!'

They looked up to see standing before them a fine looking gentleman whose handsome face was adorned with a grey, well-curled moustache and twinkling blue eyes. Bob hardly knew where to put his face but Melanie was quite unconcerned. 'Why, Jeffrey, so nice to see you. We were so busy fucking that neither Bob nor I heard you come in. Bob, let me present Mr Jeffrey Green, the local magistrate around these parts and one of Killarney's leading country gentlemen – with the accent on the cunt, if he will forgive my saying so! Jeffrey, may I introduce a very dear old friend of mine, Mr Bob Goggin.'

'A pleasure to meet you, sir,' stammered Bob, shaking hands with Mr Green, who seemed quite unconcerned about the nudity of his uninvited guests.

'But not so much a pleasure as fucking young Melanie,' laughed the magistrate. 'But, as the poet writes, *is there anything in this wide world so sweet, as the vale where the thighs of a pretty girl meet?*'

Melanie smiled and stroked the bulge which had outlined itself in Jeffrey Green's trousers. She turned to Bob and said: 'I think our host's cock needs urgent attention. Would you mind if I administered some appropriate relief?'

'Not at all,' said Bob politely, gathering his clothes together and putting them on a nearby chair as he slipped on his drawers and began to get dressed. 'Very kind of you, I'm sure,' said Mr Green who quickly divested himself of his clothing to reveal a tough hairy torso and a strong thick weapon of a very passable size which stood stiffly to attention against his stomach. Melanie reached out for this firm truncheon and held it between her long, tapering fingers.

'Truly a fine shillelagh, Jeffrey Green, and I suppose you'd like nothing better than to cudgel me with that monster.'

'Sure I would love to stretch your divine little pussey with it for I've been dying to fuck you ever since I came in and saw you two performing on the couch. Is a fuck on offer, Melanie, my little rogue?' he enquired.

'Thanks to Bob Goggin, I'm really in the mood,' she said. And so, without ado, he covered her mouth with a burning kiss and slid his hand between her legs, feeling her hairy crack, tickling her clitty and which soon roused her to fresh peaks of desire. She moaned with pleasure as Jeffrey Green tenderly opened her yielding cunney lips, sliding his fingers into her dainty quim which was already sopping wet with a liquid mix of Bob Goggin's sperm and her own love juices. As he frigged her cunt with one, two and then three fingers she took hold of his magnificent Irish cock with both hands and, lowering her pretty blonde head, she leaned forward to receive the fierce red dome of his knob between her lips. He kept his fingers buried in the sticky moistness of her pussey as she sucked lustily on his huge staff, her soft tongue rolling over and over and without losing their position they lay down gently on the rug. Bob hurried across and thoughtfully placed two plumped up cushions under Melanie's buttocks. Jeffrey Green was now on his knees with his cock now fully ensheathed in Melanie's mouth but when she slipped her hand under his ballsack and squeezed, he groaned: 'Oh no! I can't hold on!' and plunging his prick as far forward as he could without choking the girl, he shot his load of creamy jism flooding into her mouth. As he withdrew he spurted the remainder of his copious emission upon her heaving breasts and she hastily rubbed the pearly essence around her jumped-up red nipples.

He sat down heavily and banged a fist into his open palm. 'Damn and blast it! I would have far rather spunked in your pussey but you sucked me so sensually I just had to let go. Please forgive me,' exclaimed the magistrate, flipping his now flaccid member over his thigh.

'Don't blame yourself, it was my fault for squeezing your balls whilst sucking your cock,' insisted Melanie. 'Never mind, Jeff, you can fuck me tonight at Sir Harold Brown's villa. We can always do with a new cock to liven up the proceedings.'

'Ah, there's a party at Abroch House then? Splendid news – in fact Harold sent me round a note yesterday asking me to pop round tonight after the police committee meeting but I thought it was only for a rubber of bridge. I won't let you down tonight, I promise, as members of the committee are taking supper at the Northwick Park Hotel and I'll order half a dozen oysters as a starter.'

The sun was now shining brilliantly and so after Melanie had dressed herself, she and Bob continued their interrupted walk. Melanie explained that the name *Cill Arne* means 'The Church of the Sloes' and it stood for the whole of the mountainous district around the lakes. 'We must go to one of the lakes at dawn tomorrow,' said Melanie. 'I want to try and capture in a photograph the peculiar, haunting loveliness of the spirit of the mists which brood over the waters. Of course the waters look best in the splendour of a summer's day but I also need to take some photographs when the weather is inclement.'

She fumbled for a sheet of paper in the pocket of her dress. 'Here, let me read what my friend James Everleigh writes about his feelings during a storm: *On dark days when a threatened storm breaks and the water blackens under the rain and races into great waves before the wind, then, too, Killarney is beautiful with a beauty which is wild but not terrible. Killarney's woods and waters may inspire awe when the thunder is rumbling among the hollows of the hills and lightning is cutting slices out of the livid sky, but it never inspires terror. Its angers are the hot furies of a friend, not the forbidding wraths of an enemy.'*

'He certainly has a way with words,' remarked Bob as they trudged back to Abroch House. 'I don't think I've met James Everleigh but his name is very familiar.'

'Oh you've probably read his cousin Jenny's diaries *['The Intimate Diaries Of Jenny Everleigh' were amongst the most popular of all the underground magazines of this time – Editor]* as she waved to Sir Harold Brown and Colonel Piers Rankin who she saw in the distance were also making their way back home after their round of golf.

'Did you have a good game?' called out Melanie and Sir Harold answered with a broad grin on his face as they approached. 'Well, to be honest we only got as far as the fourth green when Piers filled a different kind of hole with his niblick.'

Over tea the golfers explained exactly what had happened on the course. Said Colonel Rankin: 'There were no caddies available but as it's only nine holes we carried our own bags. We sheltered during the fierce shower after playing the third hole but it was still rather wet when Harold teed off at the fourth. His shot was short but straight along the fairway. Unfortunately I sliced my shot quite badly and the ball shot off into the rough at an acute angle to my right. So I shouted out to Harold to play his shots and I would meet him on the green once I had found my ball. I really had hit the ball with some force but I thought I had tracked its path fairly well as it curved its way through the air although it was sure to be some distance away. I came to a hidden clearing between two trees where I thought my ball had landed and to my horror, I saw a young girl lying apparently unconscious on the ground with my golf ball lying beside her.

'I put down my bag and rushed towards her. By a strange coincidence I had been introduced to the girl only the day before at a reception given by the Mayor of Killarney for distinguished summer visitors to the town. I recalled that the name of this very pretty girl was Maggie Blake and she was staying with the parents at the Lake Hotel. I patted her cheek and whispered in her ear: "Maggie, Maggie, wake up!" – but to no avail. So remembering my first aid training I loosened her clothing, undoing her jacket and unbuttoning the top button of her blouse. This had the desired effect for her eyes fluttered open and she gave a tiny smile. "Why, it's Colonel Rankin, what are you doing here? How kind of you, sir, to help me. I was taking a short cut through to the road when I was hit by a golf ball." I pulled my bag of clubs over so that she could rest her head upon it.

'"My dear girl, I'm afraid that I am responsible for the accident. I stupidly sliced my shot and my ball must have struck you on the head. Let me see if there is any bruise," I replied and gently let my fingers weave their way through the soft strands of her light brown locks. "No, really, Colonel, I am quite recovered now," she said, sitting up and drawing her knees to her chest. "The ball only struck me a glancing blow and I fainted from shock rather than from pain. I'm just a wee bit giddy but I'll be all right in a moment. You can leave me and finish your game."

'"Certainly not," I said warmly. "Look, I have a hip flask in my bag, let me offer you a medicinal sip of brandy." She looked at me with a merry look in her attractive hazel eyes and put a hand on my arm. "Oh, there is no need whatsoever to qualify the offer by making it medicinal. I just adore a really good brandy." And so I fished out my flask and we polished off the contents as we chatted gaily about this and that. Maggie told me how much she was enjoying her Irish holiday. "A pity, though, that there are few young men here of your own age," I commented but she waved away this objection. "I don't care about that at all," she commented. "Candidly, I prefer older men, they are more careful and considerate than young bucks who only want to pull down your knickers and even if you let them, they are so un-schooled in fucking that a girl hardly has time to get her pussey wet before they've gone and spunked. Oh dear, I've been rather free with my words haven't I – forgive me, it was that very nice brandy which made me be so rude but you know what they say about brandy."

'"A double brandy makes you randy," I suggested and this witticism made Maggie giggle as she drew me closer towards her. "It *does* make me randy," she admitted, as we cuddled even closer together. "Undress me, Piers," she whispered and I obeyed her sweet command, aiding her to shrug off her blouse and skirt and I helped to pull off her boots and she after removing her chemise lay in the bracken in only a brief pair of frilly cream knickers.

'I smoothed my hands over her beautifully rounded breasts and tickled her along a wispy line of fluffy body hair which began at her navel and trailed down her flat tummy, widening slightly as it disappeared underneath her knickers. The insides of her firm, marble thighs were also lightly covered with a down that provocatively contrasted with her pale skin and widened upwards before being hidden by her panties. I leaned forward and kissed the darker welcoming bulge of pussey hair through the cool linen knickers. She trembled as I knelt between her parted legs and began by flicking the delicate hair of her thighs which sent electrifying shivers up into her pussey. Then I worked my way upwards, my tongue flitting over the thin tight material of her knickers and up to her stomach, tracing the hair line up to her belly button and when I burrowed my tongue in her navel she moaned with pleasure, swaying gently to the rhythm of my probe.

'It was time now to remove her knickers and my mouth soon reached the elastic. I managed to insert my tongue underneath it to nuzzle the hidden brown bush and then I grasped the elastic band in my teeth and tugged them down. She lifted her bottom to let me work the band down her thighs and expose her moist cunney lips. I raised my hands to fill them with her smallish but beautifully formed breasts and I rubbed her erect nipples between my fingers as I nuzzled my cheek over her curly thatch of pussey hair.

'I took my time in loving her gorgeous pouting cunney lips. Already her cunt was oozing drops of love juice which I flicked up with my tongue, nipping the hairs with my teeth. I buried my face between those swollen lips, parting them to expose her excited little clitty. Her thighs twined themselves around my head as I sucked on this cuntal delicacy and lapped up her flowing juices and then I slipped a finger round behind to frig her wrinkled little bum-hole while I continued to nestle my mouth in that glossy nest of brown curls, kissing and tonguing her cunney as with a cry she shuddered into a violent spend, her legs twitching convulsively with joy.'

Sir Harold Brown cleared his throat. 'Perhaps I should add that at this stage of the proceedings I had tired of waiting on the green for him and had decided to come back and see if I could help find his lost ball. But when I saw him gamahuching this lovely girl, like the bedouin shepherd, I silently folded my tents so to speak and slipped quietly away back to the clubhouse for a whisky and soda.'

'Yes, I am sure that Maggie and myself are both extremely grateful to you for your discreet behaviour, Harold,' continued Colonel Rankin. 'Anyhow, Maggie gasped: "Piers, I'm ready for you now." My head jerked up from between her thighs and with my eyes alight with eagerness for this tender young creature, I swiftly undressed and then stretched myself on top of her. She reached down between our bodies and guided my raging cock into the slippery entrance to her honeypot. Every fibre of my being tingled with excitement as the swollen knob of my shaft teased the folds of her juicy wet love furrow. Slowly but surely I edged my prick deeper inside her warm cavern as waves of sheer ecstasy washed over me. I let my hands rove freely across the *rondeurs* of her bottom as I fucked her, first in a slow rhythm but then increasing my speed in some good old-fashioned hard fucking until my cock was hammering like a piston and my balls were beating a tattoo against her arse.

'This was perhaps the best fuck I've had since the

summer of '99 when I found myself in bed with the
Laurie twins, Jennie and Julia, after Count Gewirtz's
Ball during the All-England Lawn Tennis Champion-
ships at Wimbledon. But I digress – Maggie was
winding my body up tighter and tighter until finally I
rammed my rod into her yielding cunney in a climactic release as I shot my hot, sticky juice deep into the
shivering girl who was writhing beneath me, her hips
rotating wildly as I clutched her bum cheeks, digging
nails into the soft flesh as she lifted her buttocks off
the ground to obtain the maximum contact with my
cock. Her cunt throbbed as it milked my lusty prick
which was spurting jet after jet of sticky jism inside
her.

'Maggie raised herself up and threw her arms
around me, saying: "Piers, you are a marvellous old
fucker! You beat all the young boys hands down.
Please fuck me again when you've recovered." This
was an offer I hated to refuse but it was neither
the time nor the place so I tickled her under the
chin and said: "Look, I've a better idea. Can you
slip away from the hotel after dinner? If you can,
come round to Abroch House, Sir Harold Brown's
residence where I'm staying. There are some like-
minded people staying there and I'm sure you'll have
a wonderful time." She gave me a mock salute and
said: "I'll be there, Colonel Rankin. Will medals be
worn?"

'"I don't think that there will be very much being
worn by the time you arrive, Maggie," I said as I rose
up to search for my drawers which I had so hastily
discarded. "I'll be there then without fail," she promised, giving my glistening prick a final friendly pull

before slipping her knickers back on. "Just make sure you keep your powder dry for me."

'So there we are, my friends, we will be joined by Miss Maggie Blake of the Lake Hotel, Killarney and Upper Street, Islington, London, tonight. Harold, I must beg your pardon for so cavalierly extending your hospitality to a lady you have not actually met,' concluded Colonel Rankin.

'My dear chap, think nothing of it,' beamed Sir Harold. 'An extra pussey is always welcome here and it so happens we really do need her to make up the numbers as I've just received a note from Jeffrey Green to confirm that he'll be delighted to join us after the police meeting this evening.'

'Oh, are we to have the pleasure of fucking with another gentleman tonight? I'll tell Amanda, she's always pleased to entertain a new thick prick,' said Susie who had just entered the room.

'But you'll also have some competition from another girl,' teased Sir Harold. 'Her name's Maggie Blake and she's staying at the Lake Hotel with her parents but will join us after dinner for the revels.'

Susie clapped her hands together. 'Maggie Blake? Is she from Islington? How lovely, she's an old friend of mine. I haven't seen her for some time, not since Count Gewirtz took her to Italy last September to the wedding of the Duke of Tuscany.'

'Ah, that explains a lot, doesn't it, Piers? If she's a friend of Johnny Gewirtz [see 'Cremorne Gardens' – Editor] it's no wonder she is so experienced in fucking,' exclaimed Sir Harold.

As Susie de Vere Forrester was to record in her

diary the next day, the arrival of Maggie Blake was to add to the enjoyment of all concerned. The frolics actually began during dinner when as the guests were tucking into plates of mouth-watering roast beef they were disturbed by a piercing scream of ecstasy that resounded from the kitchen. 'Good grief, what's going on in there? It sounds as if someone's murdering the cook,' gasped Bob Goggin, standing up at the table, ready to lead a rescue party to the servants' quarters. 'Nothing to worry about, young man,' said Sir Harold kindly, as a further ear-piercing yell emanated from below stairs. 'It's only Freda being fucked. She's a marvellous cook but is simply incapable of fucking in silence and usually I insist on her entertaining friends only when the house is empty. But her current *amour*, Patrick the painter, leaves town tonight to work in Dr Cooney's house down near Bantry Bay for the next three weeks. I didn't have the heart to refuse her permission to be fucked this evening before he catches the train.'

'Quite a screamer, isn't she,' remarked Colonel Rankin, offering Amanda Crombleigh the horse-radish. 'Even louder than Lady Brenda Fitzcockie of Finchley, wouldn't you say, Harold? Amanda, I hope the noise is not disturbing you,' as a further yell resounded from the amorous cook.

'I don't mind the noise,' said Amanda. 'The sounds of someone really enjoying a good fuck are quite exciting really. I don't suppose I could have a look, could I? Piers, perhaps you would escort me.'

'With the greatest of pleasure,' said the gallant

Colonel Rankin. 'Come with me, m'dear. It would be polite to be discreet but if Freda is like any of the screamers I have fucked she will be far too engaged in her fuck to notice whether there are any spectators present.'

He led the way down the stairs and at the kitchen door, which was half open, he paused for a moment to whisper: 'You go in front of me now and you'll see what's going on.' He opened the door wider and they had a clear view of a delightful erotic tableau. Freda, still in her cook's uniform but with her knickers dangling from one of her ankles, was spreadeagled on top of the well-scrubbed wooden kitchen table. Her legs were raised and widely parted. Patrick the painter (known locally as Pat the Prick) was standing in front of her, his trousers and drawers on the floor, holding one of the thickest cockshafts Amanda had ever seen, which he had just withdrawn from the cook's cunney.

To complete this lewd tableau the two young footmen, Leonard and Paul, stood each side of the table, their pricks being frigged by Freda as she awaited the re-entry of Patrick's mighty prick into her willing wet pussey. 'Aaah, bang in that big chopper, Pat, let's be having you now,' howled Freda and Amanda's eyebrows rose as she noted the immense size of Patrick's cock which gleamed snowy white in the gas light before he plunged the entire length into Freda's love tunnel.

Amanda Crombleigh and Piers Rankin watched in breathless silence as Patrick applied himself with a will, holding his blue-veined monster in both hands and placing it between Freda's love lips before warning the cook to 'brace yourself, me beauty, here it comes'. Then, after cramming home his loglike shaft, he began to fuck her in an even-paced rhythm whilst Freda drew breath and started to groan and moan as she twisted and turned like a dervish, holding on to the two bursting young tools in her hands for dear life.

This stimulating exhibition so affected the two unseen spectators that Colonel Rankin's prick began to push forward against Amanda's rounded bum cheeks which were nestling against it, an action that by no means displeased his fellow eavesdropper. He clutched at her, his hands closing over the swell of her firm high breasts and Amanda started to rotate her backside against the Colonel's cock to the rhythm of Freda's fucking so that his shaft was soon provoked up to its fullest extension. As soon as she felt his staff nudging against her, Amanda slipped a hand behind her to unbutton his trousers and release his prick from the discomfort of its imprisonment. Without taking her eyes off the coupling on the table which was now going at full swing, Amanda unbuttoned her dress so that the Colonel could feel the softness of her bare flesh and the hardening nipples through the fine material of her silk chemise.

Now Freda emitted a loud yell as together Leonard and Paul shot their loads, sending cascades of spunk splashing over her flushed face (and unfortunately in the case of Paul into a bowl of fresh fruit salad). Piers Rankin threw up Amanda's skirts to discover to his delight that the naughty girl was naked under her petticoat. Without further ado he took her doggy-fashion, thrusting his rampant tool deep into her cunney from behind, his balls jiggling against her beautifully rounded bum cheeks. The clever contracting of her cunney muscles on his enraptured cock spurred him to jerk his hips to and fro. Amanda's slippery pussey stretched to accommodate its welcome guest as the aroused girl threw back her pretty head and joined Freda in letting out a yowl of delight as Piers slicked his shaft in and out of her juicy pussey. Amanda joined Freda in screaming out her joy as her lover spunked copiously, filling her love box to overflowing with his thick hot spurts of sperm.

Meanwhile, Freda was now clutching the edges of the table to steady herself under Patrick's fierce fucking and her cries of delight echoed throughout Abroch House as he rammed his great shaft in and out of her capacious cunt. He was now battering into her with such force that the table shuddered and the pans hanging on the wall jangled as they picked up the vibrations caused by this tremendous fucking. The cook suddenly drew in a great breath and there was a moment's breathless silence before she shattered the silence with a deafening cry.

'Fuck me, I'm coming again, I'm coming, Patrick, *Eeeee!*' she screamed, her cheeks flaming to a redness as she waited for the final inward thrust which would send her to heaven. Patrick did not disappoint for he drew in a huge breath and with a lusty shout, jammed his enormous cock forward with all his might, burying it to the hilt as he discharged a hot sticky torrent of frothy sperm which drenched Freda's love funnel, thrilling her to the very core as she too enjoyed the supreme ecstasy of a celestial climax and her own nectar flowed down her thighs. Locked together, the couple thrashed around to the left and to the right in their excitement. Indeed, this led to them actually rolling off the table but to their great good fortune they were saved from serious injury by young Leonard the second footman who caught the flailing fuckers in his arms, a brave and timely action which, though sending the lad tumbling down with them, broke the fall for Freda and Pat and none of the three were injured as they sprawled, winded but unhurt.

Amanda and the Colonel decided to retire from the scene at this stage and made their way back upstairs. However, when they arrived back in the dining room they saw that the sensuous sounds from the kitchen had so affected the other guests that Melanie and Susie were locked together in a passionate embrace on the couch, the two aroused girls each undressing the other, rubbing their bare, hard-nippled breasts lasciviously as they crushed their bodies together, kissing and cuddling unashamedly. Sir Harold and Bob watched fascinated, paying the closest of attention as Melanie reached gently down and unbuttoned Susie's skirt which fell silently to the carpet. Like Amanda, Susie was not wearing any knickers and her truly beautiful reddish-haired bush was completely exposed in all its glory to the appreciative audience.

Susie lay back as Melanie wriggled out of the rest of her clothing and then the blonde girl reached down to fondle and curl the dense hair of the other girl's exquisite chestnut thatch whilst she brought her head up to press her lips to Susie's soft pearl-like ear-lobe.

She washed the tiny orifice for a moment with the tip of her tongue and then whispered: 'What a delightful little pussey you have, Susie. Why, my fingers and my tongue simply ache to taste the sweetness of your cunt just like I know your lips are yearning to suck upon my blonde pussey. But wouldn't you like me to suck out your love juice? Your cunney will tingle and throb as I slide my tongue all along your love crack and nip on your clitty. Would you like that, Susie? Would you?'

For answer, Susie reached out and took one of Melanie's long nipples daintily in her fingers, rubbing it lazily as it rose and hardened to her touch. Melanie responded by sliding her mouth down the front of Susie's quivering body as the girl lay on her back, her head resting on the arm of the settee. She paused at each delicious rounded breast, sucking up the engorged red nipples to erectness before kissing her way down the trembling flesh of the white midriff, past the small indenture of her navel before reaching the soft, light red pussey hairs. Carefully, Melanie swung herself round to position her head between Susie's parted thighs, placing one hand under her bottom and the other on her thigh so she could spread her coral cunney lips with her thumb and forefinger.

Melanie placed her lips over the engorged little clitty which had burst forth from Susie's pink cunney and sucked it into her mouth where the tip of her tongue seductively explored it from all directions. Melanie could feel it swell inside her mouth as Susie's legs drummed up and down on the cushions in her excitement. Artfully, Melanie let her teeth nibble gently over Susie's clitty as her tongue teased her sopping cunney, teasing her crack with long, rasping licks. 'Oh, your juices taste divine, darling,' gasped Melanie as she continued to play with Susie's love button and pussey with her fingers. Then she dived back again and ground her face right into the wet mound which made Susie arch her body and scream out. Melanie inserted a forefinger into her bottom-hole and within moments received a sudden flow of love juice between her lips. The tangy liquid shot out in spasms which allowed her time to gulp down a mouthful before the next rush of tasty fluid began.

Now Melanie swung herself around, throwing her legs across Susie's face, crouching on her knees and wriggling about until she had brought her blonde fringed cunt in front of Susie's lips. This position, facing Susie's feet, also gave the other girl a chance to caress Melanie's firm bum cheeks and suck her pussey at the same time. Susie immediately splayed open the two rounded spheres, making room for her lips to lick and lap between the ripe white globes. She tickled the rim of Melanie's wrinkled little rear dimple before moving her lips down to the smooth skinned crease of her cunney which opened out under the probing of Susie's tongue that slithered past the plump outer lips before delving into the small inner orifice of her cunt.

'Oh! Oh! Oh!' squealed Melanie, gripping Susie's knees as she leaned forward to allow the girl fuller access to her dripping pussey. 'Oh, that's heavenly, Susie! Don't stop, don't stop till I spend!'

Tremors racked her body and she was about to repay Susie by muff diving into her pussey for a second time when Sir Harold Brown moved across and, tearing open his trousers, brought out his throbbing tool and thrust the purple mushroom helmet into Melanie's hands. She played with his cock at once, sliding her hand up and down the sturdy shaft before tightening her grip and bringing his knob to her lips which she opened to suck in the crown of his cock into her mouth. She pulled his legs towards her, drawing in the hot velvet flesh until she could cram in no more of his rigid rod between her lips. Then she moved her head back and her eyes glistened as she looked at the pulsating prick in her hand, now gleaming with its coating of her saliva. She ran her tongue along its length to catch a sticky drip of pre-spend liquid which had formed on Sir Harold's knob. Then she moved her lips around his helmet and began to suck vigorously upon it. Sir Harold Brown groaned as he fucked her mouth, pushing his noble prick in and out as Melanie sucked greedily upon his thick cock. He rolled his hips to move his staff steadily backwards and forwards and Melanie's hand stole up to squeeze his dangling hairy ballsack. Almost immediately he spunked a stream of creamy white froth which she swallowed with delight, gulping down every last drop of his jism.

'Why did Melanie make him come so quickly?' wondered Bob aloud and he was answered by Amanda. 'Harold can usually keep his stiffie up for a second round without too much trouble,' she explained and, sure enough, their host's penis was still almost fully erect as he took it out from between Melanie's lips. Meanwhile Susie was still manfully sucking on Melanie's pussey whilst finger-fucking her cunney. She was rewarded when the blonde girl yelped out her delight as she spent over Susie's face, her body quivering all over as her juices cascaded down into Susie's mouth, splashing down her chin as she tried to lap up as much of the salty love-liquid as she could.

Melanie moved round to sit next to Susie, who giggled: 'Shouldn't we now give Harold the pleasure of a double fucking?' The blonde girl's face lit up at the lewd thought and she asked Sir Harold if he were game for such a rich second helping. It hardly took any gift of persuasion to make him agree! 'My cock is at your disposal, dear ladies,' he said as he pulled down his trousers and began to undress.

When he had finished the girls sat him down on the sofa and lay him down upon his aristocratic back. Melanie sat astride his knees whilst Susie perched upon his chest. Melanie started the ball rolling (in every sense of the phrase!) by moving her mouth to his now fully erect cock and taking his knob between her full red lips, while Susie moved her pussey over his face until his tongue could reach her pouting pussey lips.

The three of them throbbed in unison; Susie sighed in ecstasies of lust as Sir Harold's wicked tongue skilfully probed her pussey. His thick prick proved to be more than a mouthful for Melanie as she frigged his shaft up to a steel-like stiffness. When she felt that his pulsing cock was at the peak of its height and girth, she shifted herself and straddled his body until she could lower her lubricated cunney over his magnificently powerful erection. She slid down his pole until it penetrated the furthest reaches of her cunt and she bounced happily away, giggling and squealing with satisfaction as she wrapped her arms around Susie, grabbing her uptilted titties and rubbing the stalky red nipples against her palm.

The others had been so glued to this fine performance that none of them had seen Jeffrey Green make his entrance. 'By god, this beats the bloody police committee meeting any day of the week,' he exclaimed in surprise. 'Is this a private fuck or can anyone join in?' he cried and, without waiting for an answer, the magistrate threw off his jacket and tore off his tie. Once he had shucked off the rest of his clothes Mr Green positioned himself behind Sir Harold, whose head was trapped between Susie's thighs as he licked voraciously on her sopping slit. The magistrate presented his huge stiffstander to Susie who leaned forward to circle her willing tongue round the edge of his uncapped crown, paying particular loving attention to the sensitive ridge. Without using her hands at all, she sucked his entire prick up inside her mouth so that his whole shaft was enveloped in her mouth right down to his bushy pubic thatch and then she stuck out her tongue to lap at his balls in quick, darting movements.

'Susie, doesn't Jeffrey Green's cock taste good? I sucked him and he tit-fucked me this afternoon. Be careful though,' warned Melanie, 'because he spouts oceans of spunk.' As she spoke she let her tingling love funnel slide down Sir Harold Brown's twitching tadger for a further thrilling ride.

'He can't have too much jism in his bollocks for me, I just adore the taste of spunk,' mumbled Susie through a mouthful of Mr Green's rock-hard shaft.

This rude talk so stimulated Sir Harold Brown that he spurted a jet of boiling sperm into Melanie's cunney as he moved his hands to rub Susie's clitty and finish her off. The two girls came together as Sir Harold's cock popped out of Melanie's cunt and slid crazily up across his belly, his knob spurting the remainder of his creamy emission all over her downy wheaten coloured pussey hair. Susie's love juices flooded down onto Sir Harold's face as she too shuddered into a climax as Jeffrey Green followed by loosing a great wash of spunk into the back of her throat and she drank it eagerly in great gulping swallows before giving his shrinking shaft a luscious farewell kiss on his knob.

Just as the participants in this grand fuck were refreshing themselves with a bumper of champagne, Paul the fair-haired young footman announced the arrival of Miss Maggie Blake. Colonel Rankin rose to his feet and welcomed her to the party. 'My dear Maggie, let me first introduce Mr Bob Goggin and Miss Amanda Crombleigh,' said the Colonel and she shook hands with Bob and Amanda.

'I dare say you can find a variety of limbs to shake on the couch, though the cocks and cunnies may be somewhat moist,' he added with a grin. 'The heap of naked flesh you see before you belongs to Miss Melanie Marley, Miss Susie de Vere Forrester, Mr Jeffrey Green, the magistrate of this locality and Sir Harold Brown, our esteemed and revered host.'

'Susie de Vere Forrester, why, she and I have enjoyed some marvellous experiences together. Oh yes, if you know Susie like I know Susie . . .' her voice trailed off as Jeffrey Green waved his prick at her in salutation. 'Perhaps you would like to join your friend a little later when we have recovered.'

'Recovered? Does this mean that I am cockless? Piers, I hope your old wedding tackle is ready for action,' Maggie said as she unbuttoned her skirt and let it fall to the ground. 'I'm afraid I am still *hors de combat* as well,' said Colonel Rankin regretfully, 'but perhaps Mr Goggin would care to offer his thick prick for your delectation.'

'I would like nothing better than to oblige but I did promise Melanie that I would allow her the first taste of my shaft this evening,' said Bob politely. 'No matter,' said Maggie, continuing her undressing by slipping off her chemise to reveal her high, beautifully rounded breasts. 'Just look at the bulge between the legs of that young footman – what's your name, Paul, isn't it?'

'That's right, ma'am, Paul O'Toole,' he stammered, moving his hand across his lap in a vain effort to hide the swelling bulge. 'Don't be bashful,' laughed Maggie. 'Come here and fuck me. You're not a virgin, are you?'

Paul blushed to the roots of his fair hair when before he could reply, Amanda remarked: 'Possibly, though Piers and I can vouch that he's not totally inexperienced for, with our own eyes, we saw him being tossed off by the cook earlier this evening.' She swept off the remainder of the cutlery from the table and Maggie climbed on top of it whilst Amanda ripped open the young servant's trousers to bring out a throbbing red-headed cock, as stiff and as hard as marble. She frigged it up until it looked fit to burst. Quickly she assisted him to shake off his clothes and he climbed up on what was fortunately a strong well-made dining room table.

'Paul O'Toole is aptly named,' murmured Amanda as the pair gazed at each other with lustful expectancy. Paul was no mere common Irishman but a scion of an old Killarney family who worked during the summer to support himself through his studies at Trinity College, Dublin, and it would be hard to conceive of a more beautiful couple, Paul being a fine young strapping fellow with fair hair and blue eyes whilst his brunette companion's complexion was almost a counterpart of his; the base of his prick was covered by a light downy growth though Maggie's cunney was well shielded by its covering of curly brown hair.

Colonel Rankin planted two soft cushions on the table and Maggie placed one under her head and the other under her bottom as she lay down to receive this sturdy young penis in her love channel. But first she drew Paul down on his knees as she took hold of his erect truncheon. She drew back the foreskin to reveal fully the fiery purplish knob which glowed like a ruby as he presented it to the lips of her pussey which were already slightly open. He rubbed the bulbous head up and down her pouting crack until her cunt was damp enough for him to enter without discomfort to either of them and he sucked her firm upraised nipples as Maggie's hand found his ivory hard tool and began working its way up and down the shaft.

Drawing on his wide experience of many forms of fucking, Colonel Rankin now decided that Paul would spunk too swiftly if Maggie did not let the boy begin his journey to Elysium inside her honeypot so he took hold of the lad's cock and nudged the tip between the folds of Maggie's cunney lips.

The happy young man now rolled over this lewd little minx and slowly he inched his shaft inside her willing wet cunt as it sucked in his throbbing shaft. He fucked her with long smooth strokes as he hovered above her, supporting himself on his forearms. His balls slapped in slow cadence on her inner thighs as he moved down, up and down again, increasing the pace as he thrust with intensity cheered on by the assembled company who were greatly impressed with his prowess.

This erotic tableau fired the blood of Jeffrey Green, who found his magisterial cock responding to the sights and sounds of Maggie and Paul fucking on top of the table – the squeals and pantings, the groans of ecstasy and the rhythmic squelchings of fervent fuckery. Susie de Vere Forrester (who was still naked as were Sir Harold, Melanie and Jeffrey Green himself, the other participants in the whoresome foursome which had just ended) was also similarly affected and she grabbed Mr Green's hand and placed it onto the nude dampness of her awakening quim. Whilst Paul continued to piston Maggie with his sinewy young cock, Susie and Jeffrey Green moved closely together and she slid one hand across his broad chest and with the other took hold of his bare cock, enjoying the feel of the bouncing jerking shaft in her fist. She was already very wet between her legs and she held his knob in position so that her cunney lips just touched the tip of his helmet as she rubbed the purple dome along her slit and on to her clitty.

'Let's fuck,' murmured the magistrate and as they were practically the same height, it was quite easy to make love standing up. Even so, the feel of his pulsating prick pushing into her cunt almost buckled Susie's legs as she leaned against the table. Waves of pleasure swept through her so that she had to put her arms around Jeffrey Green's neck to balance herself, pressing her warm soft body as close to him as possible, her long, erect nipples crushing themselves against his manly frame. To steady her he put his hands around the cheeks of her lovely bottom so to ensure that every last inch of his prick was embedded inside her. Now he squashed Susie's gorgeously supple buttocks as she slipped her hand down to caress his heavy ballsack.

'Aaah! Aaah!' Susie sighed. 'Your big fat cock is kissing my pussey. Oh, Jeffrey, rub your divine prick against my clitty, you naughty man!' They slid drunkenly down onto the carpet and Susie rolled on top of him. For an aching moment his cock left her cunt but quickly she repositioned herself, kneeling naked in front of his bright eyes as he massaged her firm young breasts while she lowered herself upon his rampant shaft. She moved up and down on his iron-hard rod but then, to Susie's astonishment, Jeffrey Green moved her hips upward and took out his gleaming vein-gnarled staff – but only to slide her further up his torso so that he was able to rub his mouth against her cunney lips. He pushed his tongue right through the dripping crack and Susie moaned in delight as his tongue moved in ever quickening circles over her clitty.

Susie thrashed around as if demented and demanded to be fucked then and there. Ever the gentleman, he flipped her onto her back to receive his love trunchon. Above them, a scream from Maggie and a hoarse cry from Paul signalled that the footman had expelled a fountain of his sticky essence in Maggie's cunney. This spurred on Jeffrey Green who fucked Susie with long, slow strokes, gradually increasing the tempo until he corectly judged that they both desired their release and he started to pump faster and faster as the pair approached the point of no return. Suddenly his body stiffened and Susie could feel his climax approaching within her cunt. He exploded a fierce jet of frothy spunk, a rush of liquid fire which set off instantly a huge climax for Susie as her saturated clitty sent ripples of bliss throughout every fibre of her body. As he felt his prick deflate, the always thoughtful Mr Green decided that she could spend a second time. So he eased out his shrivelling shaft from her cunt and replaced it with his tongue, flicking the tip in and out of her pussey which caused a further spurting of juice to cascade out between her cunney lips while he greedily slurped her spendings into his mouth.

Whilst these two splendid jousts were taking place Melanie Marley had sidled up to Bob Goggin and had started to undress him. He too was now in a state of nudity as, unresistingly, he let himself be led to the sofa. The beautiful blonde girl was soon in his arms, engaging in the most passionate of embraces. There was an audible hiss of breath being sucked in from Colonel Rankin and Sir Harold Brown as Bob's hand roved over Melanie's alabaster white breasts, moving his hands over the large pink-circled aureoles and raised cherry nipples. He gently squeezed those succulent morsels up to a standing perfection whilst she cupped her hand around his naked cock. His prick was not yet fully erect as she rubbed her hand up and down the glistening shaft, but when she rolled down the foreskin to expose the red, moist mushroomed helmet, his shaft shot up ramrod straight under her touch.

Melanie freed herself from Bob's arms and laid herself face downwards on the sofa to explose her firm, exquisitely rounded bottom cheeks to Bob and the attentive spectators. She then scrambled up on her knees and pushed out her pert backside, opening her legs to give Bob the opportunity, as the snooker player puts it, to pot either the pink or the brown. She turned her head and saw Bob clamber up behind her and she reached out to take hold of his hot-skinned hard cock and neatly position it in the cleft of her bum.

Bob grasped the delicious *rondeurs* of her bottom and opened wide the crevice to place the tip of his knob at the entrance of her wrinkled little bum-hole. He wet his prick with some white wine kindly provided by Colonel Rankin so there was only a slight momentary discomfort for the trembling girl as Bob's cock slowly enveloped itself between the in-rolling cheeks of Melanie's beautifully proportioned bottom. A little hesitantly in case he hurt the lovely lass, Bob pushed in slowly at first but soon he realised that he was well absorbed into her tight little rear-dimple. He worked himself in with vigour and once he was fully ensconced in her warm, tingling bum he pushed his entire body forwards and backwards, making

Melanie's buttocks crack against his belly as she cried out lewdly: 'Go on, fuck my bum and fill me with your juice, you big-cocked man!'

He leaned over Melanie to fondle her luscious breasts and play with her erect red nipples as she waggled her bottom whilst he fucked her rear entrance. There was no doubt of her total enjoyment of Bob's thick prick pounding in and out of her bottom as she gasped: 'Go on, Bob, fill me with spunk, empty your balls, you rascal.' And almost immediately he obediently flooded her arsehole with such vibrant shoots that Colonel Rankin swore that he could actually see ripples of orgasm run down Melanie's spine as she shuddered to a tremendous climax, artfully wiggling her bottom as spout after spout of creamy sperm filled her hole until with an audible 'pop', Bob uncorked his still stiff shaft and sank back on his haunches. Melanie turned round and, still on her knees, dropped her head down to suck his cock, eagerly lapping up the last drains of his spend, her hands jerking up and down his shaft to coax out its last drops of jism. Then, when she had milked his shrinking prick dry, she sat sedately on his lap with her hands around his neck.

This superb bottom fuck fired the guests into forming a final fucking chain with Sir Harold Brown fucking Amanda whilst she sucked Maggie's pussey as the English girl licked and lapped at Bob Goggin's prick who was in turn busy finger-fucking Susie whose head was buried between Colonel Rankin's legs, sucking lustily on his cock whilst Jeffrey Green (after smearing his huge shaft with butter) sank his prick into her bum-hole.

* * *

The next morning Bob was roused at nine o'clock by Susie and Amanda who gently but forcefully tugged at his shoulder until he was awake. 'Come on, Bob, rise and shine,' said Amanda. 'Show a leg – or something more exciting if you like,' added Susie brightly.

'What's the rush, girls, aren't we on holiday?' asked Bob sleepily. 'Sorry, Bob, but we need your cock,' said Amanda bluntly, coming straight to the point as she lightly patted his cheeks. 'We have a crisis in the kitchen. Freda simply refuses to cook anything this morning until she gets fucked and in the absence of Patrick the painter, we thought we would ask you to do the honours.'

'Why me?' he demanded sleepily. 'Well, because the two footmen were only employed for the night and have gone home as have Jeffrey Green and Maggie Blake. Sir Harold is still fast asleep and it would be bad form to wake our host whilst Colonel Rankin is at present being gobbled by Melanie who came in here earlier wanting to be fucked but you were slumbering so peacefully that she didn't have the heart to wake you up.'

'But you two don't mind disturbing me,' said Bob crossly, stretching out his arms with a big yawn. 'Oh come on, Bob, we're hungry and anyway, we want to take you out this morning to see the ruins of Aghadoe. It's very important that you go there this morning so do get up and fuck Freda.'

Why was it so important to visit Aghadoe this morning, Bob wondered and Susie answered: 'Well, the Kerry branch of the Priapic Order Of Perpetual

212

Indulgence is holding their secret harvest festival ceremony there at lunchtime. It's strictly by invitation only, of course but Harold has procured tickets for the three of us. No more questions now, please go down to the kitchen and do your duty.' As if to emphasise her point she threw back the cover and the girls discovered that Bob slept naked. Amanda rubbed his limp shaft and the touch of her warm fingers soon made his penis swell up until it stood as proudly stiff as the flagpole on top of nearby Dunloe Castle. Amanda licked her lips but Susie shook her head and said: 'No, love, restrain yourself. Listen, I would also love to suck Bob's cock but he must first fuck Freda or we'll never get out this morning.'

Bob heaved himself out of bed and slipped his feet into a pair of slippers. 'My head feels muzzy after that wild party last night,' he grumbled. 'A good fuck will clear your head,' said Susie briskly. 'Come on, Bob, Freda is hardly an unattractive lady and you should feel honoured that she has chosen your tool to cream her pussey.' He smiled at her rebuke and held up his arms in surrender. 'Fair enough, I deserved that for being so ungrateful. Look, I'll just clean my teeth and get washed and I'll be downstairs in less than five minutes.'

He was as good as his word and as promised, very soon after this exchange Bob padded downstairs in the beautiful white towelling bathrobe provided in each guest room by Sir Harold. He owned a large factory on the outskirts of Dublin which supplied linens and absorbent fabrics to all the top hotels in Britain, Belgium and France. Freda was also wearing one of Sir Harold's robes as she waited impatiently for him in the kitchen and as soon as he entered she greeted him with a quick: 'Good morning, sir,' and proceeded to pull open his robe and grasp his cock in her left hand.

'Who's a big boy, then?' she joked as with her right hand she loosened the belt of her dressing gown. She released his swelling shaft just for a brief moment as she slipped out of her robe to stand naked in front of him. Bob passed his tongue over his upper lip as he gazed at the cook's firm, rounded breasts and blunt raspberry red nipples. He covered her right tittie with his hand and drew his fingers around the soft curves and felt the nipple harden up between his fingers. At the same time her grasp on his prick became firmer and she pulled his face down to suck on each nipple in turn whilst she slowly manipulated his stiff staff with her hand. Then, still holding him by his cock, she led him into the morning room where they sank down on the carpet where she lay on her back and Bob slid his shaft into her already lubricated cunney.

Freda drew breath and screamed her delight as she wrapped her legs around Bob's waist and shrieked: 'Fuck me! Fuck me! Fuck me!' as he started to pump in and out of her juicy love channel. With each thrust she counter-thrust with an uninhibited yell which could be heard throughout Abroch House. Upstairs, Susie looked thoughtfully at Amanda and said: 'I think that Freda has found a position that suits her.'

'A well-filled position, I would say, by the sound of it,' replied Amanda. The girls burst into laughter whilst Freda's yells reached a crescendo as Bob plunged his prick in and out of her sopping cunt in a wild frenzy of lustful passion.

'Aaah! Aaaah! Spunk over my titties, you fat-cocked fucker!' screamed the cook as she felt Bob's sinewy penis throb hard in her cunt. So he pulled out his prick and Freda grabbed hold and rubbed the bucking shaft fiercely, directing the fountain of spunk that shot out from the knob all over her large breasts until it dribbled to a stop. She massaged the sticky jism onto her nipples as her body writhed in delicious torment from the series of tiny shocks of her spend which spread rapidly through her body.

'Oh, how marvellous, it's still stiff! You have the staying power, I see, Mr Goggin,' enthused the cook as she got down on all fours and pushed out her backside towards him. Her arse was gorgeous, like a ripe peach which parted gently down the centre. Bob stroked the soft, rounded buttocks as Freda turned her head and said: 'Stick that grand cock into my cunt, please, sir. I love being fucked doggy-style but I'd rather you didn't go up my arse, if you don't mind, as I reserve my bum hole for Patrick.' 'Very well,' Bob replied politely, pushing her legs apart and rubbing the thick helmet of his cock against her slick cunney lips. Once he was comfortably positioned, he mounted her from behind causing them both to moan together in sheer, intense pleasure. He began to piston his prick in and out, holding her lovely bum cheeks as his body slewed one way and then the other. Freda pushed back her bum eagerly to meet every hot thrust of Bob's excited tool. She creamed again as her pussey spent not once or twice but three times as she squeezed his shaft in her cunney. Bob heaved and shoved, nipping his cock delightfully as they ran the familiar course. Again, the peace of the house was shattered as Freda yelled out her ecstasy until at last Bob spurted out his sticky libation of frothy white spunk into her cunney.

After they had recovered they slipped on their bathrobes and Freda began to bustle about the kitchen to prepare breakfast. Bob staggered upstairs where Amanda and Susie were waiting to greet him. 'You did very well, Bob,' said Susie, as they walked back with him to his bedroom. 'At least now we can all have something to eat. I suggest you stoke up and have a hearty breakfast as you must be hungry after all that strenuous exercise, and because, assuming you want to enjoy some more fucking today, there should be plenty of new pussies to suck and fuck at Aghadoe after luncheon. Oh, that reminds me, we must ask Freda to make up a hamper for us.'

Their genial host, Sir Harold Brown, joined them at breakfast and on hearing of their plan for the day, offered them the services of McGinty and a small carriage to take them to Aghadoe. 'I wish I could join you myself but I promised Jeffrey Green I would walk over to his place this morning and help fuck the O'Cooney girls. He's been having his wicked way with them since they were eighteen but that's four years ago and frankly he can't satisfy them on his own any more, so I said I would lend a hand.'

'Or rather a prick,' corrected Amanda as she munched a piece of hot, buttered toast.

'Indeed,' agreed Sir Harold with a grin. 'However, if I can, I'll try to meet you after luncheon although I thought I'd stroll round with Melanie to Maggie Blake's hotel to see what's going on there.'

'Perhaps the girls and Colonal Rankin would like to

join us,' suggested Bob but Sir Harold shook his head. 'I very much doubt if they'll have the time,' he said regretfully. 'Melanie's working this morning, you know, taking some more photographs for this new book for travellers to Ireland. Then this afternoon she planned to take some shots of Piers Rankin fucking Maggie Blake for publication in *The Oyster* so I don't think she'll be able to fit in a visit Aghadoe. Anyhow, she's seen the pagan fertility rites before, though I'm sure she'll agree that you must see them whilst you're here.'

'Absolutely,' said Melanie who had just come downstairs with Colonel Rankin. 'But don't wear yourself out too much, Bob, because I want a nice thick pressing of spunk in my honeypot tonight. You were sleeping so soundly this morning that I didn't have the heart to wake you but, as I have to go to Cork tomorrow, I want a good farewell fuck tonight.'

By eleven thirty the three adventurers were ready and waiting in Sir Harold Brown's landaulette *[a small four wheel carriage with a folding hood over the passenger seats and an open driver's seat – Editor]* and McGinty drove first through the magnificent Deer Park where all is wild and natural and where the flowers and ferns abound in the dells in the typical fashion of the area. They left the carriage to walk through the Fairy Glen, that charming wooded dingle with a gurgling stream which has rhododendrons and evergreens growing on its banks and with trees which have ferns growing right up their mossy trunks. After walking upstream, they rejoined the carriage at the bridge and made their way to Aghadoe which was only two and half miles distant.

'The name Aghadoe means "field of two yews",' explained Amanda as they looked out at the mountains and the lakes. An even better view awaited them when they arrived for Aghadoe stands on high ground and on a clear day such as they had the good fortune to experience the views are simply superb. 'What a splendid sight. See, Bob,' said Susie, 'over there is Killarney with Carrantuohill beyond on the left but if we climb a little further you can get a glimpse on the opposite side of Dingle Bay and its mountainous shores.'

As the ceremony of the Priapics Of Perpetual Indulgence was not scheduled to begin till after luncheon, it left time for the girls to show Bob around the ruined round tower, church and castle. Few and broken as the walls were, Bob appreciated the beauty of an architectural gem in the western wall of the nave, a Romanesque eighth century doorway with fine mouldings and four recessed archways. In the south wall of the nave lay a stone marked with the curious angled writing system of the ancient Celts.

Although the sun was now partially hidden by light clouds, it was still perfectly warm enough for a picnic and Bob helped McGinty carry the two hampers to a nearby field while Susie told the coachman that he need not return until four o'clock. The girls set a white cloth on the ground and brought out huge plates of devilled chicken, cold beef, fresh salads and a selection of sandwiches plump with egg and cress, strawberry jam and cucumber.

'We certainly won't starve,' laughed Susie as she set down a luscious seed-cake whilst Bob opened up a bottle of ginger beer. 'No wine?' queried Amanda.

'Well, I'm not entirely surprised. We'll imbibe tonight at the dinner Harold is giving for Piers Rankin – it's his birthday tomorrow but as he has to leave for England by noon, Harold is giving a surprise party for him tonight and obviously Freda wants to keep Bob in tip-top condition for tonight – and of course, tomorrow morning.'

'Oh no, you mean I will have to fuck her every morning!' groaned Bob. 'It isn't exactly a chore but just occasionally I do like to choose where I am going to place my cock.'

Susie wagged her finger at him. 'Gosh, don't start complaining again, Bob. Look, I'll let you into another secret. Count Gewirtz of Galicia is coming to Killarney this evening for the party. Now if I know Johnny Gewirtz, he'll won't be coming empty-handed.'

'Quite right, he specialises in unusual birthday presents, doesn't he?' nodded Amanda as she passed a heaped plate of food to Bob. 'Do you remember how he arranged for the chorus of the Italian Opera Company to sing at Lady Caroline Fotheringham's twenty-first birthday celebrations and then presented her with a ticket to travel first class with a friend to New York on the *S.S. White Falcon*. There's no doubt about it, he's an extremely generous man.'

'Yes, but remember he does own the ship, Amanda, and he did fuck Lady Caroline later that evening as well as making love to five of her friends who also fancied a trip to America.'

'Six actually, Susie, as I sucked off the Count just before he retired upstairs with the Duchess of Camden.'

'Did you? Goodness, well in that case I may as well admit I brought the numbers up to seven as I stayed overnight and we sucked and fucked just before breakfast the next day.'

'Did he live up to his reputation as one of the best exponents of fucking in Europe?' enquired the blonde girl idly. 'I ask because I really enjoyed sucking his circumcised cock. He enjoyed it too and, to his credit, he was dying to spend but although I was madly finger-fucking myself, I just couldn't come. So he waited for as long as he could before spunking and I managed to finish myself off in the end.

'I was very grateful for this courtesy for you well know, Amanda, how much I love sucking pricks myself. But few of the men I've ever met can hold back from coming after more than three of four minutes after I've begun to tongue their cocks. Mind, I always get a thrill when the boy spurts out his spunk, it's so exciting when it shoots into my mouth. There's nothing so invigorating and that tastes so fresh and clean either but it's so nice to let one's tongue wash over the knob of a good good-sized prick and feel the shaft throb as you take it between your lips. But I say, I've yet to meet a man who can really hold back long enough for me. Nevertheless, I found sucking the Count's cock extremely satisfying. What was he like between the sheets?'

'Johnny Gewirtz is a very good fuck indeed,' replied Susie, a smile now playing around her lips as she fondly remembered the occasion. 'What I found so impressive was that I knew he'd just fucked Lady Caroline so when he found an excuse to take me into one of the bedrooms I thought we would just kiss and cuddle for a little. But he has great stamina and I could see the outline of his stiffstander form in his lap as he stroked my bosoms. Anyhow, hardly before I knew what was happening he had unhooked my dress and pulled it down to expose my naked breasts to his delighted eyes.

'He squeezed my globes lightly and started to play with my titties which became as stiff as two miniature little cocks against the palms of his hands. As if drawn by a magical plower over which I possessed no control, I dropped my fingers over that huge bulge which threatened to damage his black trousers as I stroked the hard shaft I could feel pulsating violently beneath my touch.

'The Count pulled me into his arms and rained eager kisses on my mouth. I was almost fainting from excitement when he tugged open his fly buttons and brought out his enormous meaty dick, so thick that I needed both hands to encircle fully the pulsating monster. "Oh Johnny, are you really going to stick that huge cock in my cunt?" I sighed. "I sincerely hope so," he replied with a twinkle in his eyes as he finished undressing me. He then hastily shed his own clothes and I admired the powerful masculinity of his muscular body, his strong shoulders, his deep chest and, as he turned to lay his clothes on the floor, the suppleness of his white bottom. But then as he turned back my eyes fastened upon his massive prick that looked so juicy and inviting. It throbbed as I stroked his huge shaft and I marvelled at the pretty pattern of blue veins running along the length.

'A piercingly hot sensation now made itself felt

between my legs as my pussey began to ooze its juices. I grasped this magnificent cock and with an almost animal passion I lay down on the bed and guided the tip of the red knob between my cunney lips. So far so good, but how Johnny Gewirtz stretched my love channel with that big prick of his! He gave a great thrust forward and I shrieked aloud in delicious agony as I opened my legs as far as I could and then, aaaah! I quivered with pleasure as my cunney cleverly adjusted itself to this gigantic cock. Our nude bodies rolled in ecstasy as we thrashed around on the soft mattress, my legs now twisted around his back to ensure that every inch of his colossal cock stayed in my engorged cunney. I felt a tightness in my pussey as its little muscles quivered as his shaft slid excitedly between the grasping flesh of my cunney lips, its swollen red head appearing briefly before plunging back inside my yearning lovebox.

'I can't recall if we spent together but I do remember that Johnny came in a glorious climax, propelling his prick in and out of my sopping slit until, in three fast, powerful spasms, he spurted out what felt like gallons of warm, white spunk into my now capacious cunt. Amazingly, when he took out his shaft as I flopped back panting with exhaustion, I saw that he was still hard.

'"I'd heard you were a hard man, Johnny, but I thought the remark was about your business life," I said, which made him grin as he leaned over me, his knees on either side of my body, and presented his majestic cock to my mouth. The sight of his round domed helmet just inches from my face sent fresh sparks of lust shivering through me. "What a lovely big cock," I murmured and he replied: "I've been reliably informed that it tastes as good as it looks. Would you like to find out for yourself?" I didn't have to be asked a second time and I eagerly opened my lips and swallowed as much of his shaft as possible, which was of course nice and wet from my own tangy love juices. I lustily sucked for all I was worth and the Count slid in his shaft all the way to the back of my throat as I rolled his balls around in my hands. His prick was so thick that it strained my jaw so I massaged the underside with my tongue, moving my head up and down and this soon sent him to heaven. His cock went rigid and then out of his knob came a second libation of sticky froth which I swallowed and swallowed until at last even Johnny Gewirtz's mighty penis could no longer retain its iron hard stiffness and began to deflate in my mouth.

'Mind, this wasn't the end of our love-making – we were at it hammer and tongs for another hour or so. He came inside me twice and I managed to suck him back to stiffness so that we could end with a *soixante neuf* that finished beautifully. Seconds after my receptive cunney poured forth its juices into his mouth, he expelled a third rivulet of delicious sperm between my lips which I greedily swallowed down with relish.'

Bob cleared his throat and commented: 'I take it you'll be looking for a repeat performance from Count Gewirtz tonight? I could be mistaken but I would think that the best birthday present you could give to Colonel Rankin would be to allow him to fuck you this evening.'

'I'm sure you're right, Bob. In fact what Melanie,

Amanda and I plan to do is to surprise Piers while he is dressing for dinner by marching in together stark naked. Then we'll pull him down on his bed and engage in a three-way fuck. Piers can fuck me as he licks out Amanda's lovely blonde pussey whilst at the same time he dips his fingers in and out of Melanie's juicy honeypot.

'We'll change round again and again until he can take no more,' she added brightly. 'Won't that be a delightful present for his forty-fifth birthday?'

'It would be a delightful present for any birthday over the age of sixteen,' agreed Bob, whose own well-proportioned boner was now sticking up between his legs. Amanda and Susie saw the protuberance in his lap and they exchanged a knowing glance. 'What shall we do about dear Bob's aching prick?' asked Amanda as the wicked girls snuggled up to each other. 'Let's hold a conference to discuss the matter further,' answered Susie with a giggle. At first Bob smiled as he thought that, at least, he would be able to rely on one of the two pretty minxes taking out his bursting cock and tossing him off.

But Susie and Amanda had other ideas. Bob groaned with frustration as, after the two girls had ensured that they could not be seen from the nearby Aghadoe ruins, they undressed with great speed and then locked themselves together in a fiery embrace, their moist lips pressed together and their tongues sucked into each other's mouths.

They rocked to and fro and the sight of their beautiful naked bodies sent shivers of desire hurtling along every fibre of poor Bob Goggin's being. His hand stole down to unbutton his trousers and release

224

his aching stiffstander as he watched the two tribades smooth their hands over each other's dazzling bodies. Susie's full breasts stood firm, topped by her proud, elongated brown nipples. Her thick thatch of pussey hair that covered her love mound contrasted so excitingly with Amanda's fluffy blonde pubic bush which nestled so invitingly between her long, slim legs.

Dear God, how much would I give to be the meat in that sensual sandwich, thought Bob, as his hand flew up and down his throbbing shaft and Susie eased her hand from Amanda's nipples down across her flat white tummy to her cunney. She caressed her clitoris so expertly, tickling her fingers round the hood of her love button, that in moments Amanda's fleshy clitty protruded stiffly between her pussey lips. Their breasts shook with desire now as they ground their pussies together, gurgling with pleasure. Susie lowered her head and, by craning forward, Bob could see the tip of her pink tongue slip through the cleft of Amanda's cunt, prodding her clitty and tonguing right into the ring of her cunt, licking round the quivering walls before withdrawing it and then reentering again deeply in rapid rhythm until she brought Amanda off in a delightfully sharp series of peaks.

Now their hands were everywhere, grabbing, squeezing, and rubbing as their bodies demanded release. Susie kept her head between Amanda's splayed thighs and buried her mouth in the damp padding of silky blonde hair. She kissed the erect clitty that now protruded quite three inches and began to dip her forefinger in and out of Amanda's juicy cunt. Then she took this glorious clitty in her mouth, rolling her tongue around it and playfully biting it with her teeth. 'A-h-r-e! A-h-r-e! I'm going to spend if you do that, my darling!' cried Amanda as Susie relentlessly frigged her cunt and clitty until the coltish girl twisted her body in a violent shudder and spent profusely all over Susie's mouth and chin. Susie continued to move her tongue along the velvety grooves of her cunney, licking and sucking the aromatic juices. With each stroke of her tongue Amanda arched her body in ecstasy, pressing her erect clitty up against Susie's flickering tongue. 'Pull my clit! Hard! You won't hurt me,' urged Amanda and so Susie replaced her tongue with her fingers and tugged vigorously as Amanda writhed her hips wildly beneath this lewd stimulation.

'It's my turn to fuck you now,' whispered Amanda as Susie lay back and opened her legs. 'Would you mind letting Bob do it,' said Susie, jerking her head towards the young man who was sitting on his knees, his prick in his hand. 'He should not be forced to endure such an erotic scene without having the opportunity to take part himself.'

'Yes, you're quite right,' agreed Amanda. 'It would be unfair to tease him by showing the sweetmeats and then whipping away the goodies without his being able to taste them. No, I don't mind at all giving way.'

'Bob, would you like to come over here and fuck Susie?' she called out.

'Yes, please!' he exclaimed and threw off his clothes before striding over to the girls. In his haste, however, he stumbled and fell forward almost straight on top of Susie who managed to break his fall with her arms. 'Oh, I'm sorry,' he gasped but Susie said: 'No harm done, Bob, let me feel your cock – you haven't hurt your balls have you?' 'No, no, not at all,' he assured her as the lovely girl took hold of his iron-hard tool and, ensuring that the foreskin was fully drawn back, without ado inserted the uncapped ruby knob between her pouting cunney lips. Susie possess-ed the magical gift of contracting her cunt muscles so that her love channel took hold of Bob's shaft like a delicately soft hand. She wriggled and met his energe-tic thrusts as he moulded her uptilted breasts with his hands, inclining his neck to suck at her erect tawney titties.

Her legs came up and around his back as their lustful fucking increased in pace and Bob drove home his hard cock deep inside her squelchy honeypot, exploring the inner cavities of her cunt, plunging his prick into the glistening wet crack until his ballsack slapped against her bottom. Suddenly she stiffened and gave a startled cry: 'Come with me, Bob, I'm going to spend!'

He was ready to let go and a rush of semen shot up along his shaft from his balls to squirt thickly out of his knob. He pushed hard to ram his tool inside her sopping cunney which was now awash with her own juices. Susie screamed with happiness as the hot, creamy spunk flooded into her and Bob felt her shuddering through a tremendous orgasm as she drained the sperm from his pulsating prick. They kept glued together until his shaft started to lose its stiffness and fell out from the juicy folds of its nest.

Amanda would have very much liked to continue the game by sucking Bob's penis back up to its erect state but, as ever, *tempus fugit* and instead they dressed themselves as Susie consoled her friend by saying that Amanda would have first choice of all the cocks which would be available at Colonel Rankin's surprise party that evening. They put back the remains of their picnic into the hampers and Susie added: 'Let's go round to see the ceremony now. We can leave the hampers here without any worry – the local people are so honest that no-one will touch them and if we're not back by four o'clock, McGinty can take them back onto the carriage by himself.'

'You'll enjoy this, Bob,' said Amanda as they walked towards a nearby wood. Susie led the way along the narrow track into a thick grove and they walked for about half a mile until Bob heard a low chatter of conversation from behind a clump of trees to their left. Susie motioned to a gap between two clumps of arbutus shrubs and, following the girls, Bob found himself in a small hidden clearing. Benches had been placed around the edges of the site and about forty people were already sitting on them waiting for the ceremony to begin. A man wearing a purple toga approached them. 'May I see your tickets, please,' he said and Susie produced their invitations. 'Ah, Sir Harold Brown's party – let me show you to your places.' To their delight they found themselves in the front row on the far side of the grassy stage. Bob noticed a strange circular mound to his right and Amanda explained that this was a rath which some superstitious peasants still believed held fairy tenants which they termed *Sidhe* or people of the hills.

A small group of musicians now gathered at the side of their bench and struck up a familiar tune –

dum, de *dum*, de dum, dum, dum, dum dum; *dum*, de dum, de dum, dum, dum, dum, dum and Bob whispered across: 'What is that nice little piece? I've heard it so often but I've never found out who composed it.'

'It's the Minuet and Trio from Boccherini's Quintet in E Major, it's always been popular but sadly poor Boccherini died in abject poverty,' answered Susie.

A portly gentleman also dressed in a purple toga with the addition of a golden sash now took centre stage. 'Good afternoon, everyone. Welcome to the twenty seventh meeting of the Kerry branch of the Priapic Order Of Perpetual Indulgence of which I have the honour to be Grand Master. We shall now reenact the ancient prehistoric pagan fertility rites which were held here in days of yore. We trust that you will be entertained by our enactment. Now do bear in mind that one of the very oldest Celtic sayings, and one with which you may be familiar, is that to get the full value of joy, you must divide it with someone. So if you wish to participate in the proceedings, please feel free to do so, safe in the knowledge that you are all members of an invited audience who have sworn to keep secret everything that they will see this afternoon. We rely on your total discretion, ladies and gentlemen, as well as the fact that you or your host who purchased your ticket will stand to pay ten thousand pounds to our Order if he or his guest tells tales out of school!'

He exited to a scattered smattering of applause and two other members of the Order carried on to the nature-made stage a large double mattress on a wooden base but with a very small handmade

headboard so that the pillows on the mattress could
be fluffed up without spoiling the view of any spectators behind it. The musicians began playing a
lively minuet which Bob had not heard before. Susie
leaned across and said: 'They always begin with these
dances by Schubert which he wrote for parties when
he was only sixteen.'

'But there's nothing very prehistoric about Schubert, is there?' he muttered back at her.

'No, but it hardly matters. All the mumbo-jumbo is
simply an excuse for a hoolie with lots of fucking!'

As Bob digested this last piece of information, a
young couple dressed in flowing scarlet gowns made
their way to the mattress and to a burst of applause
bowed to the assembled throng. The Grand Master
introduced them openly as Reginald and Maude and
to a further round of applause the couple disrobed
and Bob caught his breath as he drank in the beauty of
the girl. Maude was indeed an extraordinarily lovely
young woman, a pretty brunette possessed of a most
bewitching expression of countenance, with darkly
moist eyes and a mouth which was soft and full. Her
pround body was perfectly balanced, in which were
joined the incisive lines of a slender woman with a
provocative ripeness, for her waist was very slim and
this gave a greater prominence to her large breasts
that themselves were topped with equally large aureoles and nipples. Her mound was carpeted with a
profusion of luxuriant brown hair which formed a
perfect setting for the swelling cunney lips and
glowing red chink between them that looked so
deliciously inviting to Bob and many other spectators
of both sexes.

Reginald too was a good-looking young man, tall and slim with curly fair hair and a handsome face with clear blue eyes and a wide generous mouth which he opened to reveal pearly white teeth that sparkled in the bright sunlight. Susie and Amanda gazed down lustfully at his athletic, superbly proportioned body, admiring his shapely masculine frame and especially the sturdy thick penis rooted in a thicket of wiry hair which was not fully erect but swung heavily between his muscular legs.

The couple caressed and kissed and Maude slowly slid down to her knees and took his cock in her hand and, drawing back the foreskin, made the uncapped purple knob swell and bound in her palm. Once his shaft was fully erect, Maude leaned forward and pushed out the exquisitely rounded cheeks of her backside and opened her legs to give Bob, Susie and Amanda and the front row of spectators an excellent view of her arsehole and her cunt. She gave Reginald's shaft a brisk rub to its fullest majestic dimensions and then with one gulp she swallowed in the full length of his prick until it must have been touching the back of her throat.

Slowly at first but then gradually working up to a regular rhythm, she began to suck noisily upon his throbbing cock, moving her head to and fro so that one moment the shaft was almost out of her mouth and in the next was totally engulfed between her rich, red lips which nestled in his pubic bush. Meanwhile she gently squeezed his hairy ballsack as Reginald held her head tightly in his hands, his eyes screwed up in ecstasy as the sweet girl continued to palate his thick tool.

At this point the Grand Master returned to the stage and declaimed:

'The rich folk and the poor do it,
The old folk and the young do it,
  The black, the white
  Rude and polite,
  The blind, the lame,
  The wild and tame,
The whole world loves to fuck!

Folk that were and folk that are,
And folk to come – they'll do it,
  And priest and nun
  Enjoy the fun,
  The dogs, the cats,
  The mice, the rats,
The whole world loves to fuck!'

He stayed on stage as without a word Maude moved gracefully back and he assisted her to rise back onto her feet. Reginald then swooped up the quivering girl in his arms and carried her to the bed upon which he gently laid her down. Maude lay on her back, arching herself like a sleek cat as Reginald knelt between her legs, kissing her feet, her ankles, her calves and her knees. As he began to kiss the alabaster white flesh of her inner thighs his hands wandered up to massage her divinely firm breasts. She gasped as she parted her legs as wide as she could, fully exposing her silky thatch of brown hair and a pair of pouting pussey lips between which jutted a pert, excited clitty that jutted out just like a tiny cock!

Reginald opened her cunney wider with his fingers, feasting his eyes on the glowing ruby crack before burying his head between Maude's legs and, even over the music, Bob and the girls could hear (if not see) the lad suck deeply on her open cunney which was now discharging a flow of love juice which trickled slowly down her thighs.

The Grand Master spoke again:

> 'Her bosom boasts no swell so fair
> No tints can these eclipse;
> Her head had such no lovely hair,
> Nor such enchanting lips!'

An attractive young red-haired girl sitting next to Susie craned her neck to see Reginald flick his tongue in and out between those divine cunney lips as his hand came down from her titties to roll her erect clitty between thumb and forefinger. 'Oh, what an exciting scene, Maude is such a lucky girl to have such a fine young fellow fuck her,' she murmured as Reginald continued to play with Maude's sopping cunney, licking and lapping her pussey juices whilst he slid two fingers in and out of her sticky love hole. Amanda whispered to Bob: 'Do you see that girl next to Susie? Her name is Bridget Trapes-Blockingham, a Devonshire girl who comes here every summer to be fucked by Jeffrey Green and anyone else who takes her fancy – just look at how flushed her cheeks are, and how her bosom is heaving with emotion. Why, I'll wager a thousand pounds that she'll be the first to join our friends on the bed.'

It was as well that Bob did not accept the bet for

just as he was dying to fill Maude's delicious cunt with his own bursting tool, it irked Bridget (and the other girls in the audience) to see such a fine prick as Reginald's going begging. It lay as still as a poker against his flat stomach as, on all fours, he tongued away at Maude's sopping crack. The sight of his gorgeous instrument of pleasure so affected Bridget that she stood up and began unbuttoning her blouse. In a minute she was stark naked and to the cheers of the audience, she ran up to the bed and stood behind Reginald, placing her hands upon his lean, manly buttocks. She then turned around to face Bob and the girls and acknowledged the applause before she wriggled underneath his parted knees until her head was just under his enormous organ. She kissed the shiny knob as she clasped his shaft in her hand before opening her mouth and gobbling up as much of his rampant cock between her lips as she could take, sucking it eagerly as she cupped his dangling ballsack.

This lewd spectacle was further enlived by a tall, sallow gentleman from the third row who, to the encouragement of his friends, had also stripped for action. As he ran towards the stage, his stiff cock sticking up like a flagpole with the tip of his knob against his navel, Susie chuckled: 'Good heavens, that's young Edward from the local bookshop joining the party. What a big prick he's been blessed with – he can come and catalogue my books at any time.'

Now where would Edward place himself, thought Bob, but in fact there was little difficulty as the bookseller pulled Bridget's legs out from under Reginald's body, which allowed the girl to continue sucking Reginald's cock but freed her legs and the pouting pink lips of her juicy cunt. Edward parted her legs and after wetting his prick with spittle, lay between her parted thighs and guided his knob to the folds of Bridget's pussey. With one vigorous thrust he effected a safe lodgement for his knob and then he eased forward to bury his shaft to the hilt as his balls flopped against her heaving bum cheeks. He thrust again and again, fucking her oily nook with short, sharp strokes as now a third girl, a local favourite known as Gypsy Molly, entered the fray. She was a buxom wench with jet black hair whose plump breasts jiggled enticingly as she made her way forward to enlarge the group to a quintet. She knelt down beside Edward so that he could kiss her thick dark thatched mound and superbly chiselled red gash. His tongue fluttered out and darted in between her cunney lips, exploring the moist flavour of her pussey.

Francois and Jean-Paul Marchais, eighteen-year-old twins from France staying at the Great Southern Hotel, were next to lose their inhibitions and they stood either side of Bridget who chewed on their cocks lustily, palating each in turn and then somehow stuffing both knobs in her mouth at the same time. Henrietta, a dairymaid from a nearby farm, now joined in and Bob smacked his lips as the lovely little sprite displayed her naked charms. she was finely formed with blonde hair falling down her shoulders in ringlets with small but proudly jutting breasts. In her hand she brandished a wooden dildo based, as a nearby gentleman informed Susie and Amanda, upon the prick of Martin Wellsend, a rich local landowner whio was known for his robust sexual activities. She inserted the rounded head between the cheeks of

Jean-Paul's bum and carefully pushed in the godemiche which startled the young Frenchman so much
that he almost choked Gypsy Molly as he twitched
violently, pushing his prick down into her throat.

Henrietta had time only to administer a few loud
slaps on Francois's chubby posterior, making his bum
cheeks tingle as they reddened under her smart
smacks before the seven participants in this erotic
orgy of fucking began to spend. Reginald managed to
keep slurping on Maude's pussey as he expelled great
wodges of sticky cream out of his throbbing bell end
into Bridget's waiting mouth. Almost simultaneously
Edward sent a stream of spunk into Bridget's yearning cunney just as his own mouth was completely
filled by a veritable flood of love juice that flowed out
from Gypsy Molly's excited pussey. The French twins
shot their loads of frothy sperm into her mouth
though poor Henrietta was forced to frig her own wet
slit to obtain a ride to paradise as she fucked Jean-
Paul's backside with her dildo.

Her plight was noticed by Amanda who turned to
Bob and said heatedly: 'Look at that poor girl up
there. It isn't fair that she should have to bring herself
off when all about her everyone else has enjoyed a
jolly good fucking. Bob Goggin, a true gentleman
would stride up and offer her the use of his cock.'

'I did my duty with Freda this morning,' protested
Bob. 'Surely someone else could proffer his prick?'

Amanda glanced round and said with a sigh: 'I'm
sorry to say that there appears to be a shocking
absence of red-blooded men in the audience today.
However, all is not lost – I will help this pretty girl
myself.' And she shed her clothes in double quick

time and ran across to Henrietta, waving her arm to attract the dairymaid's attention. 'Don't fret, my love, I'll bring you off, never fear. Alas, I'm afraid there seems to be a severe shortage of available stiff hard pricks just at the moment.'

'How kind of you,' said Henrietta gratefully, as Amanda held out her hand for the dildo. 'Let's get together on the bed.' The others rolled off the mattress to make room for the two girls who began to kiss and cuddle with great affection and, putting down the godemiche, Amanda then laid the dairymaid flat on her back and rubbed her hands over the ripe, white rounded globes of her breasts, making the rosy nipples harden up to peaks of hardness under her palms. Then she twisted herself over to sit across her with her bottom cheeks directly over Henrietta's face as she bent forward and picked up the dildo. She nudged the tip between Henrietta's cunney lips which made the girl tremble all over.

'Suck my cunt whilst I fuck you with this big wooden cock,' ordered Amanda as she removed the dildo to give Henrietta's furry moss a thorough licking. At the same, the dairymaid pulled out Amanda's bum cheeks and teased the long red gash open with the tip of her pink tongue. She inhaled the pungent aroma as she pushed her tongue deeper into the wet slot of Amanda's cunt. She fondled the pussey lips tenderly until a fine trickle of love juice filled her mouth. She then dipped a long finger slowly into Amanda's wrinkled brown bum-hole, which made the blonde girl yelp out in delicious agony.

Amanda's bottom jerked wildly in response to the finger-fucking of her arse and the beautiful tickling of

Henrietta's tongue. She plunged the dildo in and out of Henrietta's cunney, and this made the girl moan passionately, twisting and turning as Amanda pumped the dildo and twisted it round before slowly pulling it out of her insatiable cunt. She fucked the dairymaid's cunt faster and faster with the magic godemiche and she felt her own pussey creaming under Henrietta's tongue. In a wild explosion of delight, the two girls came together, Henrietta gulping down Amanda's love juices and Amanda lowering her head to catch the arcing fountain of liquid that spurted out of Henrietta's pussey.

This stimulating spectacle would doubtless have attracted more participants to the prurient party, but as so often happens in that part of the world, the sun had disappeared behind a thick grey cloud which had scudded up unnoticed, and a few spots of warm rain fell on the naked flesh of the young people who had enjoyed each other's bodies so uninhibitedly, if immodestly. They ran back for their clothes whilst Reginald and Maude put on their scarlet robes as the Grand Master came back on stage to intone a closing verse, which Bob recognised as coming from *Bolloxinion* by the seventeeth-century rake The Earl of Rochester.

Lifting his toga to take his meaty shaft in his hand, the Grand Master recited:

> 'Thus in the zenith of my lust I reign;
> I eat to swive, and swive to eat again.
> Let other monarchs, who their sceptres bear
> To keep their subjects less in love than fear

   Be salves to crowns, my nation shall be
      free;
   My pintle only shall my sceptre be,
   My laws shall act more pleasure than com-
      mand,
    And with my prick I'll govern all the land.'

And he ended with a final few lines from Horace:

   'Happy the man, and happy he alone
   He who can call today his own.
   He who secure within can say,
   Tomorrow, do thy worst, for I have lived today!'

Bob and the girls made their way back through the narrow path from the clearing and went back through the wood and to the field where they had left their hampers. The rain stopped as suddenly as it had begun and they had time to refresh themselves with some ginger beer before McGinty arrived to take them back to Abroch House. 'What a splendid way to spend an afternoon,' said Bob as they relaxed in the comfort of the landaulette. 'Count Gewirtz will find it hard to match such entertainment this evening.'

'Don't worry, Johnny Gewirtz usually has something up his sleeve,' advised Amanda, resting her head on Bob's shoulder.

'Yes, and always a fat prick in his pants,' added Susie salaciously.

CHAPTER FIVE
The Last Round-Up

For the moment, dear reader, let us leave Bob Goggin and the rest of the guests at Sir Harold Brown's luxurious home in the Emerald Isle as they spend the early evening resting in eager anticipation of the delights to be provided by that fabled Master of the Revels *par excellence*, Count Johann Gewirtz of Galicia. We will rejoin Cyril Totteridge and Katie Arkley who, fresh from their fucking at Gary Hornby's dinner a few days before, had returned to the West Country.

As Katie had expected, not even the excellent game of bridge during which she had been partnered by the affable Reverend Bernard Bailey, nor the passage of the hours, had fully mollified Lady Laetitia Arkley when she found out that her elder daughter had skipped away unchaperoned to London. Katie and Cyril quailed before her in the sitting room of Michael Arkley's house back in Teignmouth as she drew herself up to her full height in preparation of delivering a lecture the young couple would never forget – but before the formidable matron could begin her strictures, Michael Arkley dashed into the room.

'Hello Cyril, hello Katie, did you have a good time in London? Look here, Cyril, you've arrived just in the nick of time. Sir Paul has had a nasty accident and has hurt his back rather badly. I could do with your help in getting him into bed.'

'Doctor Aigin has told Paul time and time again that he has a weakness in that part of his body,' said Lady Arkley crossly. 'I have little sympathy if he has put his back out again. However, if you require my assistance—'

'No, no, really that won't be necessary, thank you,' said Michael Arkley hastily. 'Cyril and I will be able to cope and I'll ask Mutkin to lend a hand if necessary. Anyway, Laetitia, your visitor is waiting for you in the library. You will recall that you asked the Rector to come round this afternoon to discuss the arrangements at the summer fete at which you will be guest of honour.'

He watched Lady Arkley anxiously, as Michael Arkley had staked all on his sister-in-law being diverted by the Rector, an obsequious, teacup-passing, thin-bread-and-butter-offering yes-man whom powerfully minded women like Lady Arkley always liked at first sight. Her pretty daughter too breathed a sigh of relief when her mother nodded her head and said she would go up and see her husband after her meeting with the Rector, for Katie had no wish to face her mother's wrath alone!

'Can I help?' said Katie but her uncle held up his hand. 'I think Cyril and I will manage better by ourselves, thank you. Why don't you supervise the unpacking of your clothes?'

As they hurried out into the gardens, Cyril asked Michael Arkley why he had appeared to have wanted the women out of the way. 'I think you'll understand why when you see Sir Paul,' replied his companion drily as they approached the clump of trees which partially hid a small outhouse where Vera the housemaid ironed clothes and where a washing line was strung up between two iron posts. The reason for keeping Sir Paul's wife and daughter well away was immediately apparent to Cyril as soon as he saw Sir Paul who was lying naked, face down on a pile of white bed-linen. Squashed underneath him was the equally nude body of Vera, the lovely little housemaid who was celebrating her nineteenth birthday by being fucked by Sir Paul Arkley. (It should be noted here that the randy baronet had promised her a position in his London household in Hyde Park Gardens if, as he hinted broadly, they could agree terms).

'Good God, what on earth has been happening?' gasped Cyril.

'Use your eyes, man,' snapped Sir Paul with perhaps justifiable irritation. 'I was shagging this lovely young girl here when my back seized up and I just can't move.'

'That's right,' confirmed Vera, whose cunney was still engorged by Sir Paul's swollen shaft. She was feeling a little out of breath from having the portly baronet on top of her for so long. 'Sir Paul was shagging me beautifully, stretching my pussey with his thick prick, but then all of a sudden he went all rigid and we're stuck together like a pair of Siamese twins.'

Cyril bent down and saw that the couple were framed in a kind of still-life copulation. Sir Paul's plump penis was still embedded in Vera's cunney and his balls were hanging against her bum cheeks. The other side of an emergency is always an opportunity, thought Cyril, for if he could assist Sir Paul out of his predicament, the way should be cleared for he and Katie to continue their relationship, notwithstanding the formidable Lady Arkley.

'Let's see what we can do, Sir Paul,' said Cyril, taking off his jacket. 'Now, if I stand over you and lift you up from the shoulders whilst Mr Arkley stands at the side and lifts your legs at the same time, we can at least release Vera.'

This stratagem worked although Sir Paul cried out in agony as the two men lifted him, his body still locked in a rigidity as stiff as his cock which exited with a juicy 'pop' from Vera's cunt as he was lifted and then turned onto his back. Michael Arkley found a stepladder and this served as a makeshift stretcher upon which he and Cyril Totteridge placed the naked Sir Paul whose prick obstinately continued to stand stiffly in the air.

'We can carry you back to the house now, Paul,' said his brother but before they lifted up their burden Vera scrambled to her feet and said: 'Shall I make him come before you take him indoors? It wouldn't look right being carried indoors with his cock waggling away like that.'

'What a clever girl, you're absolutely right. Yes, I am sure you'll enjoy working for me in London,' said Sir Paul approvingly as she took hold of his throbbing tool and briskly ran her hand up and down from his balls to his knob. She knelt down and with her other hand coaxed up her red nipples to a stalky erectness. 'Come on, sir, I want you to spray my titties with your love juice,' Vera urged him as she wrapped her hand tightly around his penis. She only had to rub his shaft for a few moments before Sir Paul gasped with delight and let fly a great fountain of sticky spunk which sprayed a white necklace of sperm across the girl's bare breasts. She leaned forward and placed his jerking tool between the valley of her spheres, smearing the creamy love juice all round her saucer-shaped aureoles. She squeezed her breasts together and stuffed his shaft into her cleavage as Sir Paul cried out in ecstasy as he spurted the final remnants of his spend onto her chin.

'Well done, Vera,' said Cyril as he bent down to take up the handles of the makeshift stretcher.

'Thank you, Mr Totteridge, but if you don't mind my mentioning it, I haven't come yet and I'd love to be brought off,' she replied boldly, looking him straight in the eye.

'I'll be back as soon as possible,' promised Cyril as he took up his burden. Michael Arkley led the way back to the house saying that, if they went in through the back door, with luck they would not be seen by anybody. Alas, on Lady Arkley's recommendation, the Rector was making his way out through the garden so that he could see the flower-beds the blooms from which Lady Arkley would offer at his bazaar. He met the stretcher party on the patio and looked in horror at the naked body of Sir Paul.

At this point a scandal was averted by Michael Arkley who showed a commendably quick presence of mind. 'Ah, Rector, how nice to see you. Mr Totteridge I am sure you know, and this gentleman is my elder brother, Sir Paul Arkley. I should explain that on a visit out East he contracted a rare skin complaint which breaks out every so often and his medical advisor, the famous Doctor Aigin of Harley

Street in London, has recommended the maximum possible exposure to the sun as the only cure. Unfortunately the poor chap has just slipped and ricked his back as well.'

'Oh, my dear sir, you have my sympathy,' said the Rector with horror. 'What an unfortunate thing to happen whilst you are on holiday.'

'Yes, isn't it,' said Sir Paul, somehow forcing out a small smile between his gritted teeth. 'By the way, please don't mention that you've seen me to anyone, not even my wife. I don't want her to worry about me. I'm sure you understand.'

'Quite, quite. I won't say a word. May I take this opportunity of wishing you a speedy recovery, Sir Paul.' And with that he took his leave, to the relief of all concerned. They managed to deposit Sir Paul back on his bed without further interruption and Michael Arkley was glad to take up Cyril's offer to return the stepladder to its place in the garden.

Katie would hardly be overjoyed if he fucked Vera, thought Cyril, as he carried the stepladder back to the shed where he judged that the luscious young housemaid would be waiting for him. Still, as his old scoutmaster used to advise, one should anticipate the difficult by managing the easy and there should be few problems in placing his prick in Vera's bushy little dark-haired pussey.

As he suspected, she was waiting for him to return, lying naked on the pile of sheets and lazily fingerfucking her cunney. She looked up at him, saying: 'Why Mr Totteridge, I thought you were never coming back. Look, I've started, so will you help me finish?'

Cyril needed little further encouragement as he

tore off his trousers and knelt between her long legs. He placed his palm on her dark, thickly curled bush and she writhed in response as his questing fingers slid into the already dewy folds of her cunney, spreading her pussey lips as rivulets of female nectar ran over Cyril's hand. She undid the buttons of his shirt as their mouths met and as soon as Cyril was naked, she pulled her lips away to transfer them to the tip of his swollen cock. She flicked her tongue under the plump, purple helmet and then, bobbing her head in a deliberately slow tempo, she fucked his bursting tool with her suctioning mouth. Now with his knob in her mouth she grasped his shaft at the base and proceeded to frig it.

'Aaah! That's lovely, but I'll spend if you do that much longer,' warned Cyril as thrills of excitement vibrated out from his tingling penis. Gradually she reduced the tempo of her sucking and then lifted her head and rolled over on her back as Cyril spread her lovely legs wide and climbed on top of her. He hovered above her, supporting himself on his powerful arms to watch her take hold of his pulsating prick and feed it into her juicy love nest. He eased himself down upon her and his hairy ballsack slapped against her buttocks as he fucked the delicious girl in long, smooth strokes. Then he moved his position so that his cock entered her now sopping quim at a high angle. This brought her clitty out from its cocoon, rubbing sensitively against his knob as he increased the pace. Supported on just his fingertips and toes, Cyril thrust with a truly pile-driving intensity and, as they swiftly approached the heights, he changed the tempo of the fuck to one of short, quick jabs as Vera rotated her ecstatic buttocks on the soft, now damp-ened sheets as he pistoned in and out of her.

'I'm being well fucked,' she whispered in his ear. 'In and out of me . . . cock . . . cunt . . . fuck . . . Ohhh. . . . !' Her legs wrapped themselves around him as she flexed her body, trembled and wriggled her thighs about the fulcrum of his rod. The lewd pair spent within seconds of each other, the lovely young girl glorying in the feel of his pulsing prick as after a series of tempestuous spasms, it exploded, spurting jets of frothy warm spunk deep within her as she milked his cock with the secret inner muscles of her cunney.

As the pair lay together, blissfully exhausted in their post-fuck reverie, inside the house Michael Arkley suddenly snapped his fingers and, turning to his niece Penny who had just come back after an afternoon's croquet on the magnificent lawn of Lady Scadgers's mansion nearby, said: 'Penny, I've just remembered something that may well help your poor Papa. My old friend Colonel Piers Rankin of the Hus-sars wrote to me the other week that a most interesting lady from India would be staying at the Royal Hotel this month. Now what was her name – oh yes, Doctor Nandeep Ashreem. She is one of the most skilled practitioners of Oriental massage in the whole world. Piers met her whilst he was in Calcutta and sustained some nasty injuries after falling off his pony during a game of polo. He also suffered terribly with back pains but, after a course of treatment from Nandeep, three months later he was back in the saddle and fighting fit.'

'What brings her down to the West Country?' enquired Penny.

'She's writing a book on Eastern medicine –

frankly, Piers was supposed to come down himself as, between ourselves, I have a feeling that their relationship back in India was, how shall I put it, rather more intense than an ordinary doctor/patient relationship. Frankly, Piers is quite smitten with the lady and would have been in Teignmouth himself this week except that he had business to attend in Dublin. Whilst in Ireland, he went on to spend a few days with Sir Harold Brown in Killarney.'

'Harold Brown? Where have I heard that name before – it rings a bell somewhere, I'm sure.'

'I doubt it, my dear, as he shuns any kind of publicity. You may have heard whispers about the fast parties he is supposed to give in Ireland. His name has been linked with the notorious Count Gewirtz of Galicia *[a biography of this extraordinary roué whose escapades involved members of the royal houses of England, Italy, Spain and Portugal as well as many notable figures in France and America is currently being researched by Professor Herschel Solodowsky of Yale University – Editor]* and our own King when he was Prince of Wales.

'More important though,' he added, wishing to change the subject, for Michael Arkley had secretly attended a wild orgiastic gathering at Abroch House the previous summer, 'is that we make contact with Dr Ashreem.'

'Why don't we walk round to her hotel now and see if she can come and have a look at Papa?' asked Penny, rising to her feet.

'Why not indeed – I'll tell your Mama and we'll go straightaway.'

Lady Arkley had little faith in the idea of bringing

Doctor Ashreem round to look at her husband's back.
'Still, I suppose this woman can do no harm,' she said
grudgingly as she went upstairs to tell Sir Paul what his
brother and daughter were planning to do for him.

Meanwhile, Katie Arkley was sitting in her room
avidly reading a most interesting letter from Corinne
Cumberland, one of her closest friends from school
who was spending the summer in Italy with her
parents, Lord and Lady Nayland. The letter had been
sent on from the Arkley's London address in Hyde
Park Gardens.

Dearest Katie,

*I do hope that you are enjoying the summer
down in Teignmouth. For the first two weeks
here in Viarregio I was rather bored as there are
few young people of our age with whom to
socialise. However, last Monday morning, who
should I meet on the promenade as I walked
along with my Mama but Grahame Johnstone,
that handsome young Scottish drama student we
were both introduced to by Lady Brixton at
Stella Ponsonby's coming-out party last April.
He was here on holiday staying with a friend, a
Jewish boy from Manchester named David Arn-
stein who was studying stage management at
Grahame's college. His friend was buying ice-
creams from a stall nearby and Grahame called
him over and introduced us. David was also
very good-looking, but dark-skinned with a mop
of curly black hair and a well proportioned
body, though he was not perhaps as muscular
as Grahame who, as you know, is a great*

sportsman and has represented his country at both football and cricket.

Well, they insisted that I should take tea with them at the villa they had rented for the summer. As Grahame's maternal uncle, Lord Musselborough, is known to my parents, to my joy Mama allowed me to visit the boys without a chaperone.

Now before I continue, Katie, my only excuse for what followed is that I have not enjoyed the feel of a nice big cock in my cunney since Phil Bosinney and I decided to end our courtship four months ago. You will agree, I am sure, that sixteen weeks is more than enough for any girl to have to live through without once being fucked! I was feeling so desperate that before leaving for Tuscany I purchased a dildo from Dr Nicklee's Surgical Stores in Tottenham Court Road. Frankly, though giving some much needed relief, I found it a poor substitute for the real thing, especially as Phil's prick was generally considered to be amongst the thickest and longest in Belgravia.

But be that as it may, after luncheon I changed into a loose fitting summer dress before leaving to go to Grahame's villa which was less than half a mile down the road. I decided not to replace my knickers or my chemise as if the truth be told, it was already in my mind that I might entertain myself with at least one of the boys that afternoon. Wasn't I naughty!

Anyhow, I made my way down through the village to where the two lads were staying and found their villa without any difficulty. We sat outside in their garden under the blazing sun and I looked longingly at the cool blue water in their swimming pool. 'Oh, how I'd love to take a nice refreshing dip,' I sighed and David said: 'Well, please feel free to do so, Corrine. It's a splendid idea actually so, if you don't mind, I think I'll join you.'

'Of course, not, that'll be fun,' I replied but then my face fell as I added. 'Drat it though, I didn't bring a bathing costume with me. I'll have to walk back and get one from my room.'

'There's really not necessary,' chimed in Grahame jauntily. 'David and I always bathe in the nude. So much more healthy, you know. Have you never tried it?'

'No, not really, but I wouldn't mind having a go,' I replied with a saucy little smile. 'I'll try almost anything once.'

'That's the spirit which won the Empire,' he chuckled. 'I'll pop inside and bring out some towels.'

David and I began to undress and I took my clothes off slowly, wanting to see if this young man had the nerve to strip off completely before me. I was not to be disappointed! As I said, he was a handsome fellow with dark, liquid eyes and a full, sensuous mouth. When he slipped off his shirt he revealed a broad chest covered with a soft matting of dark hair and a flat tummy. Courteously, he turned around as he pulled down his shorts but I could not help but be aroused by his dimpled little bottom which I longed to pinch as he bent over to fold his clothes on the chair. When he turned back I had fair view of his thick circumcised cock which was already in a state of half limber. I pulled up my dress and instantly my fully naked charms were shown to him. He drew in his breath sharply in surprise for he had expected me at least to be wearing at least some underclothes! But the shock very quickly wore off and his shaft swelled up perceptibly, though I only saw it for a further brief moment as he moved away immediately and dived into the pool.

I was not quite so brave and used the steps to climb down into the water. I was swimming slowly towards David when I noticed that Grahame had already returned with the towels. When he placed them on a table he revealed that he had taken off his clothes indoors. My heart began to beat faster as I saw his remarkable cock which was already erect. Now, my dear Katie, you may well ask what was so remarkable about Grahame Johnstone's penis; I can best answer the question by saying that it was by far the biggest member I have ever seen. At first sight I estimated it to be at least nine inches long (and when I took a tape measure to it before I left them I was proved right to within a quarter of an inch) and it was almost abnormally thick. What a monster! I resolved there and then that I would have David fuck me first to exercise my cunney a bit before I tackled Grahame's gigantic weapon.

Being a gentleman, Grahame had the good manners to walk indoors when David and I finally got out the pool. The warm sunshine played on our bodies as we lightly dried off the excess moisture off our bodies and we drank glasses of chilled white wine which Grahame had thoughtfully left out for us. It was funny really, for though we had only met that very afternoon, David and I chatted away like old friends and it seemed the most natural thing in the world to raise my face and kiss him as we stood closely together. As we embraced I could feel his sturdy prick rising up against my tummy as his body pressed against me. I took hold of his rigid rod and as soon as my fingers were curled around the shaft, it began to throb and jerk wildly in my hand. I looked lovingly down at the sight of this splendid circumcised cock and I rather enjoyed pulling my hand up and down the ivory stalk without the encumbrance of a foreskin to pull back. I planted a wet kiss upon the "eye" of his mushroom knob where a small bead of spend had already formed and then I raised myself to be clasped once more in his strong arms and carried down to the easy chair where he gently lay me down. At first he simply looked with awe over my upturned nipples which were now jutting out in excitement and I rubbed my own pussey to see if I were already juicy enough (which I was) for a session of l'arte de faire l'amour.

He lay beside me, his fingers running as lightly as butterflies over my shoulders and breasts, across my flat tummy and my silky auburn pussey hair until they came to rest on my cunney lips where, as he leaned over to kiss me again, his forefinger insinuated itself between them to smooth the passage of his penis. I now desperately wanted him inside me and he must have sensed my longing, for he withdrew his tongue from my mouth and his finger from my cunt, and after kissing and sucking my rock hard nipples, he rolled over on top of me and rubbed his stiff shaft against my pussey. I parted my thighs and his helmet rested against my cunney lips. Then, raising himself upon his arms, he slowly descended upon me and his cock slid squelchily into my yearning love channel.

Still supporting himself on his forearms he fucked me with a rhythmic grace, his hips and buttocks rocking as he moved in and out of my delighted honeypot. Then he crashed down full upon me, wrapping his arms around me as I locked my legs around his waist. Our two bodies fused into one erotic mass of flesh as we fucked happily away. What joy David afforded me as his firm cock pumped to and fro, each stroke driving me onwards to the apogee of delight. I whimpered with joy at each thrust as his superb shaft slid in and out of my drenched cunney. His body began to quiver and I thrust my cunt upwards in a last effort to cram even more of that magic stiffness inside me as his ballsack banged against my bum. I tensed to receive his libation and, sure enough, he shot a fiery stream of frothy jism inside me. A fresh torrent of my own juices mingled with his spunk as I reached my own crest of utmost pleasure and we dissolved into a glorious frenzy of voluptuousness and I spent time and time again as he spurted his creamy sperm into my cunt. He left his still stiff cock in my cunney for a few moments longer and then *slowly withdrew, his shaft glistening with our mixed love juices.*

I thought I heard a sound besides us and I turned my head to see that Grahame had returned and was leaning over us, his tremendous tool waggling by my right shoulder. Yet again I marvelled at the sheer size of his instrument, at the smooth uncapped knob, rubicund and gleaming, and at the thick blue veins that knotted themselves along its rigid length. The sight was too exciting and as he nudged his knob towards my lips I opened them wide and licked and sucked this monstrous organ. 'I think it's my turn,' said Grahame politely to David who nodded silently and moved away as Grahame straddled me, his legs either side of my body so that he could bend forward and run his hands over my breasts. Holding my head still, I somehow managed to keep my lips clamped around his majestic weapon. Grahame moaned with pleasure as he fucked my mouth, moving as much of his gigantic cock as he could in and out, but I could only take about half his shaft between my lips. Sensuously, he rolled his hips as I squeezed his balls and almost immediately he shot thick jets of hot tangy jism pouring down my throat. I eagerly swallowed every last drop of tasty spunk. As I had correctly speculated, his huge shaft remained as iron-hard as before.

I enjoyed sucking his cock so much that I was torn between sucking him again or letting him fuck my pussey which was more than ready for a second joust, but Grahame settled the matter by asking me if he could follow his friend and fuck my cunney. So I gave his velvet-skinned knob a last lick and kiss and lay down on my back. His eyes now glittering with excitement, he picked up my feet and threw my legs over his powerful shoulders. This parted my legs wide and he took his throbbing tool in his hand and presented his knob to my open crack. For a brief moment, I was worried that this big prick might injure me but magically my cunney managed to absorb this terrific tadger and I cried out in delight as straightaway I thrilled to a little spend even before he had begun to stuff all of his fat sausage inside me.

Grahame was an impressive fucker, guiding his superb shaft beautifully all around my raging wetness. I twisted and turned under his commanding thrusts. I slipped my hands down his back to grasp his firm bum cheeks and, as his pelvis jabbed down, I eagerly lifted my hips to welcome the questing cock that slid so exquisitely in and out of my sopping quim. Ah, Katie, such a sybaritic euphoria pervaded every fibre of my being as the entire length of my pussey throbbed and throbbed again as Grahame's thick prick pushed deeper and deeper, exploring even the tiniest nook of my passion pit. Then he began a long, slow thrusting rhythm. Gradually I experienced a build-up of that delicious tingle which accompanies a spend. As he started to heave and buck with increasing rapidity I began my own journey to paradise as faster and faster he pounded to and fro and his big, tight ballsack bounced against my bottom.

'Now, Grahame, now! Fuck away as hard as

you can, you big-cocked fucker!' I screamed without restraint. The lusty lad obliged as, with short, stabbing strokes, he sent stream after stream of warm, white froth inside my cunney. I clapped my hands over his rounded buttocks, keeping him deep inside me until I swiftly reached the climax that my body demanded.

David was now more than ready to rejoin the party and placed my hand on his upright stiffstander. But I was concerned that if he fucked me again, I could only suck off Grahame for his cock was far too big for my other tiny orifice. 'I'll fuck you again, Corinne, whilst David prods your bum-hole. That should provide great fun for us all,' suggested Grahame and as soon as I gave my ready assent he reached for my shoulders and glued his lips to mine as I reached for his shaft and rubbed it up to its former glorious height. He sucked on my titties as he buried his shaft inside the juicy portals of my pussey and we began the old heaving and shoving – but this time we leaned to one side so that I was able to push my pert little bottom backwards. David smoothed his hands over my buttocks and parted the soft spheres, opening wide the crack between them and exposing my wrinkled little brown bottom-hole. Fortunately David's tool was not as thick as Grahame's, though it was of a good enough length for a bumfuck. With the aid of a pot of cold cream that was happily to hand he was able to push in from the start and there was only a momentary slight discomfort as the boys lustily rammed in their pricks together, with Grahame crashing into my cunney *and David into my backside. As they pushed in together I could feel their two cocks squeezing in at the same time with only the thin divisional membrane separating their shafts.*

Screaming with excitement, this brought us all to new extraordinary paroxyms of pleasure. The two boys squirted out their tributes of sticky hot sperm and I too was able to climb the summit of love before we sank back totally exhausted from this novel experience. Amazingly, David's nice-looking cock still looked heavy and, as his shaft was just by my face, I took hold of it and gently pulled him forward so that I could ease it into my mouth. I flicked my tongue against the ridge around his knob, moving my lips from balls to tip and back again, faster and faster, intoxicated by the succulent cockshaft which he was shoving down towards the back of my throat. The dear boy was so excited that in no time at all his throbbing prick released its load of hot, salty juice and I felt it course down my throat in a frothy fountain. I swallowed convulsively, lapping up every drop as I milked his cock of every drop of sperm.

Now Grahame had recovered his senses and he showed himself to be a kind and considerate lover. He realised that my pussey had been stretched by his enormous penis and so now, instead of simply ramming his huge prick back into my cunt, this time he first knelt between my open legs and deftly parted my soaked cunney lips with his fingers. I shuddered with pleasure as he smoothly massaged the insides of my love lips with his tongue, always an arousing prelude to fucking, I am sure you will agree, and a technique too rarely practised in Britain although Europeans are often skilled at this art. Indeed, Grahame had been taught to suck pussey in Paris during his studies at the Sorbonne and he had been an adept pupil. What bliss I experienced as he moved his lips to my clitty, sucking very lightly as his hands moved up quickly to my nipples, rubbing them in tiny circles which made them stand up to attention under his ministrations. Already I was floating and just when my pussey started to pulsate he slid his tongue deep in whilst one hand squeezed my titties and the other moved across to massage my clitty.

Without missing a beat, he then moved his body up over mine, pulling my legs onto his shoulders and sliding that elephantine prick into my straining cunt. He buried himself deep inside me with a powerful thrust that mashed my clitty against his pubic bone and made me spend there and then. He held us together very still, smiling as my spasms finally stopped. I lay there gasping for breath as he began to stroke his cock in and out, penetrating my pussey with lightning force and speed.

Then quite suddenly, to my surprise, he reared up over me and let his slippery pole slide out of my honeypot. He gripped his big cock, gave the shaft two or three sharp rubs and spurted a curved rivulet of spunk arcing over my breasts, splashing my nipples and fairly drenching my belly and the top of my silky bush.

We sucked and fucked the afternoon away,

Katie, and tomorrow afternoon, we plan to repeat the performance. This holiday is turning out to be one of the best I have ever taken. Now I have written frankly to you of all the details, not just for your own enjoyment (though I trust that reading of my exciting adventures has not proved too arduous a task), but also to inform you that Grahame and David will be in London on Saturday August 27th. If you are free, I thought that you might like to enlarge our trio into a quartet. You have first refusal to sample Grahame Johnstone's tremendous tadger for yourself. My parents will be away in the country for the weekend so our house in Hill Street, Mayfair will be freely available!

By the time you receive this letter we shall have returned to England and I will be staying at our country home, Cumberland Lodge in Upper Cransworth, Surrey. Do write back and let me know whether you would like to make up a discreet little gathering as soon as possible.

Love,
Corinne

Katie's cheeks were burning as she put down the last sheet of this lewd letter. At first she was cross with Corinne for thinking that she, Katie, was so short of men that she would be so interested in Grahame Johnstone's huge penis and prepared to share it with Corinne. However, on the other hand, it was kind of Corinne to offer her the first opportunity to take part in what would be a very wild affair.

* * *

Whilst Katie wondered what to write back to Corinne Cumberland, just three rooms away her poor Papa was lying helpless, flat on his back on a hard mattress and in substantial discomfort, almost unable to move. But help was now at hand, for his brother Michael and daughter Penny had located Doctor Nandeep Ashreem. The dazzlingly beautiful Indian lady had consented to see if she could help Sir Paul without delay. Her shapely figure, enchanting eyes and shiny black hair had already captivated Michael Askley. He explained to his brother about Dr Ashreem's skills and Sir Paul (ever unable to resist the opportunity of engaging into a conversation with an attractive woman) readily consented to be treated by her.

Michael and Penny waited outside whilst she examined Sir Paul. Five minutes later she came out onto the landing and said: 'Has Sir Paul engaged in strenuous exercise today? I asked him what he was doing when his back suddenly seized up but he appears reluctant to explain just what he was doing at the time.'

'I can't think why,' fibbed Michael, 'but yes, he had been exercising himself in the garden.'

'Are you quite sure about that, Uncle Michael?' queried a puzzled Penny. 'I've never known Papa ever to take any exercise at all.'

'Ah, that's probably the reason why he's in such a state now. His body is in a hypnotic spasm and we need to shake him out of it. I would suggest a homeopathic remedy. This means we treat like with like – so I will attempt to shock Sir Paul physically and this should counteract the effects of the original shock to his system.'

'What sort of shock do you have in mind?' asked Penny.

Dr Ashreem smiled and said: 'I'll think of something – there is one remedy that comes to mind which often seems to work with European gentlemen in these situations.'

'Leave it to me,' she added as she went back inside the patient's bedroom, locking the door behind her. 'I cannot imagine just what she meant by that last remark. I just hope that she is not planning anything too exotic for Papa,' mused Penny but Michael Arkley shrugged his shoulders and said: 'Please don't worry, Penny, Dr Ashreem's treatment may well offer delectations of the Orient which your father may well respond to very satisfactorily. She's an attractive woman, isn't she? I wouldn't mind being treated by Dr Ashreem myself – I could imagine that a message from her would be filled with Eastern promise.'

How perceptive was Sir Paul's brother! For the clever Dr Ashreem had already deduced that Sir Paul was a man of robust sexual appetites. She slipped off her shoes and sat on Sir Paul's bed wearing only a summer jacket and a short walking skirt. 'Well now, what can we do to make you well again, Paul? You don't mind my calling you Paul, I hope. My name is Nandeep, by the way,' she said, pulling back the sheet to expose Sir Paul's naked body to her liquid gaze. 'My, that's a nice-sized prick you have there,' she commented. 'It isn't as big as my friend Piers Rankin's but it's well proportioned and when it's ready for duty there's probably little in it between the two. Do you know Colonel Rankin, by the way?'

'No, I haven't had the pleasure,' replied Sir Paul,

whose demeanour brightened as this dark-skinned beauty from the sub-continent took his cock in her hand. She swivelled her body round to kneel directly in front of him. Forgetting the pain whenever he moved a muscle, he reached forward and placed his palms on her firm, springy breasts, fingering her stiff nipples which were easy to feel through the soft wool of her jacket. He realised from the feel that she was wearing nothing underneath and when he undid the buttons of the jacket, the lapels fell open to reveal a pair of proud, naked golden brown breasts, the nipples of which were erect dark peaks shaded by large brown aureole rings.

Sir Paul dragged himself up to get his lips around them but she gently pushed him backwards saying: 'All in good time, let your body relax now before you move again.' She lowered her head and took his bulging shaft between her lips, sucking it up to a powerful, throbbing erection whilst she undid her skirt and wriggled out of it. When Sir Paul caught sight of her silky black hairy mound he trembled all over in a frenzy of lustful excitement. Nandeep gave a swift little moistening tonguing to his domed purple knob and then sucked at least three inches of the hot thick shaft into her mouth. Sir Paul cried out loudly, not as before in pain but this time in a fever of erotic joy as Nandeep Ashreem licked the entire length of his shaft, working her full, rich lips up and down, kissing, licking and lapping until he could hold back no longer and spunked copiously into her mouth, sending globs of sticky white jism down her throat. She jammed her lips over the twitching mushroom helmet of his cock and gulped and sucked every drain of frothy essence from Sir Paul's gushing penis until at last she let his shrivelling staff out of her mouth, licking her lips as he fell back on the bed.

'It looks as if you are on the road to recovery,' murmured the doctor as she rolled over next to him and let the randy baronet squeeze her gorgeous breasts and tongue her nipples untill his prick swelled up again and was ready for a second bout. She then crawled up on all fours and stuck her lovely bottom out towards him. Brandishing his stiff shaft in his hand, Sir Paul mounted her and nudged his knob between her peach shaped bum cheeks. She gasped as he entered her dripping love hole from behind and, though he proceeded to pump his prick in and out of her juicy cunt for the next ten minutes, Sir Paul's back gave him no problems at all. 'What a marvellous fuck!' panted Sir Paul as he pushed forwards and backwards, first slowly, then quickly, then slowly again, his ballsack slapping against the back of her thighs with every stroke as he reamed her sopping slit. He climaxed with a massive burst of sperm which gushed out of his prick as she called out encouragingly as he twitched and fluttered deep inside her cunney, his cock ejaculating little afterspurts of spunk that added to the love juice from Nandeep's internal reservoir. It flowed down as she threw back her head and her shoulder shook as little quakes ran up and down her body which then exploded into an intense orgasmic release.

They lay still for a while and Nandeep wriggled herself round to look Sir Paul straight in the eye. 'Do you feel better now?' she asked.

'Oh yes, I'm right as rain. Thank you for coming so quickly, doctor,' he replied and this unwitting *double entendre* made them both laugh heartily. The sound of their mirth wafted outside the bedroom to the surprised ears of Katie Arkley, who was passing by her Papa's bedroom on her way downstairs to the writing room to compose a still unresolved reply to Corinne Cumberland. Fortunately, she had no reason to enter the billiards room, where Florrie the housekeeper was on her knees sucking Michael Arkley's prick as he leaned against the wall, his trousers and drawers round his ankles. She had grasped his cock in her fist and was pulling it up and down whilst she transferred her lips to his hairy balls, giving each a generous licking until going back to Michael's shiny uncapped knob and washing it all over with her tongue. Then she gradually eased his shaft back in, nipping it teasingly with her teeth, sucking harder as she did so and he clutched at her head as she squirmed delightedly, gobbling his cock frantically until she felt it tremble in her mouth before a gush of hot, spicy jism spilled down her throat.

Meanwhile, in the scullery, Andrew the butcher's delivery boy was lying on the floor with Vera riding upon his twitching young tool as if it were a broomstick. Upstairs Penny Arkley was luxuriating in a warm bath, with her legs over the ledge, working up a rich creamy lather of soap over her pussey, along the outside of her cunt and between her cunney lips to her erect clitty which, like her nipples, was hardening up nicely. She held her tingling love lips with her fingertips as she carefully sliced away the bristly pussey hair with a razor. Oh Bob Goggin, she said softly to herself, I can hardly wait to feel your lips, your teeth, your tongue and your glorious cock in my cunney.

* * *

Alas, poor Penny would have to wait awhile before her beloved Bob would be beside her in bed again. But before we return to see what fun and games Count Gewirtz had devised for Bob and the assembled gathering in Killarney, let us wing our way eastwards to the teeming metropolis of London, the capital city of the glorious empire upon which the sun never sets and more specifically to the back rooms of Stanley Goldhill's bookshop in Holywell Street where none other than Doctor Osbert Radley-Thatcher, the senior lecturer at St Dominic's School of Art who, dear reader, you will hopefully recall we met at the very beginning of this narrative, was peering through some explicit figure studies by the great Italian photographer, Arturo Volpe.

'These photographs are not for me, but I need them for my work with the more advanced students at the college,' he explained to Mr Goldhill who nodded understandingly. He heard similar statements of denial of personal interest in his wares at least three times a day. The lecturer smacked his lips as he turned to a book of photographs simply entitled *Sophia*. The first coloured plate showed the nude figure of Sophia Cianello *[the Genoese mistress of the King of Italy and of the Marquis d'Alba, a close friend and party-giver for King Edward VII – Editor]*. Sophia was a real beauty, lighter-skinned than many Italians with auburn hair, slightly golden in tint with deep blue eyes which were set off by dark eyebrows and long lashes. Her full mouth and richly pouting cherry lips set off a brilliant set of pearly teeth but it was her bountiful breasts, so lusciously ripe and firm,

that made men weak at the knees. The snowy promin-
ences were charmingly capped by the two red nipples
that stood out proudly out from the rounded rosy
circles of the aureoles and at the base of her soft white
belly was a finely chiselled crack with pouting pink
cunney lips peeping through a bush of curly red hair.

The second photograph showed Sophia standing
before a full length mirror, playfully parting the ver-
milion lips of her cunney with her fingers. In the third
plate she was shown reclining on a couch, working a
dildo between her protruding cunney lips whilst a
handsome naked young man stood at her side,
holding his erect prick and waiting to be allowed to
fuck her. The next picture showed the couple in
congress, with Sophia lying across his lap, her beautifully rounded backside with its milk-white globes
turned up to meet his lustful gaze as he pats her bum
cheeks whilst his cock nestles in the furrow between,
luxuriating in the soft folds of her melting pussey.

Dr Radlett-Thatcher was so engrossed as he turned
the pages of this erotic set of photographs that he did
not hear the footsteps of Victoria, a working girl
whom Mr Goldhill encouraged to frequent his shop
without payment, not only because he knew that
many of his customers might wish to avail themselves
of her professional services but also because the
kindly bookseller knew that she had been unfairly
harried by the local policemen who had demanded
free fucks in exchange for letting her ply her trade.

'Hello there,' she whispered seductively in his ear
as she smoothed her hand slowly across the lecturer's
thigh. 'I like looking at naughty pictures too – but
wouldn't it be more fun to see a naked girl in the

flesh? And if you fancy I'll do more than pose. Why, for a nice generous man I'd do almost anything. Would you like me to suck your cock? I love sucking a thick, stiff prick and from the size of that bulge in your trousers I can see that you've been generously endowed.'

Dr Radlett-Thatcher gnawed on his lower lip. The photographs of Sophia Cianello had excited him greatly and since his wife had left him for a handsome young painter three years back, he had found little solace except for the ministrations of the five-fingered widow. Victoria could see that her bait was almost taken. She let her fingertips run along his thigh and murmured: 'We can go next door to my apartment. For two guineas *[two pounds, ten pence or about three and a half dollars – Editor]* you can stay with me for the rest of the afternoon.'

'Very well, let's go,' he whispered huskily and rose up to leave, still clutching his book. He went to return it to the shelves but Victoria, who was grateful to Mr Goldhill for the free use of his shop, always insisted on her prospective client making a purchase. Dr Thatcher-Radlett paid Mr Goldhill for the photographs *[an original set of nudes by Arturo Volpe would now fetch at least fifty thousand pounds at auction – Editor]* and Victoria guided him into her suite of rooms.

'What's your name, love?' she said aimiably as she slipped off her black jacket. 'Osbert,' he muttered and she continued: 'Well, Osbert, why don't you sit on the bed and watch me take off my clothes?' She undressed quickly and he sat transfixed as she stood naked in front of him. Victoria was only twenty-five and was exceptionally attractive, with gold-dusted light brown hair, expressive large eyes, rich ruby lips and provocatively proud breasts which, though small, jutted out delectably. Her pointed ruby nipples acted as magnets to her customer's hands. 'Ah, ah,' she teased, spinning round to waggle her plump bottom cheeks at him. 'Don't be too impatient now. Why don't you get undressed too? Oh, and just pop my little present in that jar on the bedside table, would you?'

Now she moved towards him and let his fingertips touch her breasts. 'Do you like my titties, Osbert?' she asked playfully. 'Why don't you suck them for me, there's a good boy.'

There was no need for her to repeat the invitation for in a trice his mouth came down to meet the soft flesh, his hands pressing her breasts together as his tongue came forward to circle the engorged nipples. His mouth opened and drew in the rubbery erect teat which sent wild vibrations coursing through her body, for though in this instance she was fucking for business rather than pleasure, even with customers (and she could afford to pick and choose who she propositioned) Victoria usually managed to spend. She enjoyed fucking and was more than happy to be paid for opening her legs rather than work hard in a dirty little factory for less money a week than she could earn in a couple of hours on her back.

So she willingly guided Osbert's hand down over her belly to her hairy pussey and pressed his fingers against her dampening cunt whilst he continued to slide his tongue around her stiff titties. He inserted a finger into her cunney which made her juices flow freely and she reached down and tugged at his raging erection. Her face broke into a broad grin as she squeezed his thick, stubby cock. 'Oooh, I see that everything's in working order,' she said cheerily as she slowly wanked his throbbing tool.

'It's not very big though, is it?' he said gloomily. 'Never you mind, Osbert,' said Victoria firmly. 'It's standing up as stiff as a Grenadier Guardsman on parade outside Windsor Castle. Honestly, I've always preferred smaller cocks, they seem to get so much harder, honestly they do.'

He moaned loudly as she wrapped her hand around the hot shaft and stroked the hot velvet-skinned hardness. She could somehow tell that it had been far too long since he had enjoyed a good fuck so she murmured: 'Lie down on the bed.' He did so and she straddled him straightaway, sitting playfully on his thighs. 'Go on then, Ossie, love,' she giggled, planting a wet kiss on the broad, uncapped crown of his swollen staff. 'It's time to fuck me hard, you randy old goat!' He needed no further urging and she spread her thighs as he jerked his hips up and the knob of his cock battered against the soft folds of her cunt. She took hold of his straining shaft and drew her swollen cunney lips over the bulbous helmet, easing herself down until his cock was fully embedded inside her. She rode him like a bucking bronco, impaling herself on his prick as she bounced down on his stiffstander, pounding her bum against his thighs as he hammered her cunt from below.

As Victoria had expected, he couldn't last too long. With a hoarse grunt, he squirted his jism inside her with a surprising force. This had the effect of jolting her own cunney into action and she squealed as her pussey went off into a fierce spend. It was as if her clitty had been wired to an electrical current and she shivered, clenching her thighs for one long delicious moment, nurturing every last throb of her orgasm.

Osbert's prick was now shrivelled up but this lusty girl had fired his blood. As they lay together his hand slipped down to the silky bush of auburn hair between her thighs and inserted a deft finger in her soaking pussey, which made Victoria wriggle as she cooed with joy. She lay on her back with her long legs stretched wide apart and Osbert parted her soft cunney lips with his fingertips to reveal her still swollen clitty. He leaned forward and inhaled the tangy aroma of their spends as he buried his face in her hairy mound, working his mouth into the pouting cleft. Now he was down on his belly between her legs, with one hand under her bottom and the other reaching around her thigh so he could spread her cunney lips with his thumb and middle finger. Her love juices dribbled down as he flicked her clitty gently with the wet edge of his darting tongue.

'Oooh, that's lovely, what a clever boy you are,' she purred as Osbert placed his lips over her clitty and nibbled daintily at it before sucking it up salaciously into his mouth. His tongue slurped and lapped around her cunney as she slid her hands into his hair, urging him to lick harder as he tasted her sweetness, exploring her essence with his mouth. Her hips and bottom moved in synchronised rhythm and he was forced to clutch at her firm, full buttocks to maintain his hold on her pussey. Her cunney was now gushing love juice and each time he tongued her he felt Victoria's clitty stiffen perceptibly, even more eager, wanting more and more as she frantically rubbed her quim against his lips until with a little scream she climaxed and her juices splashed into his mouth and over his chin.

By now Osbert's prick had regained its former stiffness and Victoria squirmed up and pushed him down onto his back. 'Let me repay the compliment,' she smiled and, to his delight, she ducked her head. Her tousled red hair was between his legs as her lips jammed themselves around his now rampant pole. She sucked in the juicy sponginess of his knob and flicked her tongue under the swollen helmet, bobbing her head as she fucked Osbert's cock between her suctioning lips.

She sucked his delighted shaft, handling and squeezing his balls until he trembled with the approach of an oncoming spend. But before he could discharge his sperm, Victoria took out his throbbing tadger from her mouth and lay back, opening her arms to encourage him to throw himself upon her. She threw her legs over his back and, as he drove his cock into the sticky wetness of her squishy cunt, she heaved her body up and down to meet his thrusts. Despite the liquid libations of their previous jousts, her love channel was exquisitely clinging so that Osbert could feel his foreskin being drawn backwards and forwards at every shove. Her juices flowed so freely that her cunney was further oiled. This made his pumping easier as his twitching tool buried itself within the luscious folds of her delicious crack. But all too soon the spunk boiled up in his balls and, making one last lunge forward, he spent copiously inside her cunt, sending a flow of creamy white jism hurtling into her tingling pussey. He pushed and wriggled his prick around inside her as the sperm gushed out of his knob in great jets and they writhed together, enjoying the sublime bliss that only a genuinely first-class fucking can produce.

Victoria put the kettle on after they had recovered and as Osbert lay on the bed watching her put out cups and saucers he said: 'Tell me, how did –'

'A nice girl like me get to take up work like this?' she smiled, finishing his question off for him. 'Well, Osbert, the answer is really quite simple – I want the money to help support my family. You see, love, I was born and bred in Clerkenwell and we were very poor. Until his accident, Pa was a porter at King's Cross Station which didn't bring much into the house *[in those days porters received a very small wage and relied on passengers' tips to make up their earnings – Editor]* and Ma had to take in washing to make ends meet. Then Pa was knocked over by a hansom cab in Pentonville Road and was hurt so badly that he wasn't able to work any more. I was only fourteen when I went out to work in a factory with my elder sisters. We all worked long hours but earned very little and life was very hard, I can tell you. Then Marie, one of the seamstresses I was friendly with, told me about how she earned some money on the side in the West End on Saturday nights. Well, I'd lost my cherry by then and knew what men liked so I thought to myself – why am I working my fingers to the bone when I was literally sitting on a fortune?

'So I set myself up in a nice little room and put a notice in Mr Goldhill's window next door offering personal services. I've a nice regular clientele and I hope you'll come to see me again, Osbert, I only entertain clean gentlemen like yourself and if one of my regulars hadn't gone to India, I wouldn't be looking for any more business.

'He was a nice old boy – I can't tell you his name of course because I never kiss and tell – and the funny thing is that he never came here for a fuck. He'd sit and watch me take off my clothes and when I was naked he'd put me over his knee and smack my bottom. Then he'd make me lie face down on the bed and he'd toss himself off and spray my bum cheeks with his jism.'

'What strange behaviour, but I suppose that the poor chap can probably only get a hard-on that way,' commented the lecturer.

'You'd be surprised what some gentlemen like,' said Victoria, passing him a nice hot cup of tea. 'One client, and he's the son of a Lord if you please, likes to pretend he's in a restaurant and that I'm the waitress. He bought me a black uniform especially for this game. As I walk by the table with a tray in my hand he grabs me from behind, bends me over a seat and pulls down my knickers. Then before you can say Jack Robinson his trousers are round his ankles and he's shafting his cock into my pussey from behind. He can't hold on too long though and very soon he's shooting his spunk up my snatch.

'Actually, that reminds me he'll be here in an hour so I'm afraid I'll have to ask you to leave after you've finished your tea. But can I make another arrangement with you? How about the same time next week?'

Osbert consulted his diary. 'Yes, why not indeed. I'm almost always free on Thursday afternoons.'

* * *

Meanwhile, across town in the heart of the wealthy and exclusive West End, Bob Goggin's old friend Gary Hornby, who had introduced our young hero to the ecstasies of fucking with the fashionable, was himself engaged *à deux* (and later *à trois*) with Lady Estelle Bunbury whilst her husband Sir Kenton was attending an afternoon performance of *Much Ado About Nothing* in aid of the Distressed Booksellers Association at the Drury Lane Theatre.

'The title of Shakespeare's play well summarises my husband's own miserable performance between the sheets,' sniffed Lady Estelle as she toyed with Gary Hornby's erect prick as they lay naked in bed. 'Why, Gary, I doubt if I'm fucked more than once a fortnight these days. Heaven knows what I'd do without you and my ladies' comforter. I purchased a new one last week at Baum's Surgical Stores and I thought that perhaps you would like to see me use it?'

'Later perhaps,' growled the hot-blooded young man. 'Let's fuck now for our main course, and then I've a novel idea for a dessert where your new dildo will come in useful.'

Her face brightened. 'By all means,' she agreed, giving his penis a loving squeeze. He traced the outline of her nipple before running his hand lightly down the valley between her large breasts, parting them carefully as she lifted herself slightly and leaned to her side so that her breasts were brushing against his chest, their soft weight laying lightly upon him. With both hands he fondled these delicious alabaster globes and as he played with them, her nut brown nipples rose like twin projectiles, hardening with desire between his fingertips.

Lady Estelle leaned further forward and stuck out her tongue, thrusting it deep into his mouth as she grabbed his stiff, meaty shaft, which was as smooth as warm velvet to her touch. 'I need your cock inside me, Gary,' she whispered as she nibbled his ear.

Without further ado, he let his hand glide smoothly over her white skin, brushing lightly down over her belly. When he reached her thick thatch of black cunney hair, she opened her legs invitingly and his finger slipped over the moist lips of her cunt. When he found her clitty, her hand tightened further around his pulsing shaft. He rolled over on top of her and she guided his knob directly into her waiting cunney. The happy lovers revelled in the squelchy sounds of their fuck as he pistoned his prick in and out of her wet love channel. Gary adjusted his position so that he was able to feel her pussey hair rubbing along the upper side of his cock. Estelle responded to his movements, sliding herself from side to side so that her thick bush, already well dampened, rode up and down, pressing tightly against Gary's own pubic thatch.

Gary stretched out his arms around her quivering body and clutched the firm cheeks of her bottom, pressing them to him and taking control of the rhythm by moving her at a steady pace. 'A-h-r-e, that's my boy,' she crooned as his thick cock swept in and out of her dripping cunt. 'Now how about finishing me off from behind?'

'Yes, yes, yes,' he replied breathlessly and as he withdrew his prick which was glistening wet from her cunney juices, the lewd Lady Estelle turned herself over on to her elbows and knees, raising her bum cheeks high into the air. Cradling her head on her arm, she looked backwards at Gary through the tunnel of her parted thighs.

Like her breasts, her backside was well divided and Gary Hornby licked his lips as he pulled the ripe peach shaped buttocks apart to enjoy the sight of her wrinkled tiny bum hole below which the soft sopping pussey hair hung like a miniature tropical forest.

'The front door or the tradesmen's entrance?' he enquired politely.

'Either – or both!' she replied urgently.

He was sorely tempted to nudge his knob into the winking little bum-hole but finally he decided to continue to cram his cock into her juicy, lubricated cunney. Deeper and deeper, but still with a deliberate speed, he thrust back and forth inside her as she began to moan and tremble. He moved inexorably on, kneeling up, his hands holding her firmly just below her breasts as they swayed. Faster and faster he pumped as she met thrust with counterthrust. He kept a tight control on himself, determined to make this fine fuck last for as long as possible and savour every magic moment for, in all probability, this would be the last time for many months that Lady Estelle Bunbury's welcoming pussey would be available to him and any other lover. For even though Lady Estelle herself was not yet aware of the fact, there had been informed talk at the Rawalpindi Club that Sir Kenton had accepted the offer to be the new Governor of Malta following the retirement of the present incumbent.

So Gary Hornby rode on steadily, feeling her bum cheeks crash against his belly as he plunged his trusty tadger between them. But try as he might, he could no longer withstand the first familiar intimations of an approaching spend. His balls tightened as they banged against her backside. A glowing tingle announced the arrival of the first surge of spunk travelling up through his rigid rod. 'I'm coming,' he warned her and the thought of hot jets of jism drenching her cunney so excited Lady Estelle that great shudders of excitement rippled through her body and they spent simultaneously, her own love juices cascading through her cunt as the first unstoppable stream of sperm coursed its way out of his prick into her womb.

Time and time again he rammed his gushing cock between her bum cheeks, trying to fill her cunney to overflowing as jet after jet spurted out of his trembling tool. His ballsack rubbed itself stickily against her backside as Gary emptied himself inside her. She gave one final convulsive heave and then lay very still on her tummy, her legs and arms splayed out, her body quivering slightly with the energy she had expended.

They lay together heaving and panting but Lady Estelle sat up with a worried look on her face when four sharp raps on the bedroom door interrupted her post-fuck relaxation.

'Don't worry, I know who's outside,' advised Gary Hornby. 'It's only Bella, your maid. I invited her to join us this afternoon as your butler informed me last week that she is a wicked little minx with an insatiable carnal appetite.'

But alas, dear reader, here we must end this narrative. But be assured that the erotic happenings in Lady Bunbury's bedroom and the record of amazing sensual prowess which was displayed by Bob Goggin, Sir Harold Brown and the others at the exciting party given by Count Gewirtz to celebrate the birthday of

Colonel Piers Rankin will be chronicled by your humble scribe in a further volume when again we shall be spectators at some further glorious effectuations of *l'arte de faire l'amour*.

CREMORNE GARDENS

ANONYMOUS

**An erotic romp from the
libidinous age of the Victorians**

UPSTAIRS, DOWNSTAIRS ...
IN MY LADY'S CHAMBER

Cast into confusion by the wholesale defection of their
domestic staff, the nubile daughters of Sir Paul Arkley are
forced to throw themselves on the mercy of the handsome
young gardener Bob Goggin. And Bob, in turn, is only
too happy to throw himself on the luscious and oh-so-
grateful form of the delicious Penny.

Meanwhile, in the Mayfair mansion of Count Gewirtz of
Galicia, the former Arkley employees prepare a feast
intended to further the Count's erotic education of the
voluptuous singer Vaźelina Volpe – and destined to
degenerate into the kind of wild and secret orgy for which
the denizens of Cremorne Gardens are justly famous ...

*Here are forbidden extracts drawn from the notorious
chronicles of the Cremorne – a society of hedonists and
debauchees, united in their common aim to glorify the
pleasures of the flesh!*

FICTION/EROTICA   0 7472 3433 7

A selection of Erotica from Headline

EROTICA

BARE NECESSITIES	Anonymous	£3.99 □
BEDROOM EYES	Anonymous	£3.99 □
CARNAL DAYS	Anonymous	£4.50 □
ECSTASY ITALIAN STYLE	Anonymous	£3.99 □
EROS IN SOCIETY	Anonymous	£3.99 □
EROS ON THE GRAND TOUR	Anonymous	£2.99 □
EROTICON DREAMS	Anonymous	£4.99 □
INTIMATE POSITIONS	Anonymous	£4.50 □
LOVE BITES	Anonymous	£4.50 □
SWEET SENSATIONS	Anonymous	£4.50 □
THE COMPLETE EVELINE	Anonymous	£4.99 □
THE PLEASURES OF WOMEN	Anonymous	£3.99 □
THE SECRET DIARY OF MATA HARI	Anonymous	£3.50 □
THE STORY OF HONEY O	Anonymous	£3.99 □
A VICTORIAN LOVER OF WOMEN	Faye Rossignol	£3.50 □
THE FFRENCH HOUSE	Faye Rossignol	£3.99 □
SWEET FANNY	Faye Rossignol (Ed)	£2.99 □
THE TEMPTATIONS OF CREMORNE	Anonymous	£3.99 □
VENUS IN PARIS	Anonymous	£3.99 □

All Headline books are available at your local bookshop or newsagent, or can be ordered direct from the publisher. Just tick the titles you want and fill in the form below. Prices and availability subject to change without notice.

Headline Book Publishing PLC, Cash Sales Department, PO Box 11, Falmouth, Cornwall, TR10 9EN, England.

Please enclose a cheque or postal order to the value of the cover price and allow the following for postage and packing:
UK & BFPO: £1.00 for the first book, 50p for the second book and 30p for each additional book ordered up to a maximum charge of £3.00.
OVERSEAS & EIRE: £2.00 for the first book, £1.00 for the second book and 50p for each additional book.

Name ....

Address ....

....

....